Two

Jane Blythe

Bear Spots Publications
Melbourne Australia

bearspotspublications@gmail.com

Paperback
ISBN: 0-9924180-8-9
ISBN-13: 978-0-9924180-8-3

Cover designed by QDesigns

I'd like to thank everyone who played a part in bringing this story to life. Particularly my mom who is always there to share her thoughts and opinions with me. My awesome cover designer, Amy, who whips up covers so quickly and who patiently makes every single change I ask for! And my lovely editor Mitzi Carroll and proofreader Marisa Nichols, for all their encouragement and for all the hard work they put in to polishing my work.

AUGUST 12TH

11:42 P.M.

Caressing her swollen stomach, enjoying the feel of her baby kicking, she savored every second because she didn't know what the future held for either of them.

"This time is different," Brooke said aloud. "This time I'm not a scared fifteen-year-old."

Yet even as she spoke the words, Brooke knew that her age, and the fact that she had been able to think quickly on her feet and adapt to any given situation, were the only reasons she was still here.

"This time is different," she said again, welcoming the inky darkness that kept her hidden from view. "Almost time," she assured her child. "Soon I will have everything I ever dreamed of."

She gazed up at the huge brick mansion where the Everette family lived in the lap of luxury, money, and power, covering their wicked deeds as completely as the moonless night kept her covered from sight. Her gaze melted from determined to longing as she felt her mind fly back through time to her childhood. Brooke had grown up on a small farm, her father working occasional construction jobs in their tiny community to make ends meet. Her mother spent every second tending their vegetable gardens, patching their tattered clothes, and cooking enough food to feed Brooke and her ten siblings.

As a child, Brooke had felt her entire life revolved around chores. She'd rise before the sun to help with the cooking and cleaning, then off to school—a two-mile walk each way.

Returning home brought more hours of chores that ran long into the night before she could collapse into her bed, to spend just a couple of hours in blissful slumber before having to rise to start the cycle all over again. Besides the vegetable gardens, there were the chickens and cows to attend to, plus the indoor chores that Brooke had hated most of all. Cooking, cleaning, laundry, caring for her younger siblings—she had loathed every second of it. But out in the fresh air, on her own with no one to hassle her, she had been able to dream.

The Mariano family was not an unhappy one, despite their poverty. Her parents had been kind and loving, spending whatever time they could spare with their children, but Brooke had known early on that she wanted more out of life. She didn't want to wear her fingers to the bone just to survive. She didn't want to spend every single second working and toiling. She wanted to enjoy life. She wanted to have money–and lots of it. She wanted power and fame. She wanted everything she could ever dream of and she didn't want to work for it.

So the day after her fifteenth birthday, she had stashed her few bits of clothing in her school bag, retrieved the few dollars she had managed to save from her secret hiding place—the box that held her sanitary napkins which was the only spot she was sure her three younger brothers would never look—and started on the walk to school. Halfway there she had announced to her siblings that she wasn't feeling well and was going to turn around and head back home. Of course, her older brothers, seventeen-year-old identical triplets, had wanted to walk back with her to make sure she got there safely, but she had protested that the smaller children needed to get to school on time, and that they knew what a handful the younger boys, aged thirteen, eleven and nine, could be. Plus, the two-mile walk was a lot for the little girls, only seven and five, who often needed some help to make it the whole way to school.

At last, she succeeded in convincing her brothers and sisters to continue on without her. She had held her breath as she watched them disappear from sight, before literally squealing with delight when she realized her plan had worked.

Beelining to the nearest major road, she hitchhiked her way to the big city. In awe of all the big buildings and the lights and the hustle and bustle, she wandered the streets until well after dark. She had been surprised when a car had pulled up beside her, the driver asking whether she was open for business. In all her naïveté it had taken her almost a full minute to figure out what he was asking, then realizing she did not have enough money on her to pay for a place to spend the night, she had nodded and slid into the car. That first night she had been so glad of the couple of afternoon romps with her first and only boyfriend behind the school gymnasium that meant she wasn't a complete novice.

It didn't take Brooke long to figure out that sex in cars with lonely losers was never going to get her where she wanted to be. So she moved out of the Motel 6 where she'd been staying and slept on the street to save her money to buy a fake ID, some nice clothes, and take a trip to the salon. Then she interviewed for and got a job as a maid at the classiest hotel in the city, and within days of starting work there she met Logan Everette II.

A judge, who worked in the city while his wife lived out on the family estate, Logan was always on the lookout for a pretty young girl who would satisfy his manly needs. He paid her handsomely, not just for sex but also to ensure her silence. He also lavished her with gifts, expensive jewelry and clothing, and put her up in a room at the hotel so he could see her whenever he wished.

Her fifteen-year-old brain ticking over, Brooke decided that if Logan treated her this well when she was simply his mistress, imagine what life could be like as his wife. The only way she could think of to get him to leave his wife and marry her was to get pregnant, so she went to work sabotaging the supply of condoms he kept in her hotel room. A mere six weeks later when he knocked on her door in the middle of the night she greeted him with an enormous grin and announced that she was with child.

Of course, things didn't quite work out the way she had planned, but she had adapted, and this time everything was going to play out perfectly . . .

Brooke gasped as something slammed into her back, momentarily knocking the air from her lungs and sending her sprawling onto the soft grass. Before she had a chance to recover, handcuffs were snapped onto her wrists, securing them behind her back; another set were clamped onto her ankles.

As the bright white dots that danced in front of her eyes slowly dissipated, a ghostly white face hovering above her began to take shape. As she took in the features Brooke recoiled in shock, her brain flatly refused to accept what it was seeing.

"You are not going to ruin things for me," a voice growled.

Something glinted in the moonlight, but it took her a long moment to comprehend what exactly it was.

As the knife came toward her, Brooke readied herself for an agonizing burst of pain in her chest or neck, as the blade pierced her heart or sliced her carotid artery. But instead, pain erupted in her stomach.

She let out an ear-piercing scream as the knife cut a line across her middle. At least Brooke thought she let out a scream, but maybe it was nothing more than a horrified squawk.

Minutes later a pair of hands wrapped themselves around her neck, squeezing violently. Brooke tried to wiggle free from their grip, but between the restraints on her wrists and ankles and her eight-and-a-half months' pregnant belly, she was helpless to do anything.

The hands squeezed tighter and tighter, and although Brooke tried in vain to scream for help, she was unable to produce a single sound. Panic rose with each second till it flooded through her entire body; if it had been able to replace oxygen, she'd have been fine. Brooke tried to fight it, but it clawed at her, tightening its grip along with the hands around her throat.

Lungs burning, vision blackening, with her last cognitive thought Brooke wished for the first time in sixteen years that she had never left her parents' farm.

AUGUST 13TH

9:38 A.M.

"Please tell me she was dead before that happened," Detective Ryan Xander looked in horror at the body that lay before them.

"Yes, Frankie, please tell us she was already dead before someone did that to her," Paige Hood, Ryan's partner, echoed.

Francesca Marks looked up at them, her usually jovial almond-shaped, brown eyes subdued, and shook her head. "Blood everywhere. Pooled underneath her. She was alive when he did it."

Ryan shuddered and took a deep breath to try and calm himself. "Okay, well victim's name is Brooke Mariano." So long as he focused on the facts before him he'd be able to settle his racing heart. "We have to go talk to the gardener who found the body; but first, you got anything for us, Frankie?"

The medical examiner brushed a lock of straight dark brown hair out of her eyes then leaned over the body. "Looks like she died of asphyxiation, probably strangled." Frankie gestured at the red marks crossing Brooke Mariano's throat and then her eyes, probably because there was petechial hemorrhaging there.

"She didn't bleed out?" Paige asked.

"No, looks like he strangled her, but she would have bled out if he hadn't." Lifting one of her arms. "Red marks around her wrists, so she was probably restrained, made it a whole lot easier for the killer to strangle her."

"Still had to get the restraints on somehow," Ryan murmured, more to himself than to Paige or Frankie. Focusing on the top part of her body, he didn't have to think about what the killer had

7

done to his victim. Instead, he took in the dirt on Brooke Mariano's arms and under her fingernails. Despite being restrained, she had still fought valiantly for her life.

"Not sure how yet," Frankie continued. "Maybe the examination will show us how he did it. Looks like he restrained the ankles too, red marks there."

Ryan's eyes never made it to the red marks encircling her ankles, instead they were riveted on Brooke Mariano's abdomen. Before strangling his victim, the killer had cut off her clothing. The front half of her dress was discarded about a foot away; the back half remained on the ground beneath the body, and then, with her body exposed, he had proceeded to cut her unborn child from her womb.

Brooke's swollen breasts seemed almost like eyes staring up at him, the huge gaping red hole in her stomach appeared to grin mockingly like some sort of grotesque clown, and all Ryan could think of was the horrifying way that poor baby had entered the world. The infant's body was not with its mother, and Ryan wondered if the baby was even still alive.

Before he could stop it, his mind was off and running. What did a newborn think or feel? Had the baby been scared as it had been ripped from its mother's womb? Had it wondered why it no longer heard its mother's familiar voice? Was it somewhere cold and hungry and alone right now, wondering why there was nobody to care for it? Had it been scared as its life slipped away? Had it even understood what was happening?

And what about the baby's mother? Had she begged for her and her child's life as the killer had cut out her baby? What had been going through Brooke's mind as her life was squeezed out of her? Had her last thoughts been for her child? Had she apologized to her baby for not protecting it?

Ryan had no children of his own, but his younger brother had four, the oldest of which had recently won a battle with leukemia. Through the long months of treatment and hospital visits Ryan had seen the pain and suffering his brother and sister-in-law had gone through as they were helpless to do a thing to save their child. Luckily, treatment had been successful and Brian had just celebrated his sixth birthday. Ryan hoped that a happy ending might still be possible for Brooke Mariano's baby.

Clearing her throat, Frankie stood, tearing Ryan's attention away from Brooke's desecrated body to focus his gaze on the medical examiner. One look at his partner's horrified face and Ryan knew that Paige, too, had been thinking about her nieces and nephews, and the children that she and her new husband would have one day.

"I'm going to take her back to the morgue, see what her body will tell me."

Despite the hundreds of bodies forty-four-year-old Frankie had dealt with, Ryan could tell this one had deeply affected her too. Frankie had been born and raised in Japan, moving here to attend medical school. She had remained upon completing her degree and joined the medical examiner's office. Frankie was as smart as they came, and just as pretty. She and her husband had just celebrated their only child's first birthday. After years of trying unsuccessfully to get pregnant, miracle baby Tania was the light of her parents' lives.

Not envying the ME one iota, Ryan couldn't wait to be out of the presence of Brooke Mariano's corpse. "Do you think the baby could still be alive?" He wanted desperately to believe that this innocent child could still be saved.

Nodding slowly, "If it is of viable age, then yes, the baby could still be alive."

"According to the gardener who found the body, she was eight-and-a-half months along in her pregnancy."

"Then it's definitely a real possibility that whoever killed its mother is taking care of it," Frankie confirmed.

"Okay, we'll touch base later." Hoping that between whatever Frankie could learn from the body, and whatever CSU had gathered from their earlier search of the grounds, they would be able to find the baby if it was still out there somewhere before it met with the same fate as its mother.

"The gardener's waiting for us in the greenhouse," he reminded Paige, who tore her eyes away from Brooke to nod. Even his partner looked rattled by this murder, and in the four years they'd known each other, Ryan could barely recall a time where anything had caused Paige to lose her cool. She was an expert at remaining calm, no matter what was going on around her.

As he and his partner walked briskly through the perfectly manicured gardens, Ryan took a moment to study the five-story brick mansion that sat on a small hill overlooking the gardens. Ryan knew a little about the Everette family. Patriarch Logan II was a retired judge. His wife, Gloria, came from old money, the exact source of which Ryan wasn't quite sure. They had five children—three sons and two daughters—the youngest of which was rumored to be the product of an affair the judge had with a much younger woman.

There was one member of the Everette family who intrigued him more than the rest . . .

"Ryan," Paige's hand clamped down on his shoulder.

"What?" he shot her a mildly irritated frown.

"You want to take a trip to the hospital?" She gestured at the glass door of the greenhouse that, with his next step, he would have crashed straight into.

"I guess my mind was elsewhere," he shot her a grateful smile.

"I guess so."

The slight raise of her perfectly sculptured brown brow, and the slightly too understanding gleam in her calm brown eyes, had him wondering whether she knew exactly what he had been thinking about. Ryan hated to be transparent. In fact, he prided himself on his ability to keep his thoughts and feelings to himself and to separate his private and work lives. Perhaps the last few months with all the hoopla about Paige's wedding and the arrival of his newest little nephew, he had been letting some previously carefully buried longings rise to the surface.

"Tick, tock, tick, tock," Paige murmured. "There could be a baby in danger somewhere out there. Are we going in to talk with the gardener or not?"

Instantly refocused, Ryan pushed open the door and stepped into the oppressive heat of the greenhouse. At the sound of the door opening, the gardener, a short round man who appeared to be in his early to mid-fifties, bounded up and spun to look at them.

"Are you the police detectives?" he demanded, sprinting to their side, sweat trickling down a tanned, leathery face, the result of years spent working outdoors.

"Yes we are, Mr. Hannigan." Paige led him back to the small group of chairs in the corner. "Let's sit."

Twitching furiously, the gardener sat. "He cut her open," he jabbered. "He cut Brooke open, cut her open and took the baby."

"I'm sorry you had to see her like that, Mr. Hannigan." Ryan took the seat beside his partner. "Were you and Ms. Mariano friends?"

Nodding vigorously, "I've known her for years."

"What can you tell us about her?"

"She was a good girl." A slow smile spread across his wrinkled face as he remembered his friend the way she was and not as the mutilated corpse he'd last seen her as. "Very lonely, she just wanted someone to love her, she wanted to belong somewhere. She grew up as the middle of eleven children, kind of felt like she never had a place. The two oldest were girls, and very close. Then there were triplets—boys. They were close too. Then she had three younger brothers, and the last two were girls. Everyone kind of had someone but her. I guess that's why she left home at such a young age, she wanted to find her place in the world."

"How old was she when she left home?" Ryan wanted as much

information as they could gather about Brooke Mariano. Anything they learned could help them find her killer, and hopefully, her baby—alive and well.

"Fifteen."

"Why did she leave so young?" Paige asked.

Shrugging, "I think she just wanted more out of life than she was ever going to get struggling to survive on a small farm."

"She was a runaway; how did she survive?"

Blue eyes going dark, "She was smart."

"Smart doesn't pay the bills," Ryan pressed.

Sighing, "She sold her body. But she was smart about it," his gaze challenging them to disagree. "She didn't sleep with just anyone, she wanted someone wealthy."

"Judge Everette?"

"Yes," the word spat out.

"Ms. Mariano began an affair with the judge at only fifteen?" Ryan confirmed, thinking that was certainly grounds for murder. The judge's reputation would be ruined if it came to light that he had not only been having affairs, but that one of his mistresses was a teenage runaway.

"According to Brooke," a twinge of jealousy seemed to flit through the gardener's eyes.

"So is Judge Everette the baby's father?" Paige asked.

Another shrug. "She's also been having an affair with Logan Junior."

"Did Ms. Mariano know which man was the father of her child?"

"She was going to do a DNA test once the baby was born. She didn't care one way or the other; she saw that child as her ticket to a better life."

"You seem to know a lot about her, Mr. Hannigan," Ryan commented, suspecting there was more to the gardener's relationship with their victim than he was letting on.

"She used to walk the grounds; when I'd see her, I'd go talk to her," he explained, his cheeks turning a bright red.

"Were you also having an affair with Ms. Mariano?" Wondering if they had stumbled upon the killer already.

The man said nothing, but he glowered at them and his already red face managed to turn even redder.

"Is there a chance you may be the father of her baby?" Paige questioned.

Still the man said nothing.

"Maybe you didn't want her using your child to advance her social position. Maybe you didn't want her telling your wife that you two had been sleeping together. Maybe you killed her to keep her from talking and took the baby so there was no proof of what you'd been up to," Ryan suggested.

"I didn't kill her," Mr. Hannigan growled. "I'm the one who found her body. Do you really think I'd call the police if I killed her?"

"Actually, quite often it's the perpetrator of the crime who calls the police," Paige informed him calmly.

"Well, not this time," the gardener sulked.

"But you were having an affair with her, right?" Ryan prodded.

"Right," Mr. Hannigan admitted reluctantly. "But I didn't kill her. I had no reason to," he rambled, his anger replaced by earnestness. "My wife already found out about the affair. She threatened to divorce me, take everything we owned, tell our children about it. I would have lost everything. I promised her I would cut things off with Brooke. That was over a year ago, and I haven't touched her since."

"Are you willing to give us a DNA sample for exclusionary purposes?" Ryan asked. He was leaning toward believing Mr. Hannigan had nothing to do with Brooke Mariano's murder, but some criminals could be incredibly believable.

"Yes, yes, of course," Mr. Hannigan's head bobbed up and down. "Of course," he added in case they hadn't caught it the first time.

"What time did you find the body?" Paige redirected the conversation.

Eyes clouding over with pain, clearly the images of his deceased friend were once again flooding his mind. "Around four-thirty this morning, that's the time I usually get here."

"Did you see anyone about? Any cars here that shouldn't be?" Ryan asked even though he knew that with an estate this size there were any numbers of places the killer could have hidden and remained unseen.

"No, nothing, I'm sorry."

Mr. Hannigan's eyes had glazed over with shock, and Ryan knew they weren't going to get any more out of him right now. "Mr. Hannigan, I'm going to leave you my card; please call if you remember anything. However small it might seem to you, it may be important."

Once he'd pushed a card into the gardener's hand and left him in the care of an officer who would ensure he made it safely home, he and Paige made their way back outdoors. For a moment he stood, enjoying the cool breeze after the stifling heat of the greenhouse. So far, the summer had been a cool one and today was no exception. Despite the cloudless blue sky, the temperature was mild. The sun shone but seemed to have no real power to its rays. Ryan wasn't complaining; he preferred the colder weather. He loved to hike, surf, cycle, rock-climb, anything outdoorsy, and he hated the hot weather that made those activities unpleasant.

"Where to next?" Paige asked, breaking his reverie.

Tilting his gaze toward the mansion. "The big house."

* * * * *

11:03 A.M.

"I don't know what you expect to gain from talking to us. That woman was *not* a part of our family," a voice boomed, announcing

14

the arrival of Logan Everette II.

Ryan studied the retired judge as he strode into the room. The man certainly had a presence; around six foot six, he was lean and well-muscled for his age, tanned, with bright white teeth, and a very full head of snowy white hair. All in all, the man did not look even close to his seventy-two years. However, it wasn't really his physical appearance to which Ryan attributed Logan Everette's presence. It was the man's attitude. He was self-assured and brimming with confidence. He believed he was right no matter what anyone else believed, and Ryan was positive that the retired judge was used to people agreeing with him.

"A young woman was found murdered on your property, Mr. Everette," Ryan spoke calmly despite his irritation with the man. "A young woman who, while she may not be a part of your family, certainly seems to be connected to it."

Gray eyes narrowing, "I see you've been talking to the gardener. I wouldn't believe everything that came out of that man's mouth, detective. He's an alcoholic who I understand was having an affair with Ms. Mariano. My youngest daughter, Isabella, stumbled upon the two of them in the greenhouse last year. I, of course, thought it was my duty to inform Mr. Hannigan's wife of what he was doing while he was supposed to be at work. In fact, I wouldn't be surprised if Mr. Hannigan was your killer."

Deciding not to push the issue at the moment, they needed to find out as much as they could about the Everette family's relationship with Brooke Mariano, and getting the judge offside now would only result in him shutting down.

"Will the rest of your family be joining us, Mr. Everette?" Paige asked sweetly, maintaining her calm exterior. Ryan knew from the way she had her hands clasped tightly together that she was just as frustrated with the judge as he was.

Nodding briskly, "They will be here shortly, the butler was rounding them up." Logan took a seat at the head of the twenty seater mahogany dining table.

"I'm sure it must have been such a horrible shock to find out what happened," Paige cooed sympathetically, taking the adjacent seat.

"Yes, it was," Logan Everette was putty in Paige's hands. "A truly awful shock. Ah, here's my wife now."

They all turned as Gloria Everette entered the room, a flicker of resigned jealousy in her brown eyes as she spotted Paige sitting beside her husband, and Ryan wondered just how many affairs her husband had rubbed in her face.

"Darling, this is Detective Hood," Logan rose to pull out a chair for his wife. "And, uh, Detective Xander," he added.

"Detectives," Gloria nodded at them. She was not nearly as well preserved as her husband. She looked every bit her sixty-eight years, and more. Her brown eyes were sad, complexion pale, her face lined with wrinkles, her thin gray hair pulled back into a neat bun. Ryan found himself pitying the woman.

Before any questioning could begin, the dining room door swung open again and three men entered. Logan III, Lewis, and Lincoln were the spitting image of their father. All were tall and lean, tanned with bright white teeth. The only difference was their heads of full hair were red instead of white.

Once his sons were seated, Logan II made the introductions. "This is Detective Hood and her partner. Detectives, these are my sons. Logan Junior—he and his wife just returned yesterday from a trip to Europe to visit with her family. Thankfully, the children remained behind with their grandparents . . ."

"Simone is just on the phone with her mother, she will be joining us shortly," Logan Junior interrupted.

Shooting his oldest son an irritated frown, clearly the retired judge did not appreciate being interrupted. "This is Lewis," he pointed out his middle boy. "And Lincoln. And that is Lewis' wife Samantha." He gestured to the door where a timid young woman had entered unnoticed by all other than the judge. "Come and join us please, Samantha," he ordered sternly, as one might address a young child, not a grown woman. But his daughter-in-law said nothing, simply took her place at the end of the line of Everettes. "My daughters will not be joining us," Logan announced. "Isabella is too young and Sofia hasn't been well."

Ryan fought against a glimmer of disappoint at hearing Sofia Everette wouldn't be joining them. The twenty-eight-year-old was well known throughout the community as a tireless worker for charities. She ran several in her name, including one that supported families of police officers killed in the line of duty. In fact it was at a banquet dinner three months ago that she had collapsed in the middle of her speech. Ryan remembered the night well. He had been there, desperate for a chance to approach the woman and strike up a conversation. It was also the night he realized that any chance of anything happening with Sofia was nothing more than a half-formed dream in his head. A young man had been with her at the event, springing to her side when she collapsed, and carrying her from the room full of reporters, eager to advance their own careers on the misery of others.

Shaking his head to clear it, he announced, "Then let's begin." Ryan took the seat beside Paige where he was able to carefully watch each member of the Everette family. "As I'm sure you are all aware, a young woman was found murdered in the gardens of your estate. Her name was Brooke Mariano." He studied each face for signs that they may have known the victim more intimately, but all six faces stared back at him calmly.

"That woman the gardener was sleeping with?" Lincoln asked.

"Yes," Logan II nodded. "I assume he had continued to see her."

"That's brave of him," Logan III smirked. "After what his wife said she would do to him if he didn't break things off."

"Mrs. Hannigan came here to confront her husband after I informed her of his affair," Logan II explained. "Suffice it to say, she caused quite the scene."

"I'll say she did," Logan III chuckled. "She told him she'd divorce him, make sure his kids never spoke to him again, take everything they owned, leave him with nothing, and then cut off his manhood so no woman would ever touch him again."

Repulsed by their cavalier attitude toward the horrific murder that had happened in their own backyard, Ryan couldn't quite keep the reprimanding tone from his voice, "May I remind you a child's life may be at stake."

"What child?" Logan Senior asked, seemingly genuinely confused for the first time since they'd entered the room.

"Brooke Mariano was pregnant," Paige informed them.

"The gardener got her pregnant?" Lewis looked baffled.

"Apparently Ms. Mariano was unsure who the father of her child was." Ryan gave a pointed look to both Logan Senior and Logan Junior.

"I'd be speaking with the gardener's wife if I were you," Lincoln suggested. "She really did look insane that day she was here."

"Mr. Hannigan said he hasn't been intimate with Ms. Mariano since his wife was informed of their affair," Ryan told the Everette family. "According to all of you, that was over a year ago; therefore, he couldn't be the child's father."

"Well if that's what he said, it must be true," Logan III scoffed.

"Did any of you have a personal relationship with Ms. Mariano?" Paige asked.

"Of course not. I am seventy-two years old, and I certainly don't go around sleeping with girls the same age as my daughter. And I am a married man," Logan II added as an afterthought.

"I see her around the estate sometimes," a spark of something flitted through Logan III's eyes as he spoke. "Oh, for goodness' sake, come in and sit down, Simone," he snapped at his wife.

Ryan had noticed the woman entering the room several minutes ago, but had decided not to say anything. With every action and every word out of their mouths, the Everettes were helping him to learn more about them. So far, neither Samantha nor Simone had said a word, and Gloria had spoken only once. It seemed the women in the family were to be seen and not heard.

"Son," Logan Senior spoke the word so as to remind Logan Junior of his place. "We have guests."

"Who knows how she gets in," Logan III continued, ignoring his father. "I guess that stupid gardener was letting her in. Really, Father, perhaps we ought to be more careful who we employ around here."

"I've seen her around here once or twice, but I've never spoken to her," Lewis spoke up, all of them apparently deciding to ignore the oldest son, the looks on their faces implying that none of them held Logan III in very high esteem.

"I think I've exchanged pleasantries with her once or twice, but that would have been maybe eighteen months ago," Lincoln added. "I work abroad, only come home for visits every couple of years."

Ryan stored that away, wondering just what had brought the youngest Everette son home this time. "To the Missus Everettes," he addressed the three women, "have any of you had any dealings with Ms. Mariano?"

"This is ridiculous," Logan Senior inserted before Gloria, Simone, or Samantha had a chance to reply. "That woman was a slut. Anyone could have been that baby's father, so harassing my family is pointless. Perhaps you should question the local prostitutes; they might know who else Ms. Mariano has been sleeping with."

"Father!" a voice rebuked from the door.

All heads swiveled to watch as Sofia Everette wheeled into the room. Wavy red hair cascaded over her shoulders, shimmering and shining as it caught the sunlight streaming through the window. Ryan wondered briefly if it felt as silky as it looked, before catching himself and locking the thought firmly away. Sofia was already involved with someone, and besides, he already knew he was not the marrying kind.

"Isabella was right outside," Sofia admonished. "You really should think before you speak."

"I thought you were watching the girl," Logan II retorted.

"I was," Sofia shot back. "But she disappeared while I was in the bathroom." She pushed herself out of her wheelchair. Her brother, Lincoln, moved instantly to help her, but she brushed away his hands. "I can manage," she huffed.

Lincoln looked like he disagreed every bit as much as Ryan did, but no one spoke a word as Sofia made her way to the table taking the seat beside him, and he had to force himself not to breathe in the sweet lilac scent that washed over her. She already has a boyfriend, he told himself firmly. And you decided a long time ago that marriage was not for you.

"I'm Sofia," she held out a thin hand.

As he took it, Ryan noticed for the first time her amazing silver eyes. They weren't gray like her father and brothers. They were pure silver—so shiny that they seemed to emit their own glow—a glow so bright not even her milky white complexion could dull it. Realizing he was staring, "Detective Xander, and this is my partner Detective Hood."

"Nice to meet you," Sofia said with a bemused smile. "Although not under these circumstances, of course."

"Really, Sofia, you shouldn't be here," her father announced.

"I am okay," she shot him a look, daring him to disagree.

"No, you are not. You are not well, and you should be resting." Logan II looked like he wanted to spank her and send her to her room without dinner. "I told you, I did not want you to attend this meeting."

Undaunted, "And I told you that I am a grown woman," she retorted, "and asked you to tell me when the detectives arrived. It's so sad what happened to Brooke." Sofia's silver eyes were the only ones in her family to look genuinely saddened by the murder. "Brooke was pregnant, you know," she added.

"You said that a child's life was at stake," Logan II seemed to just remember the earlier statement. "Are you saying the infant wasn't killed along with its mother?"

"The baby appears to have been taken," Paige informed them, leaving out the details of just how the baby had been ripped into the world.

"How awful," Sofia said solemnly.

"You know Ms. Mariano?" Ryan asked, wondering what the rich daughter of a judge and a woman who sold her body for sex could have in common.

"Yes, she came to my women's halfway house a couple of times. I thought she wanted to make a better life for her and her baby, but she only ever came to ask me questions about my family and the estate. They told you that Isabella walked in on her and the gardener, right?"

"Yes, Sofia, we told them everything we know, and now I think it's time for you to be heading home. And for the detectives to be leaving. I'm sure they have many more people to interview about this unfortunate event." Logan II stood, and the others clearly took this as a sign of dismissal. Within seconds the room had cleared. "I'll call for one of the drivers to take you home," Logan told Sofia.

Seizing the opportunity to garner some alone time with Sofia, because she seemed like the most forthright member of the family he assured himself, and not because she stirred up needs and wants and desires within him. "Ms. Everette, I can see you safely home," he announced.

Silver eyes shone with delight. "Thank you, how sweet."

"We don't want to impose," Logan II spoke tightly, clearly annoyed but trying not to show it. "I'm sure the detectives are busy."

"It's no imposition," Ryan smiled sweetly. "May I help you to your wheelchair, Ms. Everette?"

Debating for a second then she smiled, a beautiful smile that lit her whole face. "Only if you start calling me Sofia."

"Sofia it is," Ryan smiled back. Taking her hand, he helped her stand, steadying her as she got her balance, then guided her to the wheelchair, noticing her barely perceptible sigh of relief as she settled into it.

"I'd really rather one of the drivers take you home, Sofia," Logan followed them as they started for the front door. "You're not well and I'd feel much better if there was someone to make sure you were settled safely inside. You know I don't like you living by yourself so far away from the rest of us."

"I'm sure Detective Xander will see me inside." Sofia gave her father a frustrated glare. "Now please stop trying to tell me what I can and cannot do."

As he drove off down the driveway with Sofia settled in the passenger seat, Ryan couldn't quite help a satisfied smile from lighting his lips as a fuming Logan Everette stood in the doorway watching them drive away.

* * * * *

1:21 P.M.

"He's not really worried about my health, you know."

"Who isn't?"

Detective Xander took his eyes off the road to look over at her. Sofia thought he had beautiful eyes—so very, very blue. In fact, if she was honest, Sofia thought everything about him was beautiful, or maybe handsome was a better word. His face was tanned. She guessed he spent lots of time outdoors. She loved the outdoors, or at least she had before she'd gotten sick. He was tall; he had to be almost an entire foot taller than her own five foot four, and delightfully muscled in all the right places. And he had the sweetest dimples she had ever seen. She wondered what it would feel like to be held against his hard chest, cradled in his strong arms, his gorgeous face smiling at her like she was the only woman in the . . .

"Sofia?"

Realizing she'd been daydreaming, she blinked to find he'd slowed the car and was watching her with concern. In the last few months she'd gotten very used to seeing that look.

"Are you okay? You went all glassy-eyed."

"I'm okay," she smiled, touched by his obvious concern. Maybe this sweet, handsome guy was what she had been waiting for—her knight in shining armor, her soul mate, the man she was destined to spend her life with. Putting aside thoughts of that nature for the time being, she recalled what she'd been talking about before she'd gotten distracted. "My father wasn't really worried about you taking me home because of my health; he was worried that I'm going to tell you something I shouldn't. Well at least something *he* thinks I shouldn't tell you."

"It didn't seem like you let him dictate what you do," a smile crept over Detective Xander's face.

A rush of warmth flooded through her as she realized that Detective Xander was proud of her. "No, I don't," she agreed, returning his smile. She knew he wasn't just making idle chitchat or making an attempt to get to know her better. He wanted to find out as much as he could about her family because he believed it would help him do his job, and since his job was to find a killer, Sofia was happy to oblige.

"Seems like you're the only woman in your family who doesn't keep her mouth shut; your mom and sisters-in-law all seemed scared of your dad. Doesn't he intimidate you?"

Unable to stop a laugh from escaping. "Of course, he does! You've met the judge, he has a presence. He intimidates me like crazy, I just won't allow it to over-power me. Oh, and Gloria isn't my mother," she added, growing serious.

"What?!" the car swerved wildly for a second while Detective Xander gaped at her in shock, then struggled with the wheel to get things back on track. "What did you say?" his blue eyes wide.

"Gloria isn't my mother," she repeated. "Or Logan's, Lewis', Lincoln's, or Isabella's."

"You mean you were all adopted?"

"No."

"Sofia, I know you're tired and not feeling well, but I have a killer who cut an unborn child from its mother's womb before murdering her . . ."

Detective Xander trailed off, shooting her a distressed look, but it was too late, he'd already said the words and Sofia knew she was never going to forget them. "I'm going to be sick," she rolled down the window, hoping the fresh air would calm her roiling stomach.

"Sofia, I'm sorry . . ."

"Seriously, Detective Xander, I'm going to be sick."

Seemingly taking her at her word, he pulled the car to the side of the road. The second it stopped moving, she yanked open the door and stumbled out. She managed to move a few feet from the car before falling to her knees and throwing up what little food she'd eaten so far today. The thought of someone doing that to another human being was truly horrifying. The thought of someone doing that to a poor innocent baby was beyond repulsive.

"Here, drink this," Ryan pushed a bottle of water into her hand.

She took it, her hands shaking so violently that she sloshed water all over herself as she brought it to her lips. The cold water helped to calm her a little, and after she drank some, she pressed the bottle to the pounding pulse points on her neck, allowing the water to cool her down.

"I'm so sorry, Sofia. I wasn't thinking, I shouldn't have said that. You didn't need to know what happened to Brooke and her baby."

The true repentance in his voice melted away some of the

horror that swam inside her. "I know you didn't mean to tell me."

"You're shaking," he commented, his face a picture of earnest dismay.

"I know, just give me a moment and I'll be okay." She wiggled backwards till she rested against the side of his car.

"Tell me about Gloria," Detective Xander's voice rumbled in her ear and she realized he'd sat down beside her.

"Gloria?" Her mind was stuck on an image of some faceless shadow cutting Brooke's baby from her body.

"Sofia," he gently hooked a finger under her chin and tugged till she faced him. "I'm truly sorry for telling you what happened to Brooke and her baby. I wasn't thinking. I am as horrified by it as you are, but anything you tell me might help me to find the person who did it and find that baby before it's too late."

"You really think the baby may still be alive?" She asked, trying not to fan the tiny glimmer of hope that flared up.

"Yes, I really do."

She studied his serious blue eyes, allowing them to soothe, almost mesmerize her. When she was calm enough to talk she began, "The judge wanted children right away, but Gloria couldn't get pregnant. It took her seven years before she finally conceived and carried a child to term, Logan Everette III . . ."

"Your brother?" Detective Xander interrupted, brow furrowed in confusion. "I thought you said Gloria wasn't a mother to any of you?"

"No," she shook her head a little two firmly causing a wave of dizziness to wash over her. "Logan Everette III died when he was two, some sort of drowning accident. I'm not quite sure of all the details; no one ever talks about it. Today you met Logan Everette IV. I guess after their son died, the judge decided that his wife was never going to provide him with an heir, so he took matters into his own hands. I guess he found someone who was willing to let him get her pregnant and then give up the baby. I assume he paid them to do so. That's how he got Logan, Lewis, Lincoln and me," she finished sadly. She couldn't count the number of times as a child she'd wished for her mother—her real mother—for someone who would love her and care for her and make her feel wanted.

"Gloria wasn't much of a mother to you?" Detective Xander took her hand and gave it an encouraging squeeze.

"I don't think she ever got over the loss of her son, and I'm sure she never wanted the judge to go and buy himself some babies. But he wanted heirs—heirs that were his own flesh and blood—so she went along with it. She was a mother to us in name only." Sofia hated to play the poor little rich girl, but she knew firsthand that money did not buy one happiness.

"Come on, let's get you home," Detective Xander announced after letting her sit for a moment.

"Yeah, I am a little tired." Sofia hated the illness that had basically robbed her of her life. No longer could she lead the active life she once had. She couldn't even make it through a day without having to take a nap, and she was unable to walk even short distances, let alone long ones, without getting exhausted. She'd completely lost her appetite, and as a result, a substantial amount of weight.

"Here, let me help," Detective Xander slipped an arm around her waist and practically lifted her off the ground and into the car.

Once Detective Xander had buckled her in, after patiently letting her trembling hands make several attempts at snapping the seat belt closed, she rested her head against the window and shut her eyes. The car had always lulled her to sleep since she was a little girl, and before she knew it, Detective Xander was shaking her gently and announcing that they had reached her house.

"This isn't quite where I expected you to be living," Detective Xander commented mildly as he wheeled her along the garden path to the front door.

"You expected a mansion?" she asked with a wry smile. People were always surprised when they saw her modest weatherboard cottage, but Sofia loved the little house so much more than the large estate she had grown up on. She lived alone with her cat so they didn't need much space, and the small front and back yards were a perfect size for her to manage on her own. This place was her home, her sanctuary, the one place she felt safe.

"I'm sorry. I didn't mean to offend." Detective Xander had obviously taken her silence for anger.

She tilted her head to smile up at him. "No offense taken," she assured him, standing when they reached the bright yellow door and rummaging through her purse for the key. Pushing open the door she bent down to pat Raggy, her ragdoll cat, who always greeted her with a meow and a purr. "Leave the wheelchair by the door," she instructed as she led Detective Xander down the small hall. There was a lounge room on the left with the dining room on the right. The kitchen and sitting room were at the back. "I guess you can tell yellow is my favorite color," she swept an arm around the room where everything from the walls to the furniture coverings to the décor were various shades of yellow.

"I like it," he offered her a shy smile. "Yellow always makes me feel warm, even on the coldest of days."

"Me too," she grinned back, catching the hidden meaning in his words; she didn't think he was just talking about the weather. "My father disinherited me," she explained, not quite sure why she felt such a strong compulsion to tell him private details about her life.

"He did what?" Detective Xander looked outraged.

She shrugged. It wasn't the money she cared about, it was the lack of love from the only parent she had. "I wouldn't follow his instructions on who I ought to marry."

"That man is infuriating, and I've only met him once," Detective Xander muttered.

Laughing, she agreed, "That he is, and he would be *thrilled* to hear you describe him as such."

"Are you going to be okay here by yourself? Is there someone

I can call to come stay with you?"

"I'll be fine," she assured him. "I'm used to being on my own, I kind of enjoy it."

"Well, is there anything I can do, maybe get you something to eat?"

Sofia grimaced at the thought of food. "No, thanks, I think I'll go lie down for a while. I know you're busy and probably have somewhere you need to be, and I know I've already slowed you down, but if you wouldn't mind, could you help me up the stairs? I can manage; it just takes me so long."

"Of course."

"Are you sure it's no trouble, Detective Xander?"

"Please call me Ryan, and it's no trouble at all," he assured her. She thought she caught the ghost of a wistful smile on his lips, but when she looked closer, it was gone.

Taking her elbow, he helped her take the stairs one at a time. With each step, she found herself getting more and more out of breath, reminding her once again how she hated this illness that had taken so much from her.

"I hope I'm not overstepping the bounds," Ryan said as he swung her up into his arms.

For a second Sofia was mortified, but then relief settled in, and she was simply glad she didn't have to deal with those stairs anymore. Besides, she reminded herself, he'd already seen her throw up, so after that, being carried up a few stairs was nothing.

"Which door?" Ryan asked, pausing in the hallway.

"Straight ahead," she replied. "I really need to brush my teeth."

Balancing her with one arm, he used the other to swing open the door and set her down in front of the mirror.

"Sorry, but can I ask one more favor?"

"Of course."

"Would you mind closing the drapes in my room and taking the quilt off the bed?"

"No problem." He paused by the door, "Are you going to be

all right in here on your own?"

"Yes. I promise," she added when he hesitated, then she closed the door behind him and sunk down onto the edge of the bath, resting her pounding head in her hands. As hard as she tried, she couldn't dislodge the image of Brooke Mariano from her mind. Hopefully, she'd feel better after some sleep; she usually did. Besides, she had no time to mope around and feel sorry for herself; she had another charity banquet in a couple of days, and there was still a lot to do to prepare for it. Resolutely gathering her last reserves of strength, she stood, swallowed a couple of painkillers, and gave her teeth the brushing of their lives.

Stepping into the hall, she was surprised to see one of the spare bedroom doors wide open and realized she had forgotten to tell Ryan which room was hers. Sure enough, she found him standing in the middle of the room surrounded by over a dozen expensive gowns and dresses.

"I thought your father cut you off financially?" he asked when he spotted her.

"He did. He may not like my choices, but he still expects an Everette to look a certain way in public," she explained. "I only wear these to charity benefits, my normal clothes are in my closet." He followed her to her room, staying close behind her, she guessed to catch her in the event her legs gave out. "The judge financially supports my charities; I guess he thinks it makes him look good to the public. Plus, I use my family name to attract wealthy benefactors. Thankfully, since I work for the charities full-time, I'm given a small living allowance that helps me make ends meet."

Ryan removed the quilt from her bed and closed the drapes while she pulled off her shoes and settled with a weary sigh onto the soft mattress. So thankful to be off her feet, Sofia could already feel her eyes closing and sleep pulsing at the edges of her mind.

"Do the doctors know what's wrong with you?" Ryan asked,

standing at the edge of the bed and watching her with his gorgeous big blue eyes.

Shaking her head, "No, and I have had every test you could ever imagine."

"I was at the police banquet where you collapsed." He sat beside her, perched on the edge of the bed, looking like he wanted to say more but wasn't quite sure how to get the words out.

"At first, the doctors were optimistic they would determine what was wrong, but as they crossed more and more things off their lists I guess they kind of grew hopeless that they would ever find out what was wrong with me. And so did I." Many a night in the last three months she had cried herself to sleep, so exhausted and with no glimmer of hope that her life would ever return to what it had been.

"I should be going," Ryan announced abruptly.

Tears pricked at the corners of her eyes and with sleep coming on quickly, Sofia was scared that with it would come nightmares of what had happened to Brooke. Catching his hand as he went to move toward the door, "Ryan, could you, would you mind, I know you must think I am the world's biggest baby, but if you don't mind could you stay until I fall asleep? I have very vivid dreams, especially when I'm stressed."

Face softening, "Of course I will."

He brushed a lock of hair off her face, tucking it behind her ear, then stared at her so intently that Sofia was positive he was about to kiss her, but then his gaze shifted and he pulled the blankets up, tucking her in as though she were a child. Sleep had taken over most of her mind when she realized Ryan still held her hand. She liked the feel of his warm, strong hand holding hers; it made her feel safe.

"Ryan?"

"Yes?"

She'd been debating telling him something since their earlier discussion about Gloria, but had held back, sure that it had no bearing whatsoever on Brooke's brutal murder. "I don't think it means anything, but I thought you should know…"

"Know what?"

She could feel his eyes watching her, even though hers were closed. "Brooke is—was—Isabella's mother."

* * * * *

5:18 P.M.

"We can't wait any longer, we'll have to start without him."

"No need, I'm here." Ryan jogged into the conference room and slid into the vacant seat beside Paige. "Sorry I'm late," he included the whole gathering in his apology. Things with Sofia had distracted him and he'd lost track of time, not realizing how close it was to their scheduled meeting until he'd gotten her into bed. He'd intended to leave immediately, but Sofia had looked close to tears when she'd begged him to stay with her until she fell asleep. Still feeling guilty for accidentally blurting out what the killer had done to Brooke Mariano, he had agreed. If he was honest, the fact that he was savoring every second he spent with her, because he knew he would never have another opportunity, had also had him readily agreeing. It had taken Sofia almost twenty minutes to finally fall into a fretful sleep, still tightly clutching his hand. If he concentrated carefully, he could still feel her small soft hand enclosed in his . . .

"Hey, Romeo," Stephanie Cantini threw a scrunched up ball of paper at him. "Snap out of it."

"What did you call me?" Sure he must have been mistaken, he'd never once mentioned that he had a slight crush on Sofia Everette to anyone.

"Ryan, we all know that you like her," Frankie Marks shot him a sympathetic grimace.

Recalling the look in Paige's eyes earlier today, he shot his partner a glare, "What have you been telling them?"

"Hey, don't look at me," Paige threw her hands up in surrender. "It's written all over your face."

"Yes, and the fact that you volunteer to attend every one of Sofia's charity events then spend the whole time staring wistfully at her is a tad bit of a giveaway," Stephanie grinned, her hazel eyes dancing merrily, clearly enjoying this.

"I don't like . . . I don't think . . . I never said . . ." he stuttered, shocked and horrified that he had apparently let his feelings show so openly, especially since he had always prided himself on keeping such emotions to himself.

"Awww," Stephanie reached over to pat his hand. "You thought you were hiding how you felt? That is so cute and exactly what my thirteen-year-old does."

Stephanie had started fostering Cindy when she was just two, eventually making the adoption formal when the girl was nine. Ryan had met Cindy several times and thought she was a nice smart kid, but he certainly did not appreciate being compared to her in such matters as crushes. A horrifying thought occurred to him; perhaps he had let these feelings show while he was with Sofia. She must have been so uncomfortable, probably wondering if she should remind him she was involved. Yet she hadn't mentioned anything of the sort and had instead reached out to him for comfort. He wondered what that meant.

"Ryan, is this going to be a problem?" Lieutenant Belinda Jersey studied him closely.

"No," he replied firmly. He hoped his boss believed him. He did not want to be taken off this case, and he felt he owed it to Brooke Mariano to find her child. Thankfully, Belinda was smart, probably the smartest person Ryan had ever met. Single and never married, Belinda's job was her life, and yet she still managed to make sure she took time to get involved in other activities so she didn't get worn out. She was an avid reader, a horse rider, and a fantastic baker. "Besides, Sofia is already involved with someone, so there is zero, I repeat, *zero*," he shot his colleagues a pointed look, "chance of anything happening between us."

Belinda's black eyes continued to study him, and Ryan squirmed uncomfortably. Belinda was black, with shoulder length black hair, and a penchant for wearing black suits with a black shirt. The only break in all the black were the whites of her eyes.

Eventually, his boss gave a brief nod. "All right, let's get started then. We'll begin with the victim. What do we know about Brooke Mariano?"

"She was thirty-one years of age, no driver's license, no social security number, no bank accounts, and no hits on her prints in AFIS. If we didn't get an ID on her from people who knew her, we'd probably still have no idea who this woman was. She was a fifteen-year-old runaway and it seems like she managed to keep herself completely off the books. Since the gardener was able to ID her, and she still used her real name, I was able to notify the family," Paige summarized.

A twinge of guilt surged through him as he realized that Paige had been informing Brooke's parents of her murder while he had been savoring his time with Sofia. He would definitely have to make this up to his partner.

"Parents give you anything helpful?" Belinda asked.

"No, not really," Paige shook her head. "Pretty much said the same things the gardener had already told us. That Brooke was a lonely kid, never really felt like she had a place in the family, that she didn't like life on a small farm, that she always wanted something more." Paige's usually serene brown eyes grew sad. "They hadn't heard a word from her since she left home. They looked and looked for her but never had a single lead, neither did the police. They weren't surprised to hear that Brooke was dead, just that she had lasted so long out on her own with no way to make a living."

"All right, let's try to find some more people who may know Brooke, and see if we can find out who she spent her time with.

Maybe they can give us something to go on." Belinda turned her attention to Stephanie, "What do you have for us?"

Stephanie Cantini was Ryan's all-time favorite crime scene tech. When he'd seen her driving away from the Everette estate this morning as he and Paige had been arriving, he had at once been relieved that Brooke and her baby had the best people working their case. If there was something there to find, Stephanie would find it.

"Not a lot, I'm afraid," Stephanie folded and refolded her hands on the table, clearly frustrated she didn't have more to offer. "There were no defensive wounds on the victim, so no chance there at getting the killer's DNA. The canvass of the crime scene turned up no hairs, fibers, footprints, nothing. Plus, the killer took whatever tools he used with him, so no chance at getting fingerprints either. I'm sorry."

"Not your fault." Belinda moved her gaze to the ME, "Frankie?"

"I have a few things," Frankie announced. "First off, cause of death was strangulation, manual strangulation."

"Quite an up close and personal method of murder," Ryan mused. "It takes a lot of effort and determination to wrap your hands around another human being's throat and squeeze until they stop breathing. Anyone who would do that has to be filled with a lot of anger and hate."

"Second," Frankie continued, "the wounds to the abdomen where the killer removed the baby looked like someone who had technical knowledge, but no hands-on experience at caesareans. I would guess the killer did some research, made sure he knew where the incisions should be made so as not to injure the fetus, but had never actually done it before, so I would say we can count out anyone with a medical background."

"Do you know what was used to make the incisions?" Belinda asked.

"My guess would be surgical instruments, but they are not hard to come by, so I don't think that will be of any assistance to you. As Stephanie pointed out earlier, there were no defensive wounds on the victim, but I did find faint marks on her back. It's possible the killer delivered a blow to stun her while he restrained her with the handcuffs. There's something else I found odd," Frankie paused. "There was breast milk."

"Breast milk?" Paige echoed.

"Yes," Frankie confirmed. "A trail of it dribbled down her stomach. A pregnant woman can start producing milk around the sixth month. Brooke was eight-and-a-half-months along. Since the killer took care to learn how to safely remove the baby and to apparently procure sustenance, I'm going to assume that child is still alive."

For a moment, Ryan let the thought sustain him. Immediately, he was filled with a desire to phone Sofia and give her hope that they could save Brooke's baby. He desperately wanted to make up for blurting out about what the killer had done to Brooke.

"I've sent a sample of the amniotic fluid to DNA," Frankie was saying. "Hopefully we will be able to determine the baby's paternity."

"Who are the potential fathers?" Belinda queried.

"So far we have the gardener, Mr. Hannigan, who denied having sex with Brooke in over a year, but since he voluntarily submitted a DNA sample we should be able to exclude him after we get the results from the amniotic fluid test. He's also suspect number one. He'd been having an affair with Brooke. The youngest Everette girl walked in on them and told her father, who went running to tattle to Mrs. Hannigan. Apparently, the wife made a huge scene when she found out, making lots of threats, so if Mr. Hannigan had continued the affair and Brooke wound up pregnant and was going to inform his wife, that could have led him to kill her, but also want to keep his child safe."

"And all the Everettes agreed that Mrs. Hannigan totally flipped out," Paige added. "If she wanted to kill her husband's mistress, it's feasible she couldn't kill the baby even if it was the product of Mr. Hannigan's affair. We definitely need to talk with both of them."

"According to Mr. Hannigan, Brooke was having an affair with both Logan Everette, Senior and Logan Everette, Junior. She seemed to think that one of them was the father, and she didn't care which. All she wanted was to use the kid to get herself a nice, cushy life. I think she had plans on blackmailing the family. They'd either cater to her every whim and gave her everything her heart desired, or she would go public as the mistress with the baby as proof. Killing her certainly neutralized that threat, and hiding away the baby would mean that the proof suddenly went poof. With all the money they have they could definitely arrange to have the child spirited out of the country and cared for by nannies until things calmed down. I'm not sure Logan Everette, Junior is smart enough to pull all of this off. I got the impression that the rest of the family didn't really think much of him. But the judge could definitely have done all of this," Ryan summarized. "Paige and I will bring both of the Logans in tomorrow morning to interview them."

"I guess we shouldn't totally discount this being a random attack," Paige conceded. "As unlikely as it seems, given the great care that went into protecting the child, but until we know more we should at least keep an open mind."

"I think it was Logan Senior," Ryan remembered what Sofia had told him. "According to Sofia, her father has always been obsessed with procuring offspring. Apparently, Gloria was not able to provide heirs so the judge went out and found women willing to bear his child and then hand it over to him. Sofia also told me that her sixteen-year-old sister, Isabella, was Brooke's daughter. Perhaps that was what Brooke was planning on using to blackmail the family. If it came out that former Judge Everette had been involved with underage girls, then he could lose everything. I think he would kill to keep that quiet."

TWO

* * * * *

10:47 P.M.

It wasn't fair, Lewis Everette thought as he lay in bed, glancing down at his wife Samantha. He didn't love her, never had; in fact, he barely tolerated her. But his father had insisted on him marrying her. Samantha came from a wealthy Asian family. She spoke little English and she was completely compliant and obedient—exactly what his father thought a woman should be. And ever on a quest to be the perfect son, Lewis always did what his father told him to.

Unlike Logan.

His older brother made no secret of the fact that he despised his wife or of the fact that he would cheat on her with anyone in a skirt. Logan was woefully unintelligent, but it made no difference to the women who swooned at his feet. He was handsome, charming, and rich, and that was all most women cared about.

Lewis, on the other hand may have been the intelligent one in the family, but he was not handsome, nor was he charming. All the Everette children had inherited their father's looks, no surprise there since Gloria was not their mother, but not all of them had inherited an equal portion. Logan was the most like the judge. His red hair was not so bright, he didn't have as many freckles, and he was trim and muscled. Lincoln was taller than the rest of them, and gangly, but what he lacked in the looks department he certainly made up for in charm. He was funny and personable, and women seemed to love his geeky qualities.

Unfortunately, Lewis had unnaturally bright red hair, and he was chubby. It seemed no matter how many hours he spent working out he could never manage to lose even a pound. Lewis felt distinctly short changed.

With another disappointed look at his wife, Lewis rose from

the bed and stomped to the bathroom. He should have followed in his father and brother's footsteps and tried out Brooke Mariano; the woman seemed to sleep with anyone so long as they had money. But as much as he was unsatisfied with his wife, he had never once been unfaithful. Instead, he just spent as little time as possible with the woman.

Sometimes Lewis wished he was like his big brother. Logan did what he pleased, caring about no one but himself, with no regard for who he hurt so long as he was making himself happy. With a sigh, Lewis knew that wasn't true. He could never be like Logan nor, if he was completely honest, did he really want to be. Logan could be cruel and malicious, his true nature always hovering just beneath his charm.

Splashing some water over his face to cool himself down, Lewis headed back to bed, instantly aware that something was wrong the second he closed the bathroom door behind him. He paused to survey the room, searching each shadowy corner carefully for any signs of movement. Seeing none, he took a tentative step in the direction of the bed. When nothing launched itself at him, he took another step and another till he reached it. And then it hit him what was wrong; he couldn't hear his wife snoring. Samantha always snored. Every single night of their seven-year marriage. It drove him crazy, but tonight not hearing it made him even crazier.

"Samantha?" he whispered.

No reply.

"Samantha?" he whispered a little louder this time.

Once again, there was no response.

Lewis was about to lean across the bed to shake his wife when a finger tapped him on the shoulder. Spinning around in wild surprise, before he had a chance to react, something was plunged into his abdomen.

"Sorry, Lewis, I don't have a choice."

AUGUST 14TH

8:16 A.M.

"She got off a lot easier than her husband," Paige mused.

"Sure did," studying the body of Samantha Everette, Ryan agreed. The petite Asian looked peaceful in death, resting on the bed, her eyes closed, the covers tucked in around her. In fact, if it weren't for the deep gash in her neck and the large red stain on the blankets, Ryan would have sworn she was simply sleeping. "Covers don't look at all mussed; I don't think she ever woke up."

Nodding slowly, "The killer was definitely merciful," Paige agreed. "Probably approached the bed quietly and slit Samantha's throat before she had a chance to wake up and do anything about it. But he definitely wanted Lewis to know what was going on."

"The two murders are like night and day." He crossed to the other side of the bed and assessed the scene. A puddle of blood lay on the carpet right by the bed. The covers on this side were mangled and looked as though Lewis had dragged them down with him as he'd collapsed. "He wanted Lewis to suffer, but with Samantha, it seems like he just had to get her out of the way to get to her husband."

"Either Lewis wasn't in the bed when the killer got Samantha or he's a very heavy sleeper," Paige began the scenario.

"He was probably in the bathroom," Ryan took over. "He was out of the bed when he was stabbed, but there are no signs of a struggle." He took a few steps toward the closed bathroom door. "He was probably in there. The killer comes in, takes out Samantha, then hides. Lewis comes back in, heads back to bed, and the killer catches him by surprise and takes him out before he has a chance to react."

"Only he didn't kill him right away," Paige added. "With Samantha, he intended for her to die instantly, but he wanted to watch Lewis suffer."

"So he stabs him here by the bed." He crossed back over to where Lewis had received the fatal blow. "Lewis falls but doesn't die right away; the killer sits down by the window to watch the show."

"How do you know that?" Paige's brown eyes widened with surprise.

"The throw on the armchair is the only thing in the room other than the bed that isn't perfectly tidy," he gestured at the rest of the room, where every table, chair, armoire, bookcase was meticulously arranged.

Smiling, she replied, "Good catch. He didn't *just* sit back and watch, though." Paige knelt beside the smashed remains of a cell phone. "He wanted to make sure there was no way Lewis could get help before he bled out."

"And he wanted Lewis to know it," Ryan walked through the series of events. "He stabs Lewis in the abdomen at the bed, a wound designed to kill but not immediately. Lewis falls," he gestured to the blood by the bed, "then goes for the phone on the nightstand." He studied the bloody handprints on the nightstand and phone. "Only the killer had already disabled the phone, so Lewis sees his cell phone on the floor and drags himself to it." He walked beside the bloody path Lewis Everette's dying body had made as he crawled across the carpet.

"The cell phone can't have been destroyed then, otherwise why would Lewis go for it? The killer waited till Lewis was almost to the phone then stomped on it," Paige answered her own question.

"Lewis then goes for Samantha's cell," Ryan followed the bloody trail to the second mangled cell phone. "He was deliberately exacerbating Lewis' suffering, but . . ." Ryan trailed off, trying to sort things out in his head and coming up empty. "I just don't get how this fits in with the murder of Brooke Mariano and the abduction of her baby."

"Maybe Lewis saw something last night," Paige suggested. "The killer had to come back to make sure he would never talk."

"But if all he wanted was to stop Lewis from telling what he saw, why go to all this trouble?" Ryan knew there was more to it than that. "Let's say Lewis did happen to see something last night, or maybe he was able to figure out who the killer is, whatever, a simple shot to the head would have eliminated Lewis and kept the killer's identity hidden. Instead, the killer comes here, makes sure to take Samantha out of the equation quickly and painlessly, then goes out of his way to make sure Lewis suffered in his final moments. It makes no sense. If this were simply about Brooke and making sure that no one knew he was the killer, then he wouldn't have done this."

Nodding slowly in agreement. "Then we were totally off base with who killed Brooke and why," Paige murmured. "Her murder probably had nothing to do with the father of her baby wanting to keep her quiet but also protect his child. So why do it? Why kill Samantha and Lewis?"

"Maybe Lewis was sleeping with Brooke, too," he suggested. "If both his father and big brother were doing her, why not him? Perhaps Logan or Logan found out and didn't like Lewis encroaching on their territory so they take out Brooke, and then come to punish Lewis. That would also explain why they were merciful with Samantha. They needed to get her out of the way to get to Lewis, but she wasn't involved so she didn't need to suffer."

"I think it's time to bring in Logan and Logan." Paige ran a hand over her already immaculately coiffed chestnut brown hair. She hated her unruly curls and always had them wrestled under control. "Whoever did this got in and out of this house without breaking in."

"That doesn't necessarily exclude the gardener," Ryan

reminded her. "He works on the estate so he could have a key to this place. Plus, there are a number of other employees: security, housekeepers, chefs, chauffeurs, et cetera. All of them probably have keys, and it's plausible any one of them could have motive and an ax to grind against the Everettes. Hey," a thought suddenly occurred to him, something he had meant to mention earlier but gotten distracted, "doesn't it seem odd that no one in the house heard anything? We know Lewis was conscious for a while after he was stabbed. He was trying to reach the phone; wouldn't he have yelled out?"

"He'd been stabbed. He was bleeding to death so he was weak, and he probably tried calling out but wasn't strong enough to yell loud enough to be heard."

"But Logan Senior and his wife, Logan Junior and his wife, and Lincoln and Isabella all live here—surely someone would have heard his cries for help," Ryan protested, imagining Lewis dragging his dying body across the floor desperately seeking help that never came.

"It's a big house," Paige reminded him, "with five stories. They probably spread themselves out, each wanting their own privacy."

"I guess," he admitted reluctantly. "It's just two nights, three murders, and none of the people living here saw or heard a thing. The killer has been smart so far—no prints, no DNA, no fibers …nothing. How are we going to stop this guy if we can't get anything to work with?"

"He'll slip up eventually. He'll get comfortable, think he's smarter than us, and he'll make a mistake. Hopefully that's sooner rather than later," Paige gazed at the bloody track that snaked its way toward the door.

"Yeah, sooner than later," he echoed. Sofia's face floated through his mind. If someone had a grudge against the Everette family, then that meant Sofia was in danger, and with her mystery illness she was certainly in no condition to be able to keep herself safe. He reminded himself that it was not his place to be there to personally protect Sofia, but it *was* his job to find this killer before anyone else lost their life.

Absently following the smudgy red line through the door and into the hallway, he almost walked headlong into someone hovering just on the other side. Taking in the bright red hair and large gray eyes, there was only one person this could be. "Isabella?"

Studying him with the most serious eyes Ryan had ever seen, she nodded solemnly.

He wondered just how long the girl had been eavesdropping. "I'm Detective Xander and this is my partner Detective Hood," he made the introductions and held out his hand for Isabella to shake.

She hesitated for a moment then took his hand and firmly shook it.

Studying her just as she had studied him, Isabella was tall, easily five ten or eleven, and solid, perhaps bordering on overweight. The sixteen-year-old had a sober air about her, making her seem much older than her years. Ryan remembered how the girl had also been hovering unnoticed outside the dining room yesterday when he and Paige had been questioning the Everette family about Brooke's murder. Apparently, despite her size Isabella had quite a knack for moving softly, she had somehow managed to slip past the officers who were supposed to be keeping watch on the stairs to this floor. Ryan hoped she hadn't heard too much of his and Paige's pondering. He had already upset Sofia by revealing more than he should have and hoped he hadn't repeated that with her younger sister.

"I'm sorry about your brother," he told her.

Once again Isabella responded with a solemn nod.

He decided not to mention Brooke. The way in which Sofia had told him that Brooke was Isabella's mother left him wondering just how many people were privy to this information, and he certainly didn't want to be the one to break the news to the girl if she didn't already know.

"Let's move down here." Taking Isabella's elbow, he walked her down the hall, away from the bloody crime scene.

"I understand you found the bodies this morning?" Paige asked once they reached the far end of the corridor.

Another nod.

"That must have been horrible."

A smaller nod this time.

"Did you hear anything last night, Isabella?"

"No," Isabella answered in a surprisingly childlike voice.

"Is that unusual?" he asked. "I know it's a big house, but there are also so many of you living here."

"No," Isabella said again. "My parents' room is on the ground floor. My mother has arthritis and she can't go up the stairs anymore. I sleep on the top floor. When they're here, Logan and Simone have the third floor, Lincoln has the forth, and Lewis and Samantha the second. With all of us on different floors I never hear anyone, it feels like I'm here all alone. Is that my brother's blood?" she asked, trying to peer past them to catch another glimpse of the bloody trail that weaved its way down half of the hall.

Evading the question, "Can you think of anyone who might want to hurt your family?" he asked instead.

"That horrible gardener," her gray eyes went dark. "He was having an affair with that other woman who died here. Maybe she was having an affair with my brother, too, and he got jealous and came and killed him."

"Do you know Brooke Mariano?" he pushed, hoping Isabella would let them know if she was aware the woman who'd died on her family property just over twenty-four hours ago was her biological mother.

"Not really," the girl shrugged. "I've seen her hanging around the estate a ton of times, but I've never really spoken to her."

"Has there been anyone paying particular attention to your

family the last few months? Anyone hanging around? Any unusual phone calls? Anything at all that seemed strange or out of the ordinary?" Paige queried.

"Nothing I can think of." Isabella lifted her wrist to glance at her watch. "I must be going; I begin my classes at nine o'clock."

"Isabella, if you think of anything that might be helpful, please give me a call," Ryan said, holding out his card.

"I will, detectives." She took the card then soundlessly made her way to the staircase, disappearing quickly down it.

"You think she knows anything?" Paige asked.

"I think she knows a lot more than anyone thinks; she seems quite good at listening at doors."

* * * * *

10:33 A.M.

"Ryan."

He turned, blue eyes growing wide with surprise when he saw her. "Sofia, what are you doing here?"

"Is it true?" she asked when he reached her.

His eyes told her the answer before he spoke a word. "I'm so sorry."

Her head was spinning—two nights, two murders, both occurred on her family's estate. This was pure craziness. Things like this didn't happen in real life; they happened in horror movies or crime novels. They didn't happen to normal people, and they certainly didn't happen to her.

"You should sit down."

Sofia heard Ryan's words but they didn't register. Her brother was dead. Brooke was dead. Recalling what Ryan told her the day before about the killer cutting open Brooke's body to steal her child, she wondered what the killer had done to her brother? Had Lewis suffered or died quickly?

She was vaguely aware of hands firmly gripping her shoulders and pressing her down into a chair.

"Sofia?"

Again, she heard the voice but couldn't focus on it. Her mind was conjuring up a string of images of all the gruesome things the killer could have done to her brother.

"Sofia."

The voice was firmer this time, and a light slap to her cheek accompanied it. The two together were enough to snap her mind back into the moment. Ryan's concerned face was hovering in front of her. He'd sat her down in a chair and was crouching before her, his hands resting lightly on her knees. His touch was comforting.

"I think I should take you to the hospital," Ryan announced, his tanned face creased with worry.

She shook her head, "I'll be all right in a minute," she assured him.

"You passed out," he remained doubtful.

"How did Lewis die?"

"He was stabbed," Ryan replied hesitantly, his blue eyes probing. "Why did you come here?"

"I don't know," Sofia answered honestly. When Isabella had called her to say their brother and his wife had been killed, she hadn't wanted to believe it. She'd climbed into her car, despite the fact she was no longer supposed to drive since she'd been ill, intending to go to the estate, but instead she had ended up here, at the police station. Something had drawn her to Ryan, but she couldn't think about that now. She had to know who had killed her brother. "Who? Who did this?" she questioned, unable to keep the tremble from her voice.

"I don't know."

"You said this was about Brooke and her baby."

"We thought it was."

"But why would someone kill Brooke to get to her child and

then kill my brother?" None of this was making any sense at all and that scared her.

"Why don't we go talk in another room. Can you make it to the door there?" Ryan pointed to the closest room.

"I think so," she replied, but as he helped her stand, her knees gave out and she leaned in against him, grateful for his supporting arm wrapped around her waist. Tightening his grip, Ryan led her to the door of a small interview room and helped her to the nearest chair.

"I'm going to go get you something to drink," he announced once he had her settled.

Alone, Sofia tried to pull herself together. Taking several calming breaths, she forced her mind to focus and form the questions she needed answers to.

"Here you are," Ryan set a bottle of water down in front of her. He set a box of tissues beside it, "I thought you might need these too."

Brushing a hand along her cheeks, Sofia was surprised to find them wet with tears; she hadn't even realized she was crying. Once she'd dried her eyes, she focused her gaze on Ryan, who had pulled up a chair beside her. "This isn't about Brooke and her baby, is it?"

"Looking a little less likely now," he acknowledged.

"Maybe Lewis saw something the other night, and whoever killed Brooke had to come back to kill him before he had a chance to speak." Even as she spoke the words, Sofia knew that wasn't the case. The look in Ryan's eyes when he had told her Lewis had been stabbed had told her there was more to it than that. The details, however, Sofia was sure she didn't want to know.

"Maybe," he agreed vaguely.

"But you don't think so."

"What do you know about your family's connections to Brooke?" he asked instead.

"She was sleeping with the gardener," she replied cautiously, not sure how much he already knew.

"And her relationship with your father and oldest brother?"

"You know," she said flatly.

"You do too?" he asked.

"I came home to find her and Logan going at it in my lounge room one night a few months ago." Sofia shuddered at the memory.

"In your place?" Ryan repeated with a hint of incredulity.

Rolling her eyes, "Logan isn't too smart."

"And your dad?"

"My father has lots of mistresses," she shrugged.

"Who would know about the affairs?"

"Not many people. My father was always discreet; he didn't want anything to ruin his career. Logan isn't very smart, but he was smart enough to keep his affairs quiet. Why?"

"What about Lewis?" Ryan ignored her question.

"You mean, do I think he was sleeping with Brooke too? No, I don't. Lewis didn't love Samantha, but he wasn't a cheater. So you think the father of Brooke's baby killed her, took their child, and then killed my brother because he thought Lewis was also sleeping with Brooke?"

"It's a possibility," Ryan was once again being vague.

"Stop doing that," Sofia was quickly getting frustrated. To Ryan this might be just another case, but this was her family, her flesh and blood they were talking about.

"Stop what?" Ryan looked genuinely confused.

"Stop being so vague. Tell me what you're thinking, you owe me that much," she raised a challenging brow.

"Can you think of anyone who might have a grudge against your family?"

"I guess any husband who found out about their wives' affairs with my father or Logan, or maybe someone the judge crushed on his way to the top," she trailed off, the full realization of what

Ryan was implying sinking in. "You think someone is out for revenge against my family?" she asked in a small voice.

"I think that's something we can't ignore."

"Then that means . . . that means all of us could be in danger. That means *I* could be in danger," she couldn't quite keep a small sob escaping her lips.

"I'm going to find this killer, Sofia. I'm not going to let anyone hurt you, but right now I need you to stay calm. Whatever you tell me could help me find this man." The determination in his voice not only surprised her but also convinced her that everything would be okay. "I need you to tell me anything you can think of about your family that may be helpful."

"Like what? I can't think of anything that would be helpful in finding a killer."

"You hesitated," Ryan observed, his gaze narrowing. "Why?"

Sofia sighed. "I told you I had vivid dreams, ever since I was a child; sometimes I'm not sure if I dreamt something or if it really happened."

"Like what?" He couldn't quite keep the eagerness out of his voice.

"I sleepwalk. Sometimes I've woken up in other rooms of the house, and sometimes I see and hear things, at least I think I do . . ." she trailed off, unsure how much to reveal. She didn't want to implicate anyone in her family in any wrong doing, but she also didn't want anyone else in her family to die.

"What did you see, Sofia?" Ryan asked gently.

"Women—lots of them—arguing with my father."

"What about?"

"I don't know." She wasn't sure whether she had ever heard what they were arguing about or whether she had buried it away because it was something she couldn't deal with.

"What else did you see?"

"One night when I'd been sleepwalking, I woke up in the basement. Brooke was there, and she was in labor. My father was there too. I was only twelve, Ryan, and she was just a little older than me." She was starting to cry now. "Do you think my father had something to do with this? Maybe Brooke was going to come clean about Isabella; maybe Lewis knew about it. Brooke was going to write a book. I found the manuscript at my women's shelter, but she took it before I had a chance to read it all. She was going to reveal my family's secrets. What if my father found out? What if he did this? What if he comes after me next? Maybe he knows I know Brooke is Isabella's mother..." She was beginning to hyperventilate.

"Sofia, you need to calm down," Ryan gripped her shoulders, giving her a gentle shake. "I will find whoever killed Brooke and your brother, okay? Okay?" he prodded when she didn't reply.

"Okay," it came out a whimper.

"Does Isabella know Brooke is her mother?"

"No." The gravity of the situation was slowly settling on her, leaving her feeling drained and empty and terrified.

"You need to go home and get some rest," Ryan announced. "I'll call you a cab."

"I have my car here," she reminded him, pulling a tissue from the box and brushing at her wet cheeks.

"You shouldn't be driving in this condition; I'm calling a cab. I'd take you home myself, but I have a suspect to interview."

Too tired to argue, Sofia folded her arms on the table and rested her head against them. Brooke was dead. Now Lewis and Samantha were dead. Which member of her family was going to be next?

"It's going to be okay, Sofia," Ryan said softly, kneeling beside her.

His kind tone pushed her over the edge and her tears began to flow with a vengeance. Before she knew what she was doing, she had thrown herself into Ryan's strong arms and was sobbing on his shoulder.

* * * * *

11:58 A.M.

"How is she?" Paige asked.

"She's in shock, but she's strong, so she'll be okay." Ryan had just bundled Sofia into the back of a cab, with instructions to go straight home to bed. It had broken his heart to see Sofia break down in tears, and yet in her moment of need, she had turned to him, seeking comfort in his arms.

"How're you?"

"You mean am I going to mess up this investigation by getting personally involved?" Ryan couldn't quite keep a hint of bitterness out of his voice.

"I'm sorry, Ryan," Paige looked genuinely dismayed. "But we have three people dead, a missing newborn, and at least seven more potential victims, including Sofia. I understand if you can't remain objective, but we have a job to do and people who are relying on us doing it."

"I like her, okay?" he hissed, frustrated that he couldn't fault his partner's words. "But it doesn't matter. She's taken. All I can do for her right now is find this killer and make sure she's safe. Once this is over, she'll go her way, I'll go my way, and that'll be it." Ryan knew he was destined to spend his life alone. As real as his feelings for Sofia were, he knew that all love brought was pain and misery.

"Okay," Paige seemed satisfied. "Did she tell you anything helpful?"

"As a kid she sleepwalked. She said she would wake up sometimes, see things and hear things, but she wasn't sure if they were real or not. She remembered seeing lots of women arguing with her father and she also remembered Brooke giving birth to Isabella."

"Does she think her father is involved?"

"She's afraid he might be and terrified he might come after her next."

"Do you think she knows more than she told you?"

Ryan paused, considering the question before answering. "Yes, but I don't think she knows she knows it. She also said Brooke was writing a book about the Everettes, but she's not sure exactly what Brooke knew."

"Well at least we have something to use on Judge Everette." Paige gestured at the door to the interview room. "Come on, he's waiting for us."

Ryan followed Paige into the room where Logan Everette II was impatiently awaiting their arrival.

"About time," Logan snapped. "My son was just murdered. Why am I here?"

"Because your son was just murdered," Paige replied calmly. "I would think you would want to do everything within your power to help us find the person who did it."

"Of course I do," the judge rolled his eyes. "But I don't know who killed Lewis."

"You don't think it's strange that in the last two nights there have been three murders on your estate?" Ryan asked, taking a seat opposite Sofia's father.

Eyeing him shrewdly, "Of course I think it's strange, I just don't know why *I'm* here. I should be at home with my family— my wife is distraught; my daughter is traumatized."

"Who is your daughter's mother?"

Panic momentarily flickered through Logan's eyes. "What does that have to do with my son's murder?"

"Perhaps nothing," Ryan was sure it, in fact, had *everything* to do with the murders. "Maybe it has more to do with Brooke Mariano's death."

"I was under the impression you believed Ms. Mariano's death to be related to her unborn child."

"Maybe it had more to do with Brooke's first child, Isabella."

He couldn't help but feel pleased when the judge squirmed.

"Who told you Isabella was Brooke's daughter?" Logan demanded.

"Sofia did," Ryan informed him.

"And why does Sofia believe Brooke is her sister's mother?"

"She saw Brooke giving birth."

Calming, a condescending smile grew on his lips. "Sofia used to sleepwalk as a child, and she had very vivid dreams. My daughter also hasn't been well lately; I wouldn't take anything she says too seriously."

Deciding not to get drawn in by the judge's games, Ryan pressed on, "Still, it would look bad for you if it came out Isabella was the product of an affair. And by my calculations, since Brooke was thirty-one and Isabella is sixteen, that would have made Brooke just fifteen years old when you were sleeping with her."

"Even if that were true, and it most certainly is not, the statutes of limitations for statutory rape are well and truly over. Now I was nice enough to come down here without my lawyer because I have nothing to hide, so you can either charge me with something or I am going home to my family."

"Did you know that Brooke was writing a book? A book about your family."

"And who told you that?" Judge Everette shot him a withering glare. "Let me guess, Sofia again?"

"She saw the manuscript," Ryan informed him.

The judge chuckled. "Then why don't you just arrest me for these horrible crimes that Brooke Mariano discovered I was guilty of? Look, detectives, I wouldn't take anything Sofia says to you too seriously, the girl has quite an imagination."

"Don't leave town, Judge Everette, we may need to talk to you again," Ryan kept his tone treacly sweet.

With a haughty glare, Logan paused at the door, "Detective Xander, if you know what's good for you, you'll stay away from

Sofia."

"Did you see the panic in his eyes when we mentioned his daughter's mother?" he asked Paige once the door slammed closed behind the judge. "And the book. He's worried about what Brooke knew."

"Brooke is the key to all of this, I'm sure of it," Paige looked thoughtful. "If we can figure out exactly how she fits into this family then we'll know who the killer is."

"Maybe Logan Junior can shed some light on the situation."

As he and Paige headed next door to speak with Logan IV, Ryan wondered whether he should have put Sofia in protective custody. If her father was the killer, then Sofia had to be in his firing line for talking to the police. Perhaps he'd call her this evening or maybe even pop by her place to make sure she was okay.

"Was that my father leaving?" Logan Everette IV demanded the second they opened the door.

"He's been helping us with our inquiries," Paige smiled sweetly.

"What's he been saying?" Logan was edgy and fidgety.

"Why don't we sit," Paige continued to take the lead. Since Logan clearly held women in low regard they were hoping he would let his guard down and let more slip.

"Whatever he said about me is a lie," Logan reluctantly allowed Paige to lead him away from the window.

"Oh, I'm sure it is," Paige nodded sympathetically, taking a seat.

Dropping down beside her, Logan asked, "What did he say?"

"He said he thought you and Brooke had been having an affair and that you were probably the father of her child," Paige fibbed.

"How dare he!" Logan raged.

"It's true?"

"Who cares if it is?" He shrugged indifferently. "Adultery isn't a crime."

54

"Could you have been her baby's father?"

"That whore said I was, but Brooke slept around, and she was just after my money. She would totally have lied about her kid if it meant she got a nice settlement."

"Apparently Brooke was also claiming your father was a candidate for paternity."

"The old man can't keep his pants zipped, never could," Logan growled.

"So you were both sleeping with Brooke?"

"I guess."

"What about your other brothers? Is there a possibility Lewis and Lincoln were also involved with her?"

"Lewis wouldn't cheat; he was too much of a goody-goody, and Lincoln is hardly ever even in the country."

"Can you think of anyone who would want to hurt your brother?"

"Not really, but I don't really spend much time with Lewis."

"Did you kill Brooke, Logan? Maybe you got angry that she was trying to pass her child off as yours just to get money? Maybe your brother saw something, threatened to tell so you had to keep him quiet?"

"Lady, if I killed that whore, I certainly wouldn't have spared her brat," Logan said it with such calm it was chilling. "Look, I have things to do, places to be, so I'm out of here."

"Logan, we're going to want to talk to you again," Paige told him as he strode out the door.

"Whatever," he yelled through the closing door.

"He's cold," Ryan murmured. "The look in his eyes when he said he would have killed Brooke's baby was as calm as if he'd been discussing the weather."

"It could be either one of them," Paige sighed and rested her head in her hands.

"With Logan Junior's admission that both he and his father were sleeping with Brooke, we might have enough to get a DNA

55

sample from both of them so we can see if we can establish paternity. Maybe that'll give us some answers."

* * * * *

2:19 P.M.

Paige couldn't help but sigh as she watched Ryan on the phone to Sofia Everette. Her partner always thought he was so in control, carefully concealing his emotions, always serious, cautious about who he let get close to him. She knew it had to do with what had happened with his ex-fiancée, but Ryan was a good guy and he deserved to be happy. This idea he had that love only brought pain was only going to leave him miserable and full of regrets.

Despite the fact that Ryan evidently thought he had done a wonderful job of hiding his crush on Sofia, it had been common knowledge throughout the station for well over a year. The way his face lit up when he saw her, the way his eyes followed her whenever they were in the same room, it didn't take a genius to figure out that he had fallen head over heels in love.

Paige knew the feeling. It was almost six months since her wedding. She had fallen for her now husband, Elias, the second she had seen him. Even after six months she couldn't imagine her life without Elias. He brought her so much joy and pleasure and happiness, everything she wished for Ryan. If he would just open himself up to the possibility that he was wrong about love, then he could actually have everything he wanted.

"How's she doing?" she asked as Ryan approached.

"She's all right. I told her I was concerned about her being home alone with a killer out there who may be after her family. She, uh," Ryan paused to clear his throat, "she said she'd invite a friend over."

Trying to hide her wince, Sofia didn't know it but she could have been Ryan's only hope at having a life. "The boyfriend?"

"I didn't ask," he answered with an overly serene calm.

"You want to talk about it?"

He shot her a withering glare, "Belinda and the others are waiting for us."

Frustrated, Paige followed him to the meeting room. Sometimes Ryan could be so childish; he needed to accept the possibility that he had been wrong all along about what love meant so he could finally move forward.

"Let's get started," Belinda announced the second they entered the room. "Stephanie, forensics?"

"Nothing, really." The CSU tech tugged on her curly shoulder-length brown hair, looking annoyed she couldn't provide them with something to work with. "This guy is good, really good. He doesn't leave anything behind, nothing, not a single thing. We printed the room, but it's unlikely we're going to find anything other than Lewis, Samantha, and the staff's fingerprints. Unfortunately, I have nothing more to add."

"Frankie?" Belinda turned to the medical examiner.

"Samantha died of blood loss. Killer slit the carotid artery; she would have been unconscious in seconds, dead in no more than a minute or two. Lewis received two stab wounds to the abdomen. The killer managed to pierce both the liver and the spleen, again possibly pointing toward someone who had studied the theory of where best to strike. Lewis would have been incapacitated but died slowly. In fact, I think the killer underestimated how long it would take for him to bleed out. Lewis received a third wound, this time to the heart."

"Ryan and I assumed the killer eliminated Samantha quickly so he could focus on Lewis. Once he'd stabbed him, he taunted him with a cell phone just out of reach, then crushed it once Lewis was almost to it. Ryan also noted one of the armchairs had been disturbed; looks like the killer sat back and watched Lewis suffer. I guess he got scared someone would find them before Lewis was dead and had to finish him off quicker than he'd have liked." Paige still couldn't quite figure out the killer's motivation.

"So, suffering was important for Lewis, but not his wife," Belinda mused. "How does this fit into the Mariano murder?"

"We thought that perhaps Lewis witnessed something, and the killer had to keep him quiet," Ryan began.

"But then why the focus on suffering?" Belinda interrupted.

"Exactly," Ryan nodded. "So we thought perhaps Lewis was another potential candidate in Brooke's baby's paternity, but no one seems to think he was involved with her, and Brooke herself never mentioned him."

"So we're thinking maybe it's someone with a grudge against the Everette family," Paige explained.

"Where are we on the gardener?" Belinda asked.

"Mr. Hannigan was arrested for drunk driving early yesterday evening, spent the night in jail sobering up, so if we are assuming that the same person killed Brooke, and Lewis and Samantha, then he's out."

"What about the rest of the staff?"

"We talked to most of them this morning; no one stood out, no criminal records, most have been with the family for years. No one wanted to reveal too much about the Everettes; they all seemed very loyal," she summarized.

"The house has a very sophisticated security system," Ryan continued. "It wasn't breached, so whoever killed Lewis and Samantha had to have the code. Other than family members, only senior staff have access to the code, so we'll check into them in a little more detail."

"Past employees? Anyone fired recently who may have a grudge?"

"One," Paige answered. "Everyone we spoke to mentioned the same person ... a Mr. Payne. He used to be head of security."

"So he would have been able to navigate the security system," Belinda nodded, pleased.

"Apparently an entire overhaul of the security system was undertaken after Mr. Payne was fired three months ago," Ryan explained. "But since the guy's an expert in the field, I don't think it's a stretch to say he could have made it inside undetected."

"We need to talk to Mr. Payne ASAP."

"As soon as we get a current address, Ryan and I will go and see him," Paige assured her boss.

"All right, and where are we on Logan Senior and Logan Junior? Are one or both of them still suspects?"

"Both," Ryan affirmed. "We just finished interviewing them. Logan Senior unsurprisingly went with righteous outrage that we dragged him away from his family at such a sad time. He was pretty calm until we mentioned Brooke Mariano being Isabella's mother. For a split second he was completely panicked; right, Paige?"

"I agree," she confirmed. She'd seen the look in the judge's eyes, too. "He covered quickly though, especially when he heard that it was Sofia who had told us. He immediately reminded us that she's been unwell, he wanted to discredit her." She snuck a look at her partner, whose face remained impeccably calm.

"How sure is Sofia of what she saw?" Belinda directed the question at Ryan.

"She seems positive," Ryan replied mildly. "Logan Senior was quick to point out that even if he had slept with Brooke while she was underage that the statute of limitations for statutory rape is up. I don't think it's a stretch for him to have killed Brooke if he was the baby's father; she was going to talk or take him for every penny she could get. But I'm not sure why he would have killed his son, especially in such a vicious manner."

"What about Logan Junior?"

"Completely different than his father and totally creepy." Paige couldn't quite help but shiver at the thought of the cold way he had stated he would have killed Brooke's unborn child.

"Creepy how?"

"As soon as we entered the room, he assumed his father had been talking about him, trying to blame him for the murders," Ryan replied. "When we confronted him about the affair with Brooke, he admitted it, pointing out it wasn't a crime."

"He confirmed," Paige continued, "that Brooke had approached him with claims her baby could be his and that she expected a bundle of money. We asked if he killed her to keep her from exhorting money from him, and he told us that if he'd killed her, he wouldn't have spared her 'brat.' The way he said it though, it was chilling; he was so calm."

"All right, so both Logans are still under suspicion," Belinda took a moment to jot down some notes. "Ryan, I understand Sofia was here earlier, did she tell you anything helpful?"

"She said that Brooke was writing a book exposing the Everette family's secrets, but she wasn't sure exactly what they were since she didn't get a chance to read the whole manuscript."

"Does Sofia have a copy of the book?" Belinda asked.

"No, Brooke took it back. It didn't turn up in the search of her apartment, but we weren't looking for it. We should go back and search her apartment again. It might help us figure out who would want to kill her."

Nodding, pleased, Belinda asked, "Sofia tell you anything else?"

"She told me a little about her sleepwalking as a child," Ryan's voice was carefully neutral. "She said she'd wake up in various places around the house, but she wasn't sure if the things she'd seen and heard were real or dreams. One thing she mentioned was seeing her father arguing with different women. I think," he paused, "I think she might know more. I think she's locked away certain things she witnessed as a child. We should talk to her, try to help her unlock some of those memories."

Belinda considered this, "All right," she nodded. "Go and see her, see what you can get out of her. It can't hurt and maybe she'll remember something that will implicate her father or brother."

"Ryan and I will check into all the Everette employees who have access to the security code, see if we can eliminate them." Paige was sure it wasn't any of the staff that had committed the murders. She was still positive that Brooke was the key to solving this case. She was the first victim, the catalyst in the killer's twisted mind.

"The clock is ticking," Belinda reminded them. "If the killer sticks to his pattern, there will be another victim tonight."

* * * * *

11:13 P.M.

Gloria rubbed her tender arm as she wandered through the grounds to the small guesthouse nestled down the back near the orchard.

She would never again spend another night in her husband's bed. Fifty years of abuse was long enough; she would not allow that man to hurt her ever again. This feeling of newfound confidence was exhilarating. She felt like a bird soaring through the wide blue sky, the whole world laid out before her, nothing stopping her from exploring every inch of it.

Of course, Logan hadn't been pleased when she'd told him she was leaving him. He'd ranted and raged, grabbed her arm and twisted it till she was sure it was going to snap like a twig. But now Logan had nothing left to hold over her head. It was too late for his threats and his blackmail. She was finished. It was done. In the morning she would pack her bags and leave this horrible place forever.

Gloria still remembered her first day here as if it were yesterday. She had been so young, so innocent, so naïve back then. Just eighteen years old, fresh from her family home, never spent a night away from her father. Gloria's mother had died in childbirth, and with no siblings, she and her father had grown very close. Growing up without a mother had also filled Gloria with the desire to be a mother herself one day. To hold her child in her arms and give them everything she had missed out on. It was with that dream that she had entered into marriage.

One month before their wedding was the first time she had met Logan Everette II. Her father, a renowned chef who worked in the Everette family's favorite restaurant, had arranged the marriage. She'd been scared at first, of leaving her father, of taking the final step into adulthood, of committing her life to someone she didn't even know. But her father had assured her that Logan would give her everything she would ever need.

Her father had been disinherited by his wealthy family when he made the choice not to follow in his father's footsteps and take on the family business, instead deciding to become a chef. Something his family looked down upon. Still, Gloria's mother had been wealthy, too, and her father had inherited a large sum of money upon her death. Plus her father was well paid; she had lived a very comfortable existence. And yet she had still been completely blown away by the extravagance and grandeur of the Everette family estate.

The dreams and joy with which she had been filled that first day she had walked onto this vast estate had been shattered on her wedding night. Logan had sat her down, told her he didn't love her or even care about her, and that her only job in life was to provide him with an heir. She'd been shocked and confused and told him she couldn't live in a loveless marriage. He'd laughed in her face, telling her that if she ever disobeyed him, he'd ruin her father and make him suffer.

One month later he'd begun his first affair. She'd awakened one morning to find him in her bathroom moaning in delight as he was pleasured by one of the maids. The affairs, the abuse—never physical, tonight excepted, always psychological and emotional—the isolation, she was not allowed to work nor have friends, had quickly drained her lively young spirit and she had spiraled into depression. Things grew worse when she failed to carry to term, suffering miscarriage after miscarriage, until seven years later it reached a climax and she swallowed half a bottle of sleeping pills.

Waking in the hospital to find a gentle young doctor standing over her, for the first time in seven years she felt a twinge of life flutter through her. Those days in the hospital were amongst the happiest in her adult life, and when the young doctor had shyly approached her one evening she had all too eagerly fallen into bed with him.

If Logan could cheat, then so could she.

It all ended too quickly. Eleven days after her suicide attempt, Logan whisked her back to the estate and her life of drudgery resumed. But the doctor had left her with a precious gift; she was pregnant, and finally managed to carry a child to term. Logan Everette III was a perfectly healthy, beautiful baby boy. For the next two years her life was perfect. She didn't care about her husband's affairs, she didn't care that she had no friends, her little boy kept her completely happy and fulfilled.

Until that awful winter day.

She'd had the flu, been sick in bed for over a week, her bubbly, energetic toddler, desperate to escape being cooped up in the house, had finally been allowed a trip to the frozen pond with one of the maids. The icy water fascinated little Logan, he always wanted to walk along it, stopping sporadically to bend down and check it was still frozen. Many a time when she was giving him his nightly bath he talked about the pond, and how the water froze, and could she make his bath water do the same thing.

It was the frozen lake that took her little boy from her. Toddling across it, the thin ice had broken underneath him, sending him plunging into the freezing water. The maid had tried to get to him, but it was too late. By the time he had eventually been pulled from the water he was already gone.

After that, the world became a black, hollow, empty place.

Gloria had always had her suspicions that her son's death was not an accident, that Logan had discovered her affair and realized that his namesake was not his child.

After burying her baby in a tiny white coffin, his favorite stuffed bunny clutched in his small hand, she had been ready to end her own life, desperate to be reunited with her son. However, Logan had other plans. He'd sat her down, announced she was never going to provide him with the heir he so desperately desired, so he was going to find a surrogate—someone to simply bear his child. But she, and she alone, would play the role of mother. She had screamed that her child was barely cold in his grave and yet he wanted her to play mother to someone else's children. Logan had simply given her a chilling smile, and reminded her that if she didn't go along with this he would divorce her, take the money she had inherited from her grandparents and leave her destitute before ruining her father. Gloria hadn't cared about the money, but she couldn't allow Logan to hurt her father.

And so the affairs began in earnest, Logan almost consumed by the need to sire a child. Then along came Logan IV, then Lewis and Lincoln, Sofia and Isabella. He had affair after affair as her husband sought out the perfect women to bear his children and then relinquish them to him. It seemed that the older he got, the younger his women became. Gloria had played her part, been the loyal wife and mother, but she had hated every second of it. Hated her husband, hated his children, who were a constant reminder of the son that had been taken from her.

No more, tomorrow would be the first day of the rest of her life. She may be sixty-eight years old but she had some life left in her yet...

A white-hot bolt of agony erupted in her left leg and she crumpled to the ground, clutching at her leg, trying to find the cause of the agony. Shrinking away as the bat connected a second time, this time shattering her right leg. Bile rose in her throat and she threw up, coughing and spluttering and trying desperately to breathe through the pain so she could comprehend what had just happened.

Before Gloria could get a handle on the overwhelming throbbing in her legs, someone grabbed her by the arms and began to drag her through the woods. The movement had her shrieking, as her injured legs bumped over rocks and roots.

She must have passed out from the pain because when she next opened her eyes, she was down by the lake. Trying to will her fuzzy mind to focus, someone had attacked her, broken both her legs, then dragged her all the way to the lake.

Was the someone her husband?

She hadn't seen a face, just a shadow standing over her as the bat had come swinging through the air toward her. Other than her husband, she couldn't think of anyone who would want to hurt her, but then she thought of Brooke, and Lewis and Samantha. Maybe whoever had attacked her was the same person who had...

"You're a lot heavier than you look, Gloria," a voice puffed beside her.

Panic began to claw at her chest, dulling the pain ever so slightly. She dug her nails into the soft dirt, trying desperately to drag herself to safety, but when she tried to move her legs, the pain was so excruciating all she could do was sob.

Chuckling, "Not that way, Gloria."

Once again her arms were grasped and she was pulled along, this time into the lake. She sucked in a breath as she entered the freezing water, but at least the cold temporarily numbed her legs.

"Any last words?"

"You'll burn in hell," she managed to spit out.

"I'll meet you there."

Then Gloria's head was pushed under the water. She fought valiantly despite the fact she was basically immobile from the waist down.

A minute later she went still.

AUGUST 15TH

"We're family. How could you?"

"How could I what?" Sofia asked wearily. She hadn't slept well last night, haunted by dreams or memories or whatever they were from her childhood. Then she'd been awakened early with news of Gloria's death and been summoned to the mansion to partake in a family meeting.

"You've been talking to the police," her father snapped. "Or more specifically, to Detective Xander. Do you have a little crush on him?"

Sofia was frustrated by her father's tone and the underlying implication that Ryan was beneath them simply because he wasn't wealthy. She *did* like Ryan; he was sweet, kind, caring, had a big heart. But she wasn't stupid. All of those qualities meant he was more than likely already taken. Besides, what did it really matter? Someone was clearly out to get her family. Brooke was dead, Lewis and Samantha were dead, and now Gloria was dead. How long till the rest of them wound up dead, too?

"It's a murder investigation," she reminded the judge. "I only told them things I thought could be important."

"I don't want you talking to them again without my permission," her father spoke through clenched teeth.

"I'm not a child," Sofia reminded him patiently. "You can't tell me what to do anymore. If I want to speak to the police, I will and . . ."

"Why do you always have to cause trouble, Sofia?" Logan Junior asked, entering the room, Simone at his side.

"Why do *you* always have to be so stupid?" Logan Senior turned his anger from her to her oldest brother.

"What did *I* do?" Logan Junior whined.

"You opened your mouth," Logan Senior glared. "What is the matter with you two?" He turned to include her in his glare. "What have I always taught you? You never speak about private family matters with outsiders."

"You're one to talk," her brother shrugged off his wife's restraining hand. "You were blaming the murders on me to the police."

"Idiot boy," her father rolled his eyes. "That's just what the police wanted you to think. Don't be so gullible."

"I'm not an idiot," Logan pouted.

"Then why did you admit to the police that you had been having an affair with Brooke Mariano and that she claimed you were her unborn fetus' father?"

"I didn't, you already told them that," Logan Junior's face was an unnatural shade of red, his rage palpable.

"How can you be my son?" The judge shook his head in disbelief. "Try to understand this, the police were lying to you so that you would open up to them. And it worked like a charm. You couldn't keep your mouth shut if your life depended on it. And not only did you admit to having an affair with Brooke, but you told them that I was sleeping with her too, and that either of us could have been the father of her child. And if that isn't bad enough, you actually told them that if you *had* killed Brooke, you would have killed her child as well."

"Who cares if we were sleeping with her," Logan Junior shrugged unabashedly, apparently not concerned about discussing his affairs with his wife in the room. "Sex isn't illegal and neither is having an affair. You should know all about that."

"You shut your mouth, boy," the judge took a threatening step toward his namesake.

"Stop it, just stop it," Sofia shrieked, appalled by both her father and her brother and their attitude toward Brooke and this whole horrible mess, and unable to take any more of their bickering. "Brooke is dead, Lewis and Samantha are dead, Gloria is dead. We can't turn on each other now. The killer is picking us off one by one; any of us could be the next victim."

"Don't be so melodramatic, Sofia," Lincoln admonished, entering the room and taking a seat at the table.

"And you, young lady," her father turned his rage back onto her. "Telling the police that Brooke was Isabella's mother, where do you come up with these notions?"

"It's not a notion, father," she lowered her voice, aware that Isabella could well be listening from just outside the door. "I know that Brooke was Isabella's mother." Sofia remembered vividly the night she had awakened from another bout of sleepwalking to find Brooke Mariano giving birth.

"That's right," her father mocked. "You *dreamed* it, so it must be true."

"It *is* true," she insisted.

"Even if your delusional little mind believes it, that is no reason to be spreading that nonsense all over town."

"I told one person," she countered defensively. Ryan's strong, calm demeanor compelled her to open up to him about things she had never told anyone else before.

"You told a police detective, in the middle of a murder investigation. You may as well have shouted it from the rooftops," her father snapped.

"I'm sorry, father, but I thought it might be relevant," Sofia didn't feel like having to defend her decisions right now. Three members of her family, plus Brooke, were dead, she couldn't understand why finding out who did it was not her family's priority right now. "Three nights, three murders," she reminded them. "Which one of us is going to be next?"

They all remained silent, each falling into their own thoughts.

"Who hates us enough that they want to kill us all?" Sofia

asked softly.

"I don't know," Lincoln replied just as softly.

"What if it's one of us?" she whispered, expecting the full force of her father's rage to come barreling down upon her.

"No one in this room is a killer, Sofia," the judge spoke quietly.

"Really?" It came out almost a whimper. When she was a little girl and had been scared of monsters hiding under her bed, her father's stern, authoritative voice had been enough to drive those monsters away. She wished desperately that he could still have that kind of power over *this* nightmare.

"Really. Now why didn't you tell me about Brooke's book?"

She shrugged. At the time she hadn't thought much of it, just assumed Brooke was mad that both Logans had dumped her. It was only now that someone had murdered her that it seemed relevant.

"You should have told me immediately," her father reprimanded. "So I could have taken care of it." Logan Senior's stare took them all in, "The detectives will be arriving shortly to speak with us, and I do not want anyone other than myself answering questions. It is imperative that we stick together, that we show them we are a united front, that there are no weak links." He shot a pointed glance her way.

Sofia didn't want to cause problems, but she knew that she couldn't—wouldn't—keep her mouth shut. She trusted Ryan. When she had broken down at the police station the day before and thrown herself into his arms, he had held her gently, he had been warm and solid and strong and real; he was safe. "I'm sorry, father," she defiantly met the judge's eye. "I can't promise you that I'll keep my mouth shut. You only want to tell the police what you want them to know; I want them to know anything that might help them find and stop this killer before another one of us has to die."

"I'm sorry you feel that way, Sofia," her father gave a slight nod of his head, and before she knew what was happening,

Lincoln had grabbed hold of her, pinning her against his chest.

"What are you doing?" shock battled terror inside her.

"You need to learn who's in charge here," her father's eyes were cold.

"What are you doing?" she repeated, trying to wiggle free from her brother's grip. It was useless, of course. Her brother was bigger and stronger than her, and her illness left her weak, but it didn't stop her from trying. She caught sight of the syringe in her father's hand as he came toward her. "You're drugging me?"

"I won't allow you to speak badly about this family to the police. I gave you the opportunity to agree to my terms. Your refusal left me no choice."

Sofia stared at him incredulously, "You're really going to drug me?"

Preparing the syringe, her father simply stared her straight in the eye and arched an eyebrow.

"You can't drug me against my will," she protested weakly, wishing Ryan and his partner would hurry up and arrive and get her out of here. "The police will be here any minute, they'll arrest you."

Shaking his head sadly, "My poor, ill daughter became hysterical after the events of the past several days and had to be sedated for her own safety."

"Ryan will never believe that." Sofia hoped he wouldn't anyway, but he knew she was sick, and he knew that she was understandably horrified by the murders and may just buy her father's story. "Please, father, don't," she implored. She'd lost enough control over her life lately, and the thought of being drugged against her will—by her own family—was too much.

"It's for your own good, Sofia." He came at her with the syringe.

"What are you doing?" They all turned as Isabella entered the room.

"This doesn't concern you, Isabella," the judge said sternly.

"Go to your room."

"Sofia?"

"Your sister is sick," Logan Senior spoke before Sofia could say anything. "I'm just trying to protect her."

"Sofia?" the girl repeated, hovering near the door and looking to her for guidance.

Wanting desperately to beg her little sister to run for help, but conscious of the fact that the killer could well be one of those in the room with them, battling indecision; she couldn't believe that her father would really do this to her. Before she had a chance to decide on an answer for Isabella, she felt the sharp sting of the syringe piercing her arm.

"You can't keep me here, drugged, as your prisoner," she screamed at her father. As the sedative started to take effect, Sofia felt her knees buckle, then she was lifted off her feet, cradled in Lincoln's arms. Wondering whether, if her father were indeed the killer, she would ever wake up.

"I can do whatever I want," were the last words Sofia heard before unconsciousness came, and they terrified her.

* * * * *

10:08 A.M.

"Detectives," Logan Everette II greeted them as they entered the dining room.

"Judge Everette," Ryan nodded, scanning the room, where the remaining members of the Everette family had assembled, minus Sofia and Isabella. Frowning slightly, he'd been sure that Sofia would be joining them today. He'd been counting on it as she was the only member of the family who was forthcoming with information. Not to mention he was itching to see her again. "Your daughter isn't joining us today?" he asked, trying to keep his voice nonchalant.

"Sofia is unwell," the judge replied.

Raising an eyebrow, ignoring the knot in his stomach. "Oh?"

"She became hysterical this morning, after receiving the news of her mother's death. I called her doctors. They thought it was best to sedate her so she didn't hurt herself. She's upstairs asleep."

"I'm sorry to hear that." There was something about that that didn't sit right with him. Sofia seemed pretty independent, and he couldn't see her finding out about Gloria's death, getting in her car and driving here to her family's estate, only to then become hysterical and need to be sedated. Besides, the last time she'd been scared and upset, she'd turned to him. He also couldn't ignore the fact that someone in the Everette family may be the killer, and Sofia was the only one talking. It would certainly be to the killer's benefit to have her safely tucked away and unconscious. Still, for the time being, the best way to keep Sofia safe, was to not draw too much attention to her. "We're very sorry for your loss," he murmured tightly, not one of the Everettes present seemed particularly sorry that Gloria was dead.

"Thank you," the judge nodded soberly, then frowned. "Why haven't you made any progress in finding the person who is systematically working their way through killing my family?"

"We're doing everything we can, Judge Everette, but so far your family has not been very forthcoming with information," Ryan reminded him. There was something in the judge's eyes that had him worrying for Sofia's safety.

"So it's our fault that someone is killing us?" Logan Senior demanded, incredulous.

"No, sir," Paige soothed. "Of course not. But as you pointed out, someone is systematically working their way through killing your family, and we need to know anything you think could help us find this person."

He paused, considering this, "What do you want to know?"

"This feels personal." Paige led the discussion since Logan clearly preferred her to Ryan. "This is someone out to get this family for a reason. Three nights, three sets of murders, all here on your estate. Each murder was up close and personal, all seemed to be planned to increase the victim's suffering, with the exception of Samantha. Obviously the killer does not really count her as a part of your family. Now we need you to think of anyone who might have a grudge against you, a grudge big enough to cause them to commit murder."

"Now, let's start with Brooke . . ." Ryan began.

"She was *not* a member of this family," Logan Senior interrupted.

"Let's start with her anyway," Ryan continued, taking a little glee from infuriating the judge. "Now we know she was having affairs with both of you," he included the two Logans in his glance, "and possibly many others. If someone viewed her as theirs and saw the two of you as getting in between them, perhaps that would be motive to take out Brooke and get revenge on your family."

"Like the gardener," Logan Senior interrupted again. "Why don't you go and pester *him* with your ridiculous questions?"

"Mr. Hannigan has been ruled out as a suspect," Paige informed them.

"Do you know of anyone else who was having an affair with Brooke?" Ryan asked.

"We did not keep tabs on the private life of Brooke Mariano," Logan Senior shot them a withering glare. Ryan studied each face carefully for signs they knew more than they were letting on. Logan Senior looked beyond annoyed, Logan Junior looked bored, Simone looked scared, and Lincoln looked like his mind was elsewhere. No one looked like they were hiding information.

"All right then, anyone who may have had a grudge against Lewis or Samantha?" he moved on.

"Someone with a grudge against Lewis?" Logan Junior burst into peals of laughter.

"Logan," the threatening stare Logan Senior threw his son's

way was enough to shut Junior's mouth.

He wondered what had gone on between the Everette family before his and Paige's arrival that had everyone keeping their mouths shut and Sofia locked out of the meeting altogether. "What do you mean, Logan?"

He looked to his father for permission to speak. When the judge nodded, Logan Junior spoke, "Lewis was a goody-goody. He was always trying to be the perfect one in the family. I don't think that boy ever did anything wrong in his life."

So while Logan Junior was the family's bad boy and Lewis was the good son, Ryan wondered where that left Lincoln. "What about Samantha?"

Logan Senior couldn't quite hide his smirk. He was obviously pleased with his choices of submissive wives for his sons. "I'd be surprised if Samantha had any enemies,"

From their brief meeting the day of Brooke's murder, Ryan could believe that. "Okay then, on to Gloria."

"Again, detectives, I can't see anyone having a grudge big enough against my wife to start slaughtering our family."

"What about Sofia or Isabella?" Even as he asked the question, he knew what the answer would be. Sofia was too sweet for anyone to hate, and Isabella was only sixteen.

"You've met Sofia; she couldn't create an enemy if she tried. Isabella is a teenager, a quiet one at that. She is schooled here at home, she doesn't have many friends, she doesn't date, and I can't see her knowing anyone who would do this."

"Lincoln, what about you? Anyone out to get you?"

"As far as I know, no one hates me enough to kill my family," Lincoln studied him with steady gray eyes.

Ryan realized he didn't know much about the youngest Everette son. "You said you lived overseas, what do you do?"

"I'm a computer programmer."

"Got a girlfriend or maybe an ex who someone might be angry at you over?"

Unable to keep from glaring at his father, "No. No girlfriend or ex."

Ryan assumed Logan Senior was plotting the nuptials of his youngest son, against his wishes. "Well, that just leaves you two then," He stated, setting his sights on the two Logans.

"Logan Junior?"

He shrugged disinterestedly.

"We know you have a lot of affairs; any jealous, angry husband out to get you?"

Another half-hearted shrug.

"How many affairs are you having at the moment?" Ryan asked, casting a glance at Simone who sat as still as stone, her face carefully blank, but her eyes ashamed and sad.

"Maybe . . . like, four."

"Logan," the judge snapped irritably.

"What? They asked," Logan Junior whined. "I don't think any of the husbands of the women I sleep with would take it so seriously they would kill my mother and my brother."

"What about you?" Ryan turned his attention to the judge.

"I was a judge. I'm sure there are numerous criminals and their families out there who hate me enough to do this," Logan Senior answered evenly.

"On that note, we'd like to offer you all police protection," Paige informed them.

"No," Logan Senior shook his head emphatically.

"Excuse me?" Ryan narrowed his eyes, confused.

"No, thank you," Logan Senior repeated.

"Someone is out to destroy your family," Paige reminded the judge. "Four murders have already been committed on your estate. The rest of you are all potential victims; we'd like to post officers here for your own protection."

"No," Logan Senior said once again. "We have our own security staff."

"No offense, but they haven't really done a very good job so far," Ryan reminded him. "What about the rest of you?" He turned to Logan Junior, Lincoln, and Simone.

The judge shot his sons and daughter-in-law another threatening glare. "We all feel safe here. We don't want or need police protection. All right detectives, we've answered all your questions, now as you imagine, it has been a very stressful couple of days for my family, and we have several funerals we need to make preparations for, so it's time for you to leave," Logan Senior stood to dismiss them.

"I'd like to go and see Sofia before we leave," Ryan announced. He wanted to make sure she was okay before leaving her here where more than likely another member of the Everette family would be dead by this time tomorrow.

"That is out of the question," Logan Senior shot him a frustrated glare.

"The rest of you have refused police protection. I want to make sure Sofia is aware of the fact that we have offered protection so she can make her own decision." He met the judge's gaze undaunted.

"Sofia will be safe here." Logan was fighting not to let his temper out.

"With all due respect, sir, I don't believe she or any of the rest of you will be safe here."

"Sofia is resting now, but I will pass along your message when she awakens." The judge was losing his battle to remain calm. "Now it is time for you to get out of my house."

* * * * *

12:26 P.M.

"Not very forthcoming for people who are in the sights of a killer, are they?" Paige mused as she and Ryan met up in front of Alan Payne's residence.

Raising an eyebrow, "No, they're not. Something was up with Sofia. I don't buy that she was so hysterical her father had to get her doctors to sedate her."

Paige groaned silently. Her partner had it bad for Sofia Everette. That would be great if she wasn't a potential victim in a homicide investigation. Still, on this she agreed with him. "I agree."

Surprise written all over his face. "You do?"

"There was something about the way Logan Senior told us about it that didn't sit right with me." The look in Sofia's father's eyes when he'd told them his hysterical daughter had to be sedated for her own safety hadn't been one of concern, but rather one of satisfaction.

"His eyes," Ryan shuddered. "They were so cold. And pleased; he did something so we couldn't get to her because he knows Sofia will talk to us, and he doesn't want her saying anything he doesn't want her to."

"I agree," she nodded. Too bad Sofia was already involved with someone because she would have been a great match for Ryan. Sofia was strong and independent, confident and self-assured, and she seemed prepared to do the right thing, even if it cost her.

"I wish I knew that she was okay," Ryan said wistfully.

"Ryan, she's not okay," Paige reminded her partner. She didn't want to freak him out, but they also needed to face facts. "As long as she's in that house, she's in danger. And I don't just mean from her father. Even if he's not the killer, someone else is, and that someone has already gotten onto that estate undetected the last three nights."

Her partner paled. "What are we going to do, then? We can't leave her there alone and unprotected. I need her safe, Paige," he finished, the wistful look back.

"We're going to find this killer; that's what we're going to do to keep her safe," she assured him, and Ryan calmed a little. "Ryan, are you sure she's involved with someone?"

"Why?" Her partner's bright blue eyes narrowed as they studied her suspiciously.

"She likes you, Ryan, I'm sure she does." Paige was positive that Sofia did indeed like her partner.

"She's dating someone," he reminded her.

"How do you know that?" she demanded.

"He was there the night she collapsed. I saw the panic on his face; he really cares about her." Pain flashed through his usually calm eyes.

"Did you ever think that maybe he was just her friend?" Sometimes it frustrated her that Ryan saw everything as either black or white.

"What?" From the look on his face, she could see the thought had never occurred to him.

"Ryan, I've seen her look at you, and she doesn't look at you like someone who's involved. She looks at you like someone who's interested. And the other day, when she was scared and in shock, she came to you. Would you at least talk to her, find out whether she's dating someone, before you just write the whole thing off? I want to see you at least try to find happiness again." Ryan's ex, Katrina, had put such a dent in his confidence that he was scared to try relationships again.

"Come on, we have to go talk to Mr. Payne." Ryan started up the path to the apartment building where the Everettes' ex-head of security lived.

Following him, Paige hoped that she had at least prompted him to think about getting the facts from Sofia before he made any decisions. Ringing the bell, they had to wait barely a minute before the door swung open to reveal a glowering man in his fifties.

"What?" the man growled, his brown eyes narrowed at them suspiciously.

"Mr. Payne, I'm Detective Hood and this is my partner

Detective Xander," Paige began. "We need to speak with you . . ."

"About the Everettes," Alan Payne interrupted, his frown growing. "Hurry up, then."

"May we come in?" When it looked like he was wavering, she pushed. "Or we can take this down to the station."

With a frustrated sigh, he threw the door further open and walked inside, leaving them to follow. Exchanging glances with Ryan as they entered the apartment, they found Alan Payne in the kitchen downing a glass of champagne. Paige paused a moment to take in the apartment. It was well fitted out, expensive furnishings, a huge entertainment set-up in the living area. Despite recently losing his job, it didn't seem like Alan Payne was struggling financially.

"Fancy a drink?" Mr. Payne held up the bottle of champagne. "I'm celebrating."

"Celebrating what?" Ryan raised a questioning brow.

"The fall of the mighty Everette family," he snickered. "So, you're here because you think I killed them?"

"Did you?" Paige asked.

"Nope, but I can't say I was sorry to hear that Gloria, Lewis, and Samantha were dead, or that Brooke woman." Alan took his glass and went to lounge on the couch.

"Do you have alibis for the nights of the murders?" Ryan queried.

"Yep, sure do. My new lady friend sleeps here most nights," Alan smirked.

"We'll need her number," Paige told him, taking a seat in the armchair adjacent to the couch. She didn't like Alan Payne, but she wasn't convinced he was the killer. "Why were you fired, Mr. Payne?"

His smirk disappeared, replaced by a furious snarl, "Because the judge is a hypocrite."

"How do you mean?" Ryan joined them, taking the other armchair.

"Only the judge was allowed to have affairs." Alan's snarl deepened.

"You were having an affair? With Brooke Mariano?" Paige wondered how many other people Brooke had been sleeping with.

"With Brooke?" the snarl faded to shock. "No way. I was having an affair with Gloria."

Caught off guard, Paige was sure her expression was as surprised as Ryan's. "With Gloria Everette?"

Chuckling, "I bet you didn't think she had it in her. She let the judge push her around, but every now and then she gets her own back."

"How long were you together?" Ryan asked.

"Five months before the judge found out."

"He found out three months ago?"

"His blabbermouth of a daughter walked in on us," Alan Payne's snarl was back.

"Sofia or Isabella?" Ryan's eyes narrowed slightly at the potential slight against Sofia.

"Isabella." Alan's eyebrows rose at Ryan's tone. "That girl has eyes in the back of her head; she seems to see everything that goes on at that estate."

"So Logan Senior fired you when Isabella told him you were sleeping with his wife."

"Yep," Alan nodded. "Gave a whole speech and everything. All about how unity and loyalty and honesty mean so much to him, and he didn't want anyone working for his family who didn't possess those qualities. As I said, Judge Everette is quite the hypocrite."

"Sounds like motive to me." Ryan remained unconvinced that Alan Payne wasn't involved.

"It can sound like whatever you want," Alan shrugged indifferently. "But I'm telling you I didn't kill any member of the Everette family. I had no reason to. The judge may hate me, but he gave me a glowing recommendation, didn't want me airing his family's dirty laundry in public. I've already got a new job."

"Still, you lost your relationship with Gloria Everette," Paige pointed out.

Another shrug. "Gloria was good in bed but other than that she doesn't have many endearing qualities. Again, I've already moved on."

"How long did you work for the family, Mr. Payne?" Paige asked, hoping to get some insight into the Everette family from someone who knew them.

"Going on twelve years."

"What can you tell us about them?"

"Well like I said, the judge is a hypocrite. You wouldn't believe the number of times I've had to distract spouses of the women he's had affairs with. Or the people I've paid off to keep his secrets."

"Anyone you can think of who may hate the judge enough to do this?"

"No one crazy enough to kill. Mostly lawyers, businessmen, rich guys who could never have enough money, but as much as they had something over the judge, he had enough over them to make sure everyone kept their mouths shut."

"What about Gloria? You said she got her own back against Logan Senior sometimes, could there have been other affairs besides you?" Paige questioned, surprised by this side of Gloria Everette.

"Oh, I'm sure there was, but I don't know of any specifically. Most of the time Gloria was weak, and she let the judge walk all over her. Did whatever he told her to. Played the good supportive wife and mother. Put up with the judge's abuse. But sometimes she'd had enough, needed someone's arms to cry in, someone to make her feel wanted, but mostly she just wanted to talk."

"About what?"

"Mostly her son, the one who died as a toddler. She'd

attempted suicide a few years after the wedding, met a doctor at the hospital, decided if the judge could cheat, she could too, and she ended up pregnant. Unfortunately, the little boy died when he was only two. She never got over it."

"And their children?"

"Lincoln was the quiet one, but personable. Lewis was the awkward one of the family, but relatively harmless. Logan, on the other hand, was a nasty one. I never liked him. He was cruel for cruel's sake. Isabella's a sneaky one. I would never underestimate that girl. Sofia I like, the only member of the family who's actually a decent, kind person. She's a really sweet girl."

"You mentioned that a doctor was the father of Gloria's first son. Is there any chance he could have found out about her pregnancy and come back angry that his son was kept from him?" Paige thought it was a stretch but had to ask nonetheless.

"I guess," but Alan Payne looked unconvinced. "But if it was Gloria's little boy's father, why would he kill Brooke Mariano and Lewis and Samantha? Maybe he'd be angry at Gloria and the judge, but the others had nothing to do with it."

"Do you have a name?"

"Gloria never mentioned one."

She and Ryan would look into it once they left here. "Mr. Payne, based on what you know about the Everette family, do you think it's possible one of them might be the killer?"

"I assume you're really asking about Logan Senior and Junior." He studied them for a long moment. "Either of them. I wouldn't put anything past Logan Junior. And the judge, well . . ." he trailed off, seemingly debating with himself whether to continue or not.

"Well?" Ryan prodded.

"Well, Gloria always thought," he continued somewhat reluctantly, "that her little boy's death wasn't an accident."

Understanding dawning, Paige exchanged a look with Ryan. "She thought her husband killed him?"

Nodding, Mr. Payne answered, "She thought he found out

about the affair, realized the child wasn't his, and killed him. If Judge Everette can orchestrate the death of a two-year-old, then I wouldn't put anything past him."

* * * * *

4:38 P.M.

The killer moved unnoticed through the house.

So far, so good. Everything was running smoothly.

Step by step, everything was falling into place.

Brooke was dead. Lewis and Samantha were dead. Gloria was dead. And by this time tomorrow, another member of the Everette family would join them. It might have been more practical to take out the entire clan in one foul swoop, but that wouldn't have been nearly so much fun.

As enjoyable as this was, there was still a lot of work left to do.

Most important was deciding on the next victim.

It was undecided at the moment just who that would be.

The killer paused in the doorway of Sofia Everette's room. The girl was still drugged unconscious. She'd been placed on the bed and tucked under the covers, her red hair fanned out around her pale face, which even in sleep was creased in concern. Sofia was sick and weak, making her a good potential next victim. On the other hand, that meant that she wouldn't put up as much of a fight as the others, which would make her murder much less exciting.

Entering the room to sit on the edge of the bed, the killer watched the girl sleep. Sofia was too sweet, too honorable for her own good. She was going to get herself killed. This desire she had to help the police solve these murders was worrying. Perhaps taking her out next was for the best.

And yet, that could produce a new problem. Sofia's police detective admirer would likely be driven to stop at nothing to solve these crimes if Sofia was killed.

Choices, choices. So many choices.

Still, whichever direction things went next, it would be for the best.

Sometimes just going with the moment gave the most profitable outcomes.

The killer stalked outside Sofia's room and headed outside into the warm summer sunshine. Smiling, pleased almost beyond measure with how well things were working out.

Just a few more hours until the next kill.

The rush from murder was getting intoxicating. Addicting. The possibility that even after the Everette family was decimated the killing would never stop was increasing.

Still, that bridge could be crossed if or when the time came.

For now, every drop of pleasure and enjoyment that could be wrung from this would be.

Life was good.

* * * * *

7:52 P.M.

"Uncle Ryan."

Two tiny torpedoes hurled themselves at him as he opened the door to his brother's house, attaching themselves to his legs.

"How're my two favorite girls in the whole entire universe?" Ryan reached down and wrapped an arm around both his nieces, lifting the three-year-old twin girls so they sat on his shoulders. "What are you two still doing up? Isn't it past your bedtime?"

"You missed dinner," Elise looked at him reproachfully. "Daddy said we could stay up till you got here."

"I made a wand in preschool today," Eve told him, her little hand jabbing his cheek as she spoke.

"Cool," he replied as he headed for the kitchen. "Maybe you

could solve my case with your magic wand so I don't miss dinner again."

Eve giggled, "I could make you a princess."

"Actually, sweetie, I think Uncle Ryan already has a princess in mind." Mark grinned mischievously at them as they entered the kitchen.

He glared at his younger brother. "Sorry I missed dinner," he announced.

"No problem," Mark replied, although his tone implied he was annoyed by Ryan's absence from the family meal. "Okay my little princesses, Mommy is waiting upstairs to tuck you in and read you a story. Give Uncle Ryan a kiss goodnight."

Both girls planted kisses on his cheeks.

Ryan set both girls back down on the ground. "Nighty-night, superstars." He kissed their blonde heads.

Still giggling, the little girls ran up the stairs. Ryan watched them wistfully. He'd spent years convincing himself that he didn't need a wife and kids. And yet every time he'd seen his younger brother with his family he'd known he was lying to himself. Deluding himself that he wanted to be alone because he was scared to get into another serious relationship after what happened with Katrina.

"So, you finally met her."

Turning back to face his brother, Mark's grin had been replaced by a studious stare, which was mirrored in their older brother Jack's face. Ryan knew that his family had been worried about him ever since he'd decided he wanted to spend the rest of his life alone. "Is there anyone who doesn't know I have a slight crush on Sofia Everette?"

"You really thought you were hiding that?" Jack grimaced. "Man, you really need lessons in hiding your feelings."

Seemingly he'd have to give up on the notion he had been successfully hiding his attraction to Sofia. "Yes, I met her."

"And . . ." Mark prodded.

"And what?" Now he was frustrated.

"And what's she like?" Mark asked with exaggerated patience.

Perfect, Ryan wanted to reply, but it was pointless. Sofia was already involved with someone and he was getting tired of reminding people of that. He was also getting tired of reminding himself of that. It seemed like his head and his heart couldn't get in sync. In his head he knew that Sofia was off limits, and yet in his heart it didn't change how he felt. He really wanted to believe Paige when she said she thought Sofia was interested in him, but he was reluctant to get his hopes up, especially after the disaster his last relationship had ended in.

"I'm really not in the mood to talk about Sofia Everette, okay?"

His brothers exchanged glances. "How's your case going?" Jack asked.

Jack was a homicide detective too, and they often bounced ideas off each other. "It's going nowhere." Nowhere seemed to be the big destination of his life.

"You want to run it through?"

Casting a glance at Mark, as similar as the brothers looked, all three were tall, well over six feet, all had the same bright blue eyes, the same blond hair, although Jack kept his head shaved smooth, but physical resemblance was as far as it went. Mark was the quiet one, the only one who was married with a family, the only one who had broken with family tradition and not joined the police force. He didn't like to hear the gruesome details of their cases.

"Go ahead," Mark nodded with a smile. "Just leave out anything I'd rather not know."

He exhaled slowly, "There's too many avenues," he said at last. "Too many possible options and nothing to narrow it down. Judge Everette has cut down a lot of people in his career, so he has plenty of enemies. Plus, we heard some stuff about him that may indicate he could be violent. His son Logan Everette is cold, so again plausible that he could be the killer. He's also not very smart, he has a reputation for having plenty of affairs, so he has plenty of enemies too. So we have the judge, his son, any of the women or their partners who have had affairs with either Logan, or anyone the judge climbed over on his way to the top."

"What's your gut telling you?" Jack asked.

Ryan considered this even though he already knew the answer. "The baby. It's about the baby. The killer didn't have to save it."

"Maybe he just couldn't kill an innocent baby," Mark suggested hopefully.

"Okay," Ryan nodded. "Let's say he . . ." He caught himself just in time from once again blurting out that the killer had cut Brooke's unborn child from her womb. "Let's say he couldn't kill an innocent baby," he said instead, "then why take the baby with him? Why didn't he just leave the baby with the body for us to find? Or if it wasn't personal, then the killer could have just dropped the baby off at any hospital or church or anyplace safe. So far, we've had no calls on abandoned newborns. We're running a paternity test. Hopefully, once we find out if either Logan is the baby's father, we can prove that one of them is the killer. Brooke was going to tell all about their affairs and write a book about the family, airing who knows how many well-buried secrets. Killing her kept her quiet, and by taking the baby they thought they were getting rid of any links between them and Brooke."

"What if," Jack looked thoughtful, "what if it wasn't about the father protecting himself? What if it was about protecting the baby?"

"Protecting it from the Everettes?" he asked.

"Sure, why not?" Jack mused. "Someone hates the Everettes enough to kill them off one by one, but maybe they thought this baby could still be saved."

"Makes sense to me," Mark agreed.

"Okay," Ryan mused slowly. He would run Jack's theory by Paige in the morning, see what she thought. Right now though he really needed to take a break from thinking about the case for a little while. "So, how's the McKinnley case going?" Ryan cleared his mind, sat back and listened as Jack detailed how he and his partner were closing in on a man who had abducted his ex-wife and her boyfriend and kept them locked in his basement for almost a month before killing them.

* * * * *

11:11 P.M.

Lincoln had a feeling.

It was going to be him tonight.

He had considered going against his father's wishes and accepting the police's offer of protection. But when it came down to it he was more afraid of his father than he was of this killer.

Which was pathetic.

Especially for a thirty-eight-year-old man.

Lying in his bed, in the room he had grown up in, he felt like he had so many times before. Like a pitiful, useless, weak, spineless little boy.

Maybe death wouldn't be so bad. After all, his life was a complete and utter mess.

Lincoln was in debt. *Deep* in debt.

Thankfully, he'd managed to keep this from his family. Living overseas helped. It meant his father wasn't able to keep tabs on him as easily as he could on the rest of the family.

He'd tried giving up gambling, but he was in too deep. He was addicted and nothing he'd tried could lessen the hold it had on him.

His gambling debts weren't the only thing Lincoln was ashamed of. He'd slept with Brooke Mariano, too. It was a mistake. He'd known it from the second he'd fallen into bed with her. He knew she was also sleeping with his brother and father, but he'd been drunk and depressed, and Brooke was beautiful, and as it turned out, she was also great in bed.

That was over a year ago.

As far as he knew no one had learned of his fling with Brooke. So there was no reason to suspect him as a possible father to her baby; and therefore, no reason to think of him as a potential suspect.

It also meant no one suspected him as the one who had been feeding Brooke family secrets for her book in exchange for money once the book was published.

Lincoln hated himself for what he was doing, and a little piece of him died each time he gave up another secret, but he was desperate. He needed to pay off his debts and he needed money to keep gambling. He didn't have a choice.

Just like with Sofia earlier.

He rose up and began to pace the length of his room. He hadn't wanted to restrain his little sister while their father drugged her, but again, his fear of the judge overrode everything else.

Lincoln actually liked Sofia; she was sweet, loving, caring, and kind. The only member of their family who had somehow managed to turn out nice. He shouldn't have gone along with it. He should have allowed Sofia to talk with her detective friend— maybe they could have figured out what was going on and put a stop to it.

Maybe they could have saved his life.

Lincoln was scared that it was his father who was the killer.

That was why the judge didn't want them talking to the police. That was why he wanted them all staying on the estate where he could get to them. That was also why he didn't want the police staying and offering protection.

The judge had probably found out what Brooke was up to and that Lincoln was the one helping her do it. He had probably decided to destroy the family first before anyone else had a chance to do it. He had probably…

Something cold pressed to his neck and Lincoln knew he had

been right.

It was his night to die.

AUGUST 16TH

8:03 A.M.

"Okay, people, let's get started," Belinda announced wearily. "So, what do we have from the latest crime scene?"

Ryan stifled a yawn; he hadn't gotten a minute's sleep last night. He'd just laid awake and replayed his conversation with Paige, wondering whether her insistence that Sofia was interested in him could possibly be true. Still, no matter whether anything could or would ever happen with her, it couldn't be his priority right now, this case was number one. "Youngest son Lincoln was strangled."

"Strangled repeatedly," Frankie inserted.

All eyes turned to the ME. "How do you know that?" Belinda demanded.

"Multiple ligature marks on his neck," Frankie replied.

"The killer wanted him to suffer," Paige murmured. "Just like the others."

"He had to subdue him somehow first," Ryan reminded them. "We found him tied to the bed. Maybe he caught Lincoln by surprise, used something to get him under control, a gun or a knife maybe . . ."

"A knife," Frankie interrupted again. "I found a small cut on his neck."

"Okay," Ryan resumed. "So he uses a knife to get control of him, takes him back to the bed, secures him by tying his wrists and ankles so he can take his time, enjoy himself."

"Ties him to the bed," Belinda pondered aloud. "There doesn't seem to be a sexual component to any of this. There were no signs of sexual assault on Brooke, Samantha or Gloria, right, Frankie?"

"Right," Frankie affirmed.

"It's all about the suffering," Paige said, and they all nodded their agreement.

"The suffering of *certain* family members. Samantha was killed quickly," Ryan reminded them.

"But the others . . ." Paige shuddered. "That they suffered before they died was of great importance to the killer."

"Brooke had her baby cut out of her before she was strangled. Lewis was delivered a stab wound that was intended to make sure he bled out slowly. Samantha was killed quickly, mercifully, she wasn't really an Everette so the killer wasn't invested in her death. Gloria had both her legs broken before she was drowned. And Lincoln was strangled over and over. The killer probably choked him until he passed out, then waited till he came to before strangling him all over again. Any idea of how many times he was strangled, Frankie?" Ryan asked.

"I counted at least five different marks," the ME replied.

"The killer likes it up close and personal," Paige noted. "Two stranglings, a drowning, and even with the stabbing the killer hung around to watch, before finishing him off when it became clear Lewis was taking too long to die. Everything about these murders scream that it's all personal. The killer *has* to know them. Know them well. Well enough to hate them."

"Do we have any forensics at all?" Belinda turned to Stephanie, who had been sitting quietly throughout their discussion.

Stephanie shook her head, "I wish I had something to offer, but I don't. This guy is good. Really good. He's careful and meticulous. He seems to take his time and make sure he gets everything just right. I get the feeling, though, that it's more for him than for me. I don't think he's really all that worried about leaving behind any forensics. Which would certainly make sense if your guy is one of the Everettes himself or anyone who works for them. That way he wouldn't have to worry about leaving behind DNA or fingerprints, because they would already be expected to be found all over the estate anyway."

"Good point," Belinda nodded. "Any luck finding the manuscript for the book Sofia mentioned Brooke Mariano was writing?"

Refusing to allow himself to think about Sofia Everette again until this was all over, Ryan answered, "Unfortunately no. Her apartment was thoroughly checked out, no manuscript."

"Talk to Sofia and the gardener. They seem to be the two people we have who knew her the best, see if either of them can think of anywhere Brooke may have hidden this manuscript. She was sleeping with the judge and his son, she knew their secrets, she had to know that they might come after her, so it would make sense that she would want to keep it someplace safe."

Ryan could tell their boss was ready to dismiss them, but there was a theory he wanted to pose to everyone first. "What if the cases aren't linked? What if we're looking for two different killers?" he asked.

"What?" Belinda shot him a confused stare, mirrored in the faces of the room's other occupants.

"I was talking to Jack last night. He suggested that maybe Brooke's killer wasn't trying to protect themselves from being found out, but rather they were trying to protect the baby. Maybe that's why he took the child and why he hasn't dropped it off anywhere."

"Maybe he didn't drop it off anywhere because it's already dead," Belinda reminded him.

"But what if it's not? Let's just assume for the moment that the baby survived. That whoever killed Brooke has the baby with them right now. Or at least, that they know where it is," he added, thinking that if the killer was indeed Logan Senior or Junior, they could have spirited it out of the country with a nanny. "Let's say that they killed Brooke to get the baby, to protect it," he continued. "Well, I was just thinking that maybe that doesn't fit in with the other killings."

"Okay," Belinda agreed, nodding slowly. "So why kill the others?"

"Maybe we were right, and it is someone with a grudge against the Everette family. We all agree that there are plenty of possible suspects who could hate the family—what if one of them heard about Brooke's murder and decided it would be the perfect time to exact revenge and take advantage of the fact that we were distracted by the murder of a pregnant woman and the abduction of her child?"

"It's possible, I guess," Belinda acknowledged reluctantly. "But quite a big risk. Breaking into an estate with superb security, killing some pretty powerful people right under the noses of the police."

"If Stephanie is right, though, and it is someone who knows their presence and evidence of them being there isn't suspicious, then they might just be confident enough to give it a go," Ryan reasoned.

"And whoever is doing this has clearly already gone off the deep end," Paige added. "The level of suffering inflicted on the victims is evidence of that."

"All right, let's keep both options open for the time being," Belinda pronounced. "Paige, Ryan, go talk to the gardener, and then see if you can track down Sofia Everette and talk to her. See if either of them can give us any ideas as to where this mysterious manuscript might be. At the moment that seems like it might be our best shot at finding our killer or killers."

* * * * *

10:29 A.M.

"Sofia?"

She groaned as someone shook her shoulder. She didn't want to wake up. She wanted to stay right where she was, warm and comfortable inside her snugly little cocoon.

"Sofia?" the voice prodded again. "Come on, honey, wake up."

She was given another shake, which seemed to pop her eyes open almost against her will. She struggled to focus on the face hovering over her. "Edmund?" she asked, her voice sounding groggy and weak.

"Yeah, it's me," Edmund brushed a lock of hair from her face, tucking it behind her ear.

"What are you doing here?" She felt confused and disoriented. "And where is here? Where am I?"

"You're at your father's house," Edmund told her.

"Why aren't I at home? Did I pass out again?" Wondering whether she'd had another episode while she'd been here earlier. She had been here earlier, right?

"Kind of."

Edmund sounded mad. Studying him, his hazel eyes were filled with a mixture of anger and concern. "What do you mean 'kind of'? What's up, Edmund?"

"What's the last thing you remember?"

Sofia scrunched her brow in concentration, trying to force her gooey mind to focus. "My father summoned us all here after Gloria was killed."

"Do you remember what happened while you were talking to him?"

"I don't know, it's all fuzzy. What do you know, Edmund?" She was tired and not in the mood for games, her head felt like it had been filled with rocks.

Edmund sighed. "Isabella called me this morning in a panic because she couldn't wake you up. She was worried because you've been sick, and yesterday your father . . ." he trailed off

Her stomach dropped. "What did he do to me?"

Reaching for her hand, "Isabella said he drugged you."

Her head began to spin and she was glad she was lying down. Sofia wouldn't put it past her father to drug her. The judge was angry that she wouldn't do as he wanted and keep her mouth shut when it came to talking to the police. But drugging her against her will? It made her feel physically ill.

"Sofia?" Edmund was watching her with thinly veiled concern.

"Is Isabella sure?"

"She said she came in and Lincoln was pinning you against his chest, and your father had a syringe full of sedatives which he administered to you and you passed out."

"Does he intend to keep me here as a prisoner?" This house and her old childhood bedroom were filling her with an intense claustrophobia. She wanted out of this place immediately.

"I convinced him to let me take you back to your place, so long as I keep an eye on you. Which given what's going on with your family I am more than happy to do."

Forcing herself into a sitting position so she could throw her arms around Edmund's neck, she felt relieved beyond measure. "You are a life saver. How can I ever thank you enough?"

Edmund kissed the top of her head. "No need for thanks. I love you—there isn't anything I wouldn't do to make sure you're safe."

Resting against Edmund, she was tired and sleep was beginning to trickle back into her mind. She was about to give in to it when Edmund's arms tightened around her.

"Honey, there's something I have to tell you."

Something in Edmund's voice had the hairs on the back of her neck standing up. "Someone else is dead," she whispered dully. "Who?"

"Lincoln."

She let out a gasp. The last time she'd seen the youngest of her older brothers, he was holding her down to help their father drug her. This was a nightmare. She almost couldn't believe that it was happening. All that was left of her family was her father, her oldest brother and his wife, her little sister, and herself.

"Sofia? You still with me?" Edmund gently eased her back so she was lying against the pillows.

"We have to call Ryan," she murmured, wishing desperately that he was here right now. As much as she loved Edmund, she felt safe with Ryan.

"The cop who's working your family's case?"

She nodded, "He and Detective Hood were supposed to be coming by after the family meeting yesterday." As the drugs her father had given her slowly worked their way out of her system, her memory of the events of the previous day were trickling back. "That's why Father called the family meeting, because Ryan and his partner were going to come over and he wanted me to agree not to say anything to them. Only I wouldn't."

"You trust this detective?" Edmund was examining her closely.

"Yes." Sofia didn't have a glimmer of doubt about Ryan's trustworthiness.

"Okay then, let's call him, let him know what's going on."

"Not here, though." Sofia couldn't be sure who might be listening to her here on the estate, especially given the fact that her father didn't trust her.

"Agreed. Let's get you dressed and back home, then we'll call your detective. Think you can stand up?"

She grimaced, her stomach was roiling, her head was still spinning, and she felt like she could curl up and go to sleep for a million years. "I don't feel so good," she told Edmund.

"You don't look so good, either," Edmund agreed. "We'll stop by your doctor on the way back to your place, get you checked out, make sure your father didn't cause more damage with that stunt of his. Come on, let's get you dressed."

As Sofia allowed Edmund to help her out of bed and into some clothes, she found herself counting the hours until she could see Ryan again.

* * * * *

2:12 P.M.

"At least now we know she's safe," Paige assured him as they pulled to a stop in front of Sofia's home.

"For now, at least," Ryan agreed, catching himself before he could jump from the car and run to the front door. As soon as he'd received the call from Sofia asking him and Paige to come and meet her at her place they had jumped in the car and sped all the way here.

"We'll keep her safe, Ryan," his partner assured him again.

Thinking of what Paige had said yesterday, asking him if he was sure that Sofia was involved because it seemed like she liked him. He hardly dared to believe that might be true. Reaching the door, he knocked sharply. He couldn't quite convince himself that Sofia was okay until he saw her with his own eyes. A moment later the door swung open and he froze.

"You must be Detective Xander and Detective Hood," a young man with somber hazel eyes and dark blond hair, greeted them warmly. The same man that had been there the night Sofia collapsed. The same man who had frantically dashed to her side as she lay unconscious. The same man who had cradled her gently in his arms. This was Sofia's boyfriend. "I'm Edmund, please come in. Sofia's in the sitting room." He held the door open and led them down the hallway.

Seething with jealousy, it was taking every ounce of Ryan's strength to keep walking toward the sitting room rather than darting back out the door. His jealousy ebbed a little as they reached the sitting room and he saw Sofia lying on the couch, propped up against some pillows and covered with a blanket. She looked weak and exhausted but her eyes were alert and she moved to stand when she saw them.

"Don't get up," Edmund told her, pressing a hand to her shoulder to keep her in place.

"Hi, Ryan," Sofia shot him the sweetest smile.

"Sofia," he nodded. If her boyfriend hadn't been standing right beside them then he could have sworn that Paige was right and that Sofia was interested in him.

"Detective Hood," Sofia added, seemingly remembering his partner.

"Call me Paige," his partner replied.

"So, this is the cute detective you were telling me about." Edmund shot both him and Sofia a bemused smile.

"*Edmund*," Sofia's pale cheeks flushed a bright pink.

"Sorry," Edmund grinned, looking like he couldn't be less sorry if he tried.

"What?" Ryan stammered, sure he must have misheard.

Taking in his shocked face, Sofia and Edmund exchanged glances, then both began to laugh. "You thought Edmund and I were involved?" she giggled.

The look on his face must have confirmed that he did.

"Remember when I told you my father disinherited me because I wouldn't marry the man he told me to?" Sofia asked.

"Uh huh," was all he could manage.

"Well that man was Edmund. I mean I love Edmund, and he is one of the most important people in my life." She shot the other man a warm smile. "But we're just friends. We met in preschool as a couple of three-year-olds, and we've been best friends ever since. Now Edmund is married to our other best friend, Mary."

"Sofia likes you," Edmund sat beside her on the couch. "So, tell me everything about you." He grew serious, "Are you a jerk?"

"Edmund," Sofia admonished.

"Sorry." Again Edmund didn't look even the least bit repentant.

"I-I don't think so," Ryan stammered, caught off guard.

"There is no *think*. No jerks date my Sofia, so I'll ask you again:

are you a jerk?"

"Edmund," Sofia said again, this time lightly punching his shoulder.

"I'm sorry, Sofia, but I need to know what kind of guy he is since he's seemingly captured your heart."

Unable to produce an answer, less because of Edmund's inscrutable stare and more because of the knowledge that Sofia actually felt the same way about him as he felt about her.

"He's not a jerk," Paige answered.

"Good," Edmund nodded, pleased. "Sofia's not either."

"I know; she seems pretty amazing." Paige couldn't hide her amusement.

"She is," Edmund nodded. "And she deserves someone who knows it. So, Detective Xander, you know she's amazing?"

"Edmund, this is so embarrassing," Sofia moaned.

"That's not my fault," Edmund said evenly. "You're the one that cut yourself off since you got sick. She thinks she's dying, so she stopped looking for someone," he explained.

Sofia groaned and buried her face in her hands.

"Sorry, honey, but it's true." Edmund patted her arm comfortingly.

"I know she's amazing," Ryan told Edmund seriously. Sofia lifted her head and her eyes met his, hers shining with delight.

"Okay, then," Edmund's grin returned. "I'll give you my number, we'll talk some more."

"Well I almost hate to do this," Paige announced, "but we have some things we need to talk about."

Instantly they all grew serious. "My father drugged me," Sofia informed them.

"He did what?" Ryan demanded, furious.

"I hate that guy," Edmund muttered, clenching his fists.

Sofia placed a soothing hand on her friend's arm. "Yesterday, before you came, he called a family meeting. He wanted all of us to agree that we would let him do all the talking. I wouldn't, he got mad, and he . . ." Sofia's voice wobbled, "he had a syringe full of sedatives. Lincoln held me still while my father drugged me. That's the last time I saw my brother." Her voice grew panicked, tears began to trickle down her cheeks. "That's the last time I'll ever see my brother and he was holding me against my will so my father could drug me." Sobbing now, she threw herself into Edmund's arms.

Edmund held her and rubbed her back for a moment, before looking up. "Detective Xander, here you go."

Ryan took the spot Edmund vacated on the couch, as Sofia's friend gently moved her into his arms. She twisted her hands into his shirt and clung to him as she wept. "Shh," he murmured, stroking her hair. "I'm sorry, Sofia. I'm sorry about what your father did, and I'm sorry about your brother."

"I was praying you'd get there before my father injected me," she whispered against his chest.

His grip on her tightened as he held back his rage at her father's actions only because it wasn't what Sofia needed right now. "I'm sorry we didn't get there in time to stop him."

"How did you convince your father to let you come home?" Paige asked.

"Edmund." Sofia lifted her head from Ryan's shoulder to smile at her friend.

Edmund smiled back encouragingly. "I told her father I'd keep an eye on her. The judge likes me." It was clear the feeling wasn't mutual.

Sofia brushed away her tears and rested back against the pillows, embarrassment lending a little color to her pale face. "I'm sorry, I don't usually cry like that."

"No need to apologize," Ryan assured her. "After everything you've been through, you're entitled to a good cry."

She smiled at him, reaching out to take tight hold of one of his hands. "What did you talk to my family about?" Sofia asked.

"We were trying to ascertain whether any member of your

family had any enemies who may do all of this," he replied.

"Can you think of anyone who'd want to hurt you, Sofia?" Paige queried.

"No, I don't think so," she shook her head.

"Sofia, what about last year?" Edmund's face had creased in concern.

Ryan felt his own face crease with worry. "What happened last year?"

Sighing tiredly, Sofia responded, "I had a stalker."

"She's downplaying it," Edmund frowned. "The guy was hard core. Sent her letters and gifts all the time, broke into her house when she was out, kept calling her even though she kept changing her number."

"Did the police catch him?" Ryan's chest had tightened uncomfortably.

"No," Sofia shook her head wearily.

"He disappeared when she got sick," Edmund elaborated. "Everything just stopped, but it still creeps me out that he's out there somewhere, especially when she's clearly in no condition to deal with him if he comes back."

Sofia frowned but didn't disagree.

"Did the police have any leads?" he demanded, the thought of someone stalking Sofia turning his blood to ice. The fact that the stalker was still out there added to his fear a hundredfold.

"No." Sofia sank further into the pillows; she was beginning to fade.

Ryan looked to Edmund for more information. "The police have all the letters and gifts, but they had no suspects," Sofia's friend explained. "They didn't find any prints or anything from any of the break-ins either."

"If it's someone out for revenge against my family, why would they steal Brooke's baby?" Sofia asked. Her voice had gone faint and she looked like she was fighting to keep her eyes open. Ryan still held her hand but it had gone limp in his grip.

"I don't know, cupcake, but we'll sort it out," he assured her. "I think that's enough for now, though; you look like you need to rest."

"I want to help," she protested weakly.

"I know you do, but you're exhausted," Ryan reached out to tuck her hair behind her ear. Sofia caught his hand and pressed it to her cheek. Aware of Paige and Edmund's eyes on them, he self-consciously brushed his thumb along her cheekbone. "We offered police protection to your family. They refused, but the offer is still on the table for you."

"She'll take it," Edmund answered immediately.

"Edmund," Sofia looked frustrated.

"Sofia," Edmund shot back, equally frustrated. "They're offering, you take it. So you don't end up dead," he reminded her.

"I'll take it," Sofia nodded.

"Good," Ryan and Edmund murmured simultaneously.

"Now you go get some rest," Ryan told her.

"Maybe I will take a little nap before tonight," she relented.

"Sofia, you are not going to that charity event tonight." Edmund was glaring at her, daring her to disagree.

"Yes I am," Sofia frowned. "Don't try to tell me what I can and can't do, Edmund. I don't like that."

Edmund didn't back down. "Sofia, you're not strong enough to handle that tonight. Especially when there's someone out there who's killing off your family," he reminded her.

"So what do you want me to do?" Tears were brimming in her eyes but she angrily brushed them away. "You want me to lock myself away until Ryan and Paige find this guy?"

"Yes," Edmund nodded emphatically.

"And what if they never find him?" she demanded. "You want me to give up what's left of my life and lock myself away in some safe house? What about *you*?" Sofia turned her frown in Ryan's direction. "Do you think I shouldn't go tonight, too?"

Hesitating, Ryan didn't think she should go tonight, but unlike

Edmund who didn't seem to care if he made Sofia mad or not, he wasn't confident enough with her yet to upset her. "I'm not sure it's the best idea," he ventured carefully. "After your father drugged you, and another of your brothers was killed last night, maybe the safe house idea isn't such a bad one."

Growling, she wiped away the tears that trickled down her cheeks. "I'm only crying because I'm mad and tired." Lifting her eyes to Paige, "You with them? You think I shouldn't go to the charity event tonight?"

"Sorry, sweetie," Paige grimaced. "I'm just not sure you're up to it."

"Well, I'm going, and there's nothing any of you can do to stop me." She looked at them all defiantly from eyes she could barely hold open.

"Sofia," Ryan took her hands, "we're just worried about you."

She calmed a little, "Which is very sweet, but I'm going tonight. This is the first gala I've held since the one where I...collapsed," she forced the word out. "I need to go. I need to know that being sick hasn't cost me everything. So I am going to go upstairs and get some sleep, and then I'm going to get ready for tonight."

"If we can't stop you, then maybe we can use it to our advantage," Paige suggested.

"What do you mean?" Edmund was eyeing Paige warily.

"No," Ryan knew what Paige wanted to do and no way was he going to let her do it.

"What?" Edmund looked more concerned.

"Ryan . . ."

"No, Paige," he repeated more forcefully, cutting her off.

"No to what?" Sofia asked.

"She wants to use you as bait," he answered tightly. "Try to lure this guy out."

"No way," Edmund said frantically. "She can barely stand up on her own and you want to use her as bait to try and catch a killer who's already killed her mother, two of her brothers and her sister-in-law? Are you insane?" Edmund ranted.

"She'll be protected bait," Paige soothed. "We'll have officers all over the place."

"Okay," Sofia nodded. "I'll do it."

"Sofia!" Ryan and Edmund exclaimed.

Sofia ignored them, "Whatever you want me to do, I'll do; anything to make this nightmare end."

"This is stupid!" Edmund exploded. "You're upset because you feel like you've lost control of your life since you got sick, so you're going to make yourself bait for some psychotic serial killer? That's stupid, Sofia! You're being ridiculous."

"You really want to do this?" Ryan asked. He agreed with Edmund's assessment of Sofia's logic, but he decided to attempt a different route with her.

"Yes," she nodded firmly.

"Then I'll go with you; kind of like your own personal bodyguard."

"What?" Edmund whirled around to face him. "I thought you liked her; you can't possibly think this is a good idea."

"I don't," Ryan conceded grimly. "But she's going to do it regardless. The best I can do is make sure she stays safe."

"I'll go set this up, then," Paige nodded. "We've got your back, Sofia—we won't let anything happen to you."

"This is ridiculous," Edmund muttered as Paige headed out. "I'm going to call Mary, maybe she can talk some sense into you."

"Are you sure?" Ryan asked Sofia once again when they were alone.

"I have to. I can't lose any more of my life; I don't want to end up dead or locked away in some safe house." Her serious frown smoothed away, replaced by a shy smile. "So, are you only coming tonight to be my bodyguard?"

His fear for her safety was immediately replaced by a nervous anticipation. "I'd like to be more."

"Maybe you could be my date. Or at least date-slash-bodyguard," her silver eyes flickered with trepidation.

"You don't have to do this," Ryan pleaded desperately, instantly back on edge.

"Yeah, I do," she whispered, lifting a trembling hand and running it through his hair, then tracing her fingertips down his cheek.

Catching her hand, he brought it to his lips, pressing a kiss to it. "Just promise me you'll be careful."

"You'll keep me safe," Sofia murmured, her eyes fluttering closed as she drifted off, unable to fight sleep any longer.

As he settled her on the couch, Ryan prayed that her blind faith in him was well founded and he could indeed keep her safe. The possibility that she would be the next Everette to not survive the night was too horrifying to contemplate.

* * * * *

9:42 P.M.

"Come in here and take it easy for a minute," Ryan led her out of the main reception room and into a smaller, quieter room.

"I'm okay," Sofia assured him, not wanting to admit she was struggling. The charity event had been going only a little over an hour and already she was fading.

"No, you're pushing yourself too hard." He sat her gently down in a chair and began to rub her shoulders.

Sofia let his kneading hands soothe her jangled nerves. As much as she wanted to end this, and was prepared to do whatever necessary to make it happen, it didn't change the fact that she was scared. Edmund was right. She had lost a lot being sick, and she wasn't going to lose anything more because some lunatic was out to slaughter her family. If making herself bait was the only way to stop this, then she would do it. But knowing that the monster

108

who was killing off her family could be here right this second and planning on making her his next victim was terrifying. The only thing that was giving her the strength to keep it together was Ryan. He hadn't left her side; his warm, solid hand holding hers as she made the rounds, spending time talking with each of her guests. She was aware of him constantly scanning the crowd, checking for anything or anyone who could be a threat to her. It was comforting. If it wasn't for him, she was pretty sure she would have fallen apart already.

"Sofia, you should have told me you had a stalker," Ryan admonished, breaking the silence.

"We only just met a couple of days ago," she reminded him. "And it's not like the first thing I say upon meeting people is, 'Hi I'm Sofia, and I had a stalker until he disappeared off the face of the planet.' Besides, I've been a little preoccupied with what's been going on with my family. And the stalker is gone now, so it's no longer an issue."

"Did you ever think maybe he was arrested on other charges and is in jail, and that when he comes back out he'll pick back up straight where he left off?" he asked gently.

She let out a defeated sigh. "No."

"I don't mean to scare you, honey. I know you already have a lot on your plate right now." He dropped a kiss to the top of her head. "I just want you to be prepared in case he comes back."

A little thrill tingled through her as he called her honey. Other than Edmund, no one had ever used any term of endearment with her. Twisting around so they were facing each other. "You always come to my charity events," she commented, catching the surprise that flitted through his eyes as he realized that she'd noticed him. Ryan had caught her attention many months ago, the way his blue eyes studied her so longingly as he watched her every move. "I was going to talk to you that night, before I passed out."

"You were?" his brow creased in disbelief.

"Mmhmm," she nodded. "The way you looked at me, it made

me feel . . ." she trailed off, searching for the right word, "wanted. Like I was the only person in the world. So I was going to talk to you, only then I fainted, and I was sick, and it didn't seem fair to start something with you." She was still concerned about that. She was sick. The doctors didn't know what was wrong with her, and there were no guarantees she'd ever get better. It didn't seem right to drag Ryan into all of that.

Before Ryan could respond, there was a knock on the door and it swung open. "Okay, Sofia," Paige announced. "It's time for your speech. You ready?"

This was her focus now, so she pulled herself together. She would worry about Ryan and her illness later. "I'm ready."

"Are you really sure you want to do this?" Ryan's bright blue eyes were filled to the brim with concern. "It's not too late to change your mind."

"But I haven't changed my mind," she told him gently.

He gave a resigned sigh, "Then you don't leave my sight, okay? You stay where I can see you at all times, and when you give your speech, I'll be right beside you."

"Okay," Sofia replied, shivering anxiously.

Tugging her to her feet, Ryan paused, sighed, opened his mouth to say something, then apparently changed his mind and snapped it shut. Sofia was about to say something herself when his hands suddenly cupped her face, and he brought his lips to hers, kissing her softly and sweetly. Too soon he broke contact, took her hand and pulled her to the door. "Come on. Let's get this over with so we can get you home safely."

She let him lead her back through the reception room, barely stopping to give her a chance to greet well-wishers. Before she knew it, Sofia was standing at the microphone. The room grew quiet; all eyes were expectantly on her, and for a moment, she froze. Any one of the faces looking back at her could be the killer. Feeling lightheaded, she almost threw herself into Ryan's arms, but then she caught sight of Paige's calm face smiling at her encouragingly. Paige was there, as were several of Ryan's colleagues. They wouldn't let anything happen to her.

Taking a deep breath, she forced herself to calm down, and began the speech the police had given her to read. She eased her face into a well-practiced smile. "I want to thank you all so much for coming tonight. Your support means a lot, especially given what my family is going through at the moment. As you know, my family has worked tirelessly in the name of many charities, donating millions to help and improve the lives of those less fortunate than ourselves. My father . . ."

Sofia never got any further than that in her speech. A bang echoed throughout the ballroom and something pierced her chest, sending her flying to the floor.

Screams erupted from every direction.

"Sofia!" Ryan dropped to his knees at her side. She could feel his fingers press to her neck, then heard his small exhale of relief. As if to reassure himself, he quickly unbuttoned her blouse, his hands running over the Kevlar vest the police had given her to wear. He let out a shuddering breath, "You're okay, Sofia, it got the vest."

While that was true, it still hurt worse than anything else she'd ever experienced. Her chest ached and she was struggling to draw a proper breath. Her head was spinning and she'd clenched her eyes shut in a vain attempt to still it.

"Ryan?" Paige's voice.

"She's okay. I got this, Paige; go find the shooter," Ryan assured his partner. "Sofia? Open your eyes, cupcake." He was working to keep the panic from his voice.

"I can't," unable to keep the tremble from her own voice. "It hurts."

"I know it does, honey. The bullet probably cracked your ribs. EMT's will be here soon. Open your eyes for me."

Fighting to do as he asked, Sofia managed to pry her eyes open. "Did they get the shooter?"

"Not yet." Anger and fear battled in his face.

So, she'd done this for nothing. Let them use her as bait, taken a bullet to the heart which would have killed her had it not been for the Kevlar vest, all for nothing. She let her eyes fall closed again, the pain in her chest was overwhelming.

"We'll get him, cupcake," Ryan assured her. "I'm going to take you out of here, okay? We'll wait for the medics in another room; there are too many reporters in here."

As Ryan gently picked her up and carried her from the room in his strong arms, Sofia realized this was the second time from two that she'd been carried from one of her charity events to a waiting ambulance. She wondered whether it was possible for her life to spin any more out of control. Then she wondered nothing else, her mind faded to black as she passed out.

* * * * *

10:11 P.M.

That had been close.

Too close.

For a moment there it had seemed like everything was over.

That would have been a nightmare. Especially when half the Everette family was already dead. Halfway was good, but it still meant that half of that despicable family still lived. Logan Senior and Logan Junior were the worst; taking them out would be deliciously satisfying. Simone wasn't really an Everette. It was unfortunate that she was caught up in all of this, but she was, so she had to die too.

Sofia, on the other hand, well, that one was particularly unpleasant. There would be no pleasure derived from the death of Sofia Everette. The one member of the Everette family who was actually a decent human being. On the one hand, the desire to let the woman live was overwhelming; on the other, it would mean that the Everette family wouldn't be completely destroyed.

Still, appearances had to be kept up. The police expected another of the Everette family to be dead by morning and so an attempt on her life had to be made. Thankfully, the police had been on the ball enough to make sure Sofia was wearing Kevlar, and while she probably had a horrible bruise and perhaps some broken ribs, she was alive. And honestly that made...

"Isabella?"

Isabella started at the voice and sudden appearance of someone behind her. Turning, she found her sister's knight in shining armor studying her with worried blue eyes.

"How's Sofia?" she asked, genuinely hoping for good news. She sincerely wanted there to be a way to keep her older sister alive. Sofia was the only member of their family who had ever cared about her, who had ever looked out for her, who had ever loved her.

"She's unconscious, but she's stable. I just left her with the medics to come and check on you, then I'm going to ride in the ambulance to the hospital with her. How're you doing?"

Ryan Xander was watching her with such sincere concern that for a moment Isabella was almost tempted to tell him everything. The detective was a good guy and she was glad her sister had found him. Sofia deserved some happiness. And while Sofia was under Ryan's watchful care she'd be safe from their family's curse.

"I'm okay," she assured Ryan.

"Do you want to come with us to the hospital? Or I can get my partner to see you safely home if you're tired?"

"My father and brother are both here; I'm sure one of them will take me home." Isabella still had the gun hidden in her pocket, it would have been too risky to try dumping it while the place was crawling with cops. And as Sofia's younger sister, no one had given her a second thought, nor had it occurred to them to check she wasn't the shooter.

"Isabella, that house isn't safe," Ryan said hesitantly. "Why don't you come home with me and Sofia tonight; stay at her place. I'll be there with her, you'll be safe."

"That's very thoughtful, Detective Xander," forcing her usually serious face into a smile. "But I'll be fine."

He opened his mouth to argue when one of the EMT's called out to him that they were ready to leave for the hospital, so he shot her a grave stare instead. "It's Ryan. I have to go; do you still have my card?"

She nodded.

"So you have my number, call me if you need anything. Really, Isabella, for anything."

As she watched Ryan rush off toward the ambulance, Isabella decided it was a sign. She was glad that Sofia had survived; she'd never really wanted to kill her sister. The fact that Sofia had indeed survived had convinced Isabella to let her sister live. Which meant it was time to focus on the next murder. It was a toss-up between Logan Senior and Logan Junior. Whichever one she decided on, she was going to enjoy it.

AUGUST 17TH

1:36 A.M.

"We're here," a voice murmured beside her.

Where was here and why did her eyes feel so heavy?

"Sofia? Wake up, cupcake, we're home," a hand gently cupped her face, fingers brushing across her temple.

And then everything clicked. 'Here' was her house. The voice was Ryan's. And he was bringing her home from the hospital after her disaster of a charity event last night. Her chest still ached, and she had a huge bruise forming on her breast, right above her heart. If she hadn't been wearing the Kevlar, she'd be dead.

Prying open her eyes, she mustered up a smile for Ryan. "Hey."

"Hey yourself," he smiled back. "Can you walk?"

"I think so," she said, unsure whether she could or not, but determined to try.

Ryan took her hands and tugged her to her feet. He quickly moved an arm to wrap around her waist as her knees buckled. "I got you," he whispered in her ear.

Leaning into him, grateful for his strength, Sofia hoped when this was all over, somehow the doctors could manage to find out what was wrong with her and fix it so she could have this sweet, caring guy.

"Hey," Ryan's hand cupped her face again, his thumb brushing away tears from her cheek. "You're crying. You okay?"

"Just tired." She raised her hand to cover Ryan's and held it there, drinking in his warmth and strength.

"It's been a crazy couple of days," he said, bending down to

115

kiss her forehead. "Come on, you want to try a few steps?"

"Yeah," nodding tiredly, no longer sure she did, but too stubborn not to give it a go. Leaning heavily on Ryan, they started toward the house. She made it halfway before she was too breathless to take another step.

"Had enough?" Ryan asked gently.

Managing a nod, Sofia let out a weary sigh of relief as Ryan gathered her up into his arms and carried her the rest of the way to the house.

"Sofia." Edmund rushed at them the second they came through the front door, snatching her from Ryan's arms and squeezing her tightly.

"I'm okay, Edmund," she assured her friend. "I just have a bruise," *and two broken ribs* she added to herself, but didn't want to worry Edmund more by telling him.

"You," Edmund glared at Ryan, she could feel the anger bubbling inside him. "I don't like you anymore."

"Edmund," she warned. It wasn't Ryan's fault she'd been shot; it was hers. She was the one who had insisted on letting the police use her as bait.

"No, Sofia," Edmund growled. "He said he'd keep you safe, and he didn't. You were shot."

"It wasn't Ryan's fault," she insisted. "Let me go."

"No. I almost lost you tonight," Edmund said fiercely, and she could feel his whole body shudder.

"But you didn't," she soothed, pressing a kiss to his cheek.

"Edmund's right. I'm sorry, Sofia," Ryan's blue eyes were devastated.

Ryan had already apologized to her at least fifty times in the last few hours. He'd apologized when she'd regained consciousness in the ambulance. He'd apologized while he held her hand in the ER. And he'd apologized in the car on the ride home. "It wasn't your fault, Ryan," she assured him again, just as she'd assured him each other time he'd apologized.

"It was mine."

All three of their heads swiveled to Paige who stood in the doorway, her face a picture of earnest dismay.

"No, Paige," she assured Ryan's partner. "It wasn't your fault either."

"I promised we'd keep you safe and you were shot," Paige's brown eyes were dismal.

She pushed gently till Edmund reluctantly loosened his grip and lowered her to the ground. She was tired and in pain and she was getting mildly irritated with everyone for blaming themselves. She wasn't a child. She'd made her decision weighing up the risks versus the potential gain. Heading to the lounge room, she dropped wearily down onto one of the sofas. "You guys need to stop blaming yourselves. I don't blame either of you."

"Sofia . . ." Edmund begun.

"Edmund, I'm tired; please, just let it go," she begged.

He looked like he wanted to argue but wisely opted to keep his mouth shut. "Okay, I'll let you get some rest." He crouched beside her, "Mary and I will come check on you tomorrow." Edmund made it to the door then stopped, turning to face Ryan, his fury had melted away replaced by pure fear. "Don't let anything happen to her."

"I won't," Ryan promised.

"Are you two going to be okay here on your own tonight?" Paige asked once Edmund had left.

"We'll be fine," Ryan assured his partner. "No one is getting to Sofia tonight."

"All right," Paige agreed reluctantly. "Call if you need me. Sofia, try to get some sleep. We'll find this guy."

Finally, alone, they sat side by side on her couch. Sofia took Ryan's hand and entwined their fingers.

"Sofia," he began, watching her hesitantly, "I'm not good at knowing what to say. If you're looking for a guy who's always going to say and do the right thing, then . . ." he trailed off.

She frowned slightly. "Why would I need someone who always says and does the right thing?" she asked.

"Because . . ." Ryan stammered, "because you're sick, and with everything going on with your family, fragile and . . ."

Sofia let out a frustrated breath, she was *so* tired of everyone treating her like she was helpless.

"See," Ryan looked devastated. "I always say the wrong thing. I always make things worse. I just meant, you're vulnerable right now and I don't want to make things worse."

Growling irritably, she stood and paced.

"I'm sorry," Ryan was watching her helplessly.

Sofia would have been more annoyed had it not been for the panicked regret on Ryan's face. She took a calming breath, "No, I'm sorry. I didn't mean to lose my temper. I'm just so tired of being sick, of everyone being so careful around me and treating me like I can't do things for myself anymore, because . . ." she trailed off.

"Because you can't?" Ryan finished gently.

"Yeah," she sighed. "I just hate how being sick has changed my life. My father wants to use it as an excuse to get me under his thumb. Take advantage of the fact that I'm..." *weak*, she'd been going to say, but couldn't make the word come out of her mouth, even if it was true. "Not as strong as I used to be," she finished instead.

"I'm sorry, Sofia," Ryan said again. His hands balled into fists, his face a mixture of concern and guilt.

She was scared that what she was about to say was true. "You're afraid of me. Afraid you'll hurt me, afraid I'll break, afraid I'll die," she finished, watching him closely to gauge his reaction.

"Well, there is a serial killer after you," he joked weakly.

"Don't," she warned, annoyed again. "I'm serious."

"I'm sorry, Sofia," again he looked devastated that he'd said the wrong thing. She wondered what could make this gorgeous, kind, thoughtful guy so self-conscious.

"Stop apologizing to me," she glared. "I might die, Ryan," she'd thought a lot about that the last few months. "You're going to find whoever is killing my family, but the doctors might never find out what's wrong with me. If you can't deal with that, then you shouldn't get involved with me. Can you deal with it?"

"No."

She staggered back as though he'd slapped her. It was fair enough. He had every right not to get involved with her just to watch her die. But it still hurt.

He wrung his hands together. "That didn't come out right," Ryan looked distressed, like he wanted to come and hold her in his arms but was afraid of upsetting her again. "I meant just like you believe that I'm going to find this killer, I believe that the doctors are going to find out what's wrong with you."

Letting out a breath she hadn't known she was holding, Ryan's confidence brought hope to her own heart. Impulsively, she crossed back to the couch and pressed her lips against his, kissing him deeply. "I don't want you to ever be afraid of me, Ryan," she told him seriously when she finally pulled away.

"I just don't want to hurt you, cupcake; I really like you," he said shyly.

"I really like you, too," she smiled weakly, a headache was beginning to pound at her temples, her vision already starting to spin, even aside from being shot, she'd overdone it last night. "Why do you call me cupcake?" she asked.

"Oh, I didn't even realize that I did that," he responded, surprised. Then he grimaced, "It's too cheesy, right?"

"It's cheesy," Sofia grinned. "But I like it. I always wanted a cheesy pet name. Why cupcake, though?"

Ryan chuckled, "I guess because it's what my dad always called my mom. I can call you something else if you don't like it."

"No, I like it," she assured him, the term of endearment was sweet. Wearily she rested her head against Ryan's shoulder.

"You're tired," his arms came around her.

"Mmmhmm," she nodded against him, her head too heavy to lift.

"Where's your medication?"

"Bathroom cabinet," she whispered, pressing her eyes closed to try to ease the pain in her head.

Gently, he laid her back to rest against the couch, and hurried from the room. Sofia attempted some of the breathing exercises her doctor had taught her to try and quell the nausea mounting in her stomach. They weren't working.

"Here you go," Ryan murmured, slipping an arm beneath her shoulders and raising her up. He dropped her pills into her hand and held the glass of water to her lips. Once she'd swallowed them he picked her up without a word and carried her up the stairs.

As he moved to tuck her under the covers she caught his hand, "Stay with me, please. I'm scared, Ryan."

He gave her a reassuring smile, "Of more nightmares?"

"More like living nightmares. Who's going to be dead when I wake up in the morning?" Tears trickled from her eyes, "What if I'm next? The killer already tried once. What if they come back and next time I'm not so lucky?"

"Shh," Ryan soothed, stretching out on the bed beside her, his arms warm and strong around her. "I'm going to be right here, no one is going to get to you. And if you wake up scared, I'll be here to hold you. No one is going to hurt you. I'll be right here."

"Promise?" she begged.

"Promise," he kissed away her tears.

As she snuggled herself against Ryan and let her eyes fall closed, she held on to that thought and prayed for good dreams.

* * * * *

8:22 A.M.

"I'm looking forward to this," Ryan told Paige as they pulled into the driveway of the Everette family estate. About an hour ago he had been wakened from a deep sleep by the buzzing of his phone. It had been his partner, with news that the results of the paternity test were in.

Judge Logan Everette II was the father.

Based on the fact that he was the child's father, that he had lied about his affairs with her, and that he had been at home on the estate where Brooke had been murdered on the night of her death, they had enough to arrest him. And Ryan couldn't be happier. For drugging and imprisoning Sofia against her will alone, the judge deserved to lose his freedom. If he really had killed Brooke and stolen her child, then he deserved to die.

Sofia didn't yet know that her father was about to be arrested. She had still been fast asleep, her body draped across his, when he'd received Paige's call, given how emotionally and physically drained she was, he had decided to let her sleep. There would be time for her world to be tipped upside down later. So he had gently eased out from underneath her, called Edmund to come and stay with her, made sure she had two officers posted outside her front door, and then picked up Paige on the way to the Everette estate.

"I have to admit it will be pretty satisfying to snap the cuffs on him," Paige shot him a grin. "How's Sofia this morning?"

"I'm guessing sore and tired, but she was still asleep when I left."

"She doesn't know about her father?"

"Not yet."

"Don't you think you should have told her?" Paige asked.

"She needed the rest. I asked Edmund to wait until I got back to tell her. Besides, she doesn't even like her father, and after what he did to her the other day, I doubt she'll be too broken up about it," Ryan answered confidently.

"I don't think she likes people making decisions for her," Paige reminded him gently. "Especially given that she's been sick lately."

"I'm sure everything will be fine," he reiterated, but a little less confident than he had been a moment ago. "We're here."

As Ryan brought the car to a stop, both his and Paige's gazes were drawn to the enormous house. But Ryan wasn't impressed with its grandeur; instead, he was thinking about the horrors that it had seen. Both in the last week and in the past, in whatever haunted Sofia's dreams.

Brushing aside concerns about Sofia for the moment, he'd explain his reasoning to her later. Now he was going to go and arrest her father. Knocking on the front door, he was surprised when it wasn't opened by the butler, but by the judge himself.

"What do you two want?" Logan growled before either of them had a chance to speak.

"Please put your hands behind your back, sir," Ryan fought to keep the smirk from his face.

"What?" Logan demanded.

"You are under arrest for the murder of Brooke Mariano," Paige informed him.

"What?" the judge stuttered, eyeing them both like they were aliens.

"Please put your hands behind your back," Ryan repeated.

"I most certainly will not. Have you two lost your minds? Why on earth would I kill Brooke Mariano?"

"Because she was pregnant with your child," Paige informed him.

"How could you know that?" Logan glowered. "I thought the killer took the baby with them."

"We were able to run a DNA test from the amniotic fluid. You are the proud papa," Ryan couldn't quite control his snarl.

"So because I am apparently the father of Brooke's child that means I murdered her? Stole the baby? And killed two of my sons, my wife, and my daughter-in-law?" Logan looked incredulous.

"You are just under arrest for Brooke Mariano's murder," Paige told him. "Now we are not going to ask you again. If you don't put your hands behind your back, we will add resisting arrest to your charges."

Ryan wanted to add drugging and holding Sofia against her will to Judge Everette's charges, but he wasn't sure there was any proof, so there was no point upsetting Sofia more than she already would be once she found out about her father.

The judge spluttered, but, realizing he didn't have a choice, he put his hands behind his back as Ryan stepped toward him with handcuffs out. "You have the right to remain silent," Ryan began. "Anything you say can and will be used against you in a court of law. You have the right . . ."

"I know my rights," Logan spat out. "I'm a *judge*."

Continuing with a smile, "To speak to a lawyer, and have him present while you are being questioned. If you cannot afford a lawyer . . ."

"You know darn well I can afford any lawyer I want," Logan interrupted.

". . . One will be appointed to you. You can decide at any time to exercise these rights and not answer any questions or make a statement. Do you understand these rights?"

Logan just glared.

"Do you understand these rights? Sir?" Ryan repeated.

"Of course I do, I am not an imbecile," Logan snapped. "You'll be sorry for this. Sofia will never forgive you."

* * * * *

10:35 A.M.

"How could you?" Sofia demanded, storming toward Ryan.

"I'm sorry," Edmund said from behind her. "I didn't tell her.

Isabella called before I got a chance to tell her not to tell Sofia until you got back."

"Ganging up on me?" Sofia turned her glare from Ryan to Edmund. "Playing games with my life and treating me like a child, just like my father. Coming from you, Edmund, that really hurts."

"It wasn't Edmund's fault," Ryan came toward her tentatively. "I asked him not to say anything until I got back to your place."

"Now *that* I believe," she glared at him with eyes she knew were as cold as her tone.

"Cupcake, I was just trying to protect you," Ryan rested a hand on her shoulder.

Jerking herself out of reach. "Don't touch me and don't call me cupcake," Sofia snapped. It was only ten-thirty in the morning and it had already been a horrible day. Waking from a nightmare, expecting Ryan's comforting arms to come around her, wrapping her up and making her feel safe, but instead she had been alone. Dragging herself out of bed, her head aching, her chest burning, she had found Edmund in the kitchen. Her friend had been vague with her about where exactly Ryan had gone. And then Isabella had called to tell her about their father's arrest.

As soon as she had gotten off the phone with her sister, she had jumped in the car and insisted that Edmund drive her to the police station so she could confront Ryan. Ryan was a liar. He had promised he'd be there with her, but he had left. He'd promised that he wouldn't let anyone hurt her. But instead he had been the one to hurt her.

Sofia was angry. Angrier than she had ever been. Angry with Ryan for lying to her, angry with herself for believing him, angry with Edmund for conspiring with Ryan against her, angry at everyone and everything.

"Cup—Sofia, why don't you come and sit down," Ryan gestured at the nearest chair.

Ryan's apparent concern only added fuel to the raging fire burning inside her. "I don't want to sit down."

"Sofia, maybe Ryan's right, maybe you should sit," Edmund took her arm.

"After last night, I think you really need to take it easy," Ryan tried to soothe her.

"Stop it, stop it, stop it," she shrieked, aware that she was sounding hysterical. She jerked her arm free so she could glower at Ryan. "Don't you know by now that I hate for people to make decisions for me? I told you how much I hated my illness for making it easier for people to try and control me."

"I'm sorry," Ryan looked distressed. "I'm just trying to protect you."

"I don't need anyone to protect me. And how could you do it?" she demanded. "How could you arrest my *father*?"

"I didn't do it to hurt you," Ryan looked devastated that he had upset her. "The DNA test we ran showed he was Brooke's baby's father."

"I know," she snapped, ignoring Ryan's sad blue eyes. "Isabella told me. Even though you should have been the one to do it."

"You were sleeping," he protested weakly.

"And you couldn't have woken me up?"

"You needed the rest. You've been through hell the last few days."

"Yes I have, so thank you, thank you for making things worse." Battling to keep her anger afloat, the screaming agony in her head was making it difficult to concentrate. "Just because my father was the father of Brooke's baby doesn't mean he's a killer; it just means he's a cheater. Which I already knew."

"This is the man who just forty-eight hours ago drugged you and locked you up in his house. If he'd had his way, you'd still be there," Ryan reminded her gently.

Sofia didn't want Ryan to be gentle with her. She wanted him to be as angry as she was feeling. "That still doesn't mean he's a killer," she pouted sullenly.

"You told me you were scared of him," Ryan added. "You said

you were afraid your father could be the murderer."

Not really sure why she was so angry with Ryan, but right now that fury was the only thing keeping her on her feet. "I was in shock when I said that. I'd just found out that my brother had been killed. I never really believed that the man who's my father, the only parent I have, is some sort of deranged serial killer."

"I'm sorry, cupcake," Ryan was looking at her helplessly.

"I told you not to call me that," she said, but the anger was gone from her voice. Now she was simply tired and in pain and scared. And desperately wanting Ryan to hold her tightly in his arms and tell her that everything could be okay. But that was done and over with. He'd lied to her. And she was so sick of lies. Her whole life had been full of them and she wasn't going to have them as part of her future.

Ignoring her wishes, Ryan grabbed her arms and gently pushed her down to the floor. "You need to sit," he said softly as he crouched beside her.

Taking a moment to gather herself, she allowed her long red hair to form a curtain around her face so the others couldn't see the tears brimming in her eyes. "No, I need to go," she said, pushing wearily to her feet.

"Okay, maybe it would be a good idea for Edmund to take you back home so you can get some rest," Ryan agreed warily. "Maybe I could stop by and see you later?"

"Actually, I don't think that's the best idea," Sofia planned to crawl into bed as soon as she got home and stay there. She didn't want visitors.

"All right." Ryan replied, looking distressed. "I'll make sure that we keep some officers on you until this case is solved. Make sure you don't go anywhere alone. I don't want anything to happen to you."

Knowing that that was true, Sofia softened her tone, "I know, and I'll be careful, I promise." Then she turned and fled from the police station as fast as her wobbly legs would let her.

TWO

11:01 A.M.

"What was that all about?" Paige asked, coming up beside him.

Staring after Sofia and Edmund's retreating backs, Edmund turned and gave him an apologetic wave. "I'm not really sure," Ryan murmured. "She totally freaked out about us arresting her father." He turned to look at Paige, "You were right; I should have been the one to tell her."

"She's in shock right now, just give her some time."

"She asked me not to go and see her later," Ryan added, wondering how things could have gone downhill with Sofia so quickly. Just hours ago she was asking him to hold her and make her feel safe, and now she wanted nothing to do with him.

"She'll get over it," Paige assured him. "But right now you need to forget about her. You need to focus on work. We have to go and interview Judge Everette; that needs to be your priority. There'll be time to fix things up with Sofia later."

"I know that," he snapped, glaring at his partner. "I'm not stupid."

"I never said you were," Paige replied mildly.

Rolling his eyes, Ryan was annoyed that his partner wasn't going to be drawn into an argument. He wanted to let out some of his frustration, and he couldn't bring himself to do it with Sofia. Maybe she was right, maybe he was afraid of her. But he'd watched her for so long now, and dreamt so many times about what it would be like to actually be with her, that he just couldn't bring himself to hurt her. He focused himself. Paige was right. At the moment his priority had to be the case. There was no point in sorting things out with Sofia if he was only going to lose her to this killer.

"Ready?" Paige asked, watching him carefully with her calm

brown eyes.

"Ready," he nodded, heading for the interview room where Logan Everette II was waiting for them.

The judge's head snapped toward them as they opened the door. His gray eyes practically shot arrows at them.

"You've chosen to speak to us without a lawyer, is that correct?" Paige asked.

"I *am* a lawyer," Logan growled. Jingling his still handcuffed wrists at them, "Why am I still cuffed?" he demanded.

"You've been arrested for murder," Ryan reminded him.

"You can't honestly believe that I am a killer," Logan shot them an incredulous frown.

"I can and I do," Ryan told him, taking a seat.

Logan turned to Paige. "What about you? Do you think I'm a cold-blooded killer too?"

Paige eyed him shrewdly as she joined them at the table, "I think you could be."

"This is ridiculous," Logan looked honestly frustrated. "No one thinks that I am a killer."

"Well, that's not quite true," Ryan began.

"What do you mean?" Logan asked, his brow furrowing.

"It turns out that someone very close to you has always suspected you of being a killer."

The judge rolled his eyes, "Sofia again? When are you going to accept the fact that she has a very vivid imagination and is unwell? Nothing she says should be taken too seriously. And if you persist in listening to her delusional ramblings, then I'll simply have to get her doctors to write a report detailing her poor health and fragile grip on reality," Logan finished with a smirk.

Ryan bit his tongue to keep his fury in check. "You'd really do that?" he asked calmly. "You'd really have your own daughter declared incompetent?"

"I'd have her locked up in a secure psychiatric facility if it keeps her away from you," the judge said malevolently.

Breathing deeply, he had to focus. "Actually," Ryan told the judge, "we didn't hear it from Sofia; it was Gloria."

Surprise flashed across Logan's face before he could contain it. "My wife thought I was a killer?"

"Apparently, she thought it for quite some time," Ryan was enjoying seeing the judge's smug smirk wiped off his face.

"Why would Gloria think that I had committed murder?"

"Her son," Ryan answered simply.

He paled, "Which one?"

"I think you know," Paige raised an eyebrow. "The only one that was really hers."

"He died in an accident, fell through the ice," Logan spluttered.

"Or so the story went, anyway," Ryan couldn't quite keep the snarl out of his voice. If little Logan Everette III had been murdered, then he deserved justice.

"Why would Gloria have thought that the child was murdered?"

"She thought that you figured out that he wasn't yours," Ryan watched closely for the judge's reaction.

Pink stained his pale cheeks. "That witch knew how much I wanted children and she went and got herself knocked up by that doctor."

"You knew he wasn't your son?" Ryan was surprised, not that the judge had known but that he had admitted it so freely. Perhaps Logan was more worried about being arrested than he had anticipated.

"I knew," he confirmed. "I made sure that the doctor got sent far away so he wouldn't know that he had a child."

"Did you kill him, Logan?" Paige asked softly.

"I was so desperate for a child," the judge answered, his grey eyes going vacant, reminding Ryan of a shark. "She had miscarriage after miscarriage. She thought it didn't affect me. But each time she lost another baby it was like a piece of my heart died along with it. Then she tried to kill herself and came back from the hospital pregnant. Talk about adding insult to injury. But I was prepared to play her game. I let her child live with us, let him take my name, treated him like my own son."

That the judge had had numerous affairs of his own didn't seem to enter his mind. However, Ryan reluctantly noted, he did seem genuinely upset about the many miscarriages his wife had suffered. "Did you kill Gloria's son, Logan?"

His eyes cleared, "No. I am *not* a killer. I love my children. Yes, I love to control them, but I would never hurt them," he said emphatically.

"I believe you on that," Ryan conceded. "Which is why when you killed Brooke, you had to save your baby."

Logan just glowered.

"You must have hated Brooke, though," Paige added. "To rip out her baby before you killed her. Did you want her to know that she wasn't going to use your child to blackmail you?"

He gave a resigned sigh, "I didn't kill Brooke, and I can prove it."

Ryan and Paige exchanged a suspicious glance. "Yeah? How?"

"I was with a woman."

"You know we're going to need more information than that," Paige reminded him when he didn't add more.

"She's one of my...friends..."

"You mean one of your mistresses?" Ryan wanted him to admit out loud that he was a cheater.

He frowned, "Yes. We were in one of the bedrooms..." He paused as he obviously chose his words carefully. "Enjoying each other's company."

"You mean having sex?" Ryan pressed, annoyed that the judge was deliberately being vague when he was supposedly giving them his alibi to prove he hadn't committed murder.

The frown deepened, "Yes."

"No offense, Judge," Ryan wasn't completely buying this yet, "but I'm sure you could pay off any number of your mistresses to lie for you and give you an alibi."

He sighed again. "We got a little creative," his cheeks heated, this time with embarrassment. "Decided we would record ourselves." Lowering his head to his hands, "This is so humiliating," Logan muttered.

"We're going to need the name of your mistress, and some contact information for her," Ryan told him, reaching over to unlock the handcuffs.

"Yes, I know." Logan took the piece of paper and pen Paige offered and scribbled down a name and phone number.

"And we're going to need a copy of that recording," Ryan added.

"Mary-Anne will be able to give it to you," Logan handed them the paper with Mary-Anne's name and number on it.

"You won't be able to leave until we verify the recording hasn't been doctored," Ryan warned him, feeling let down. If Logan hadn't killed Brooke, then they were right back where they started.

"Yes, I am aware of that," Logan bit out.

"All right then, we'll be back once we've either confirmed or denied your alibi," Ryan was ready to be away from the judge, it looked unlikely that he was a killer, but he was still the man who, among other things, had drugged and imprisoned Sofia.

"Well, hurry up about it," the judge said haughtily.

Ignoring him, Ryan headed for the door, Paige at his heels. Once outside he turned to his partner, "Do you believe him?"

"Yeah," Paige said dismally. "Unfortunately, I do. On the bright side, that will make Sofia happy."

"Yeah, I guess," Ryan replied, wondering whether it really would. The way Sofia had looked at him earlier had made him feel like whatever they might have had was over before it had even begun. "Let's go call this Mary-Anne and see what she has to say."

* * * * *

11:43 P.M.

What a long and tedious evening it had been.

Logan Everette IV hated having to attend social functions as his family's representative.

It was his stupid father's fault.

Going and getting himself arrested.

And his father had the gall to call *him* stupid.

Logan wasn't as stupid as his family believed. But he had found over the years that it was quite a convenient role to play. And he was very good at playing roles.

Very few people knew the real Logan Everette IV.

The real Logan was cold and calculating. He didn't care about others. As far as he was concerned, people were there simply to comply with his whim. Especially women. And there had been a *lot* of women in his past. In his present, too, he chuckled.

Casting a glance at his wife, Simone was sitting quietly in the passenger seat of the car. His father had done a good job with her. Picked him a woman who was one hundred percent completely subservient to him. If anyone knew the real Logan, Simone certainly did. She was the one who took the brunt of his anger. He'd learned early on how to hurt her without leaving a mark. Bruises led to questions. Questions he didn't want to answer. He had too many secrets to have people buzzing around him.

His anger was burning brightly tonight.

He was looking forward to getting his wife up to their room. They basically had the house to themselves tonight, which meant he didn't need to take things easy. With his father in jail, Sofia back at her house, and both his brothers dead, which Logan supposed he ought to be sad about but wasn't in the least, the only one he had to worry about was Isabella. She was a weird one, that girl. But she was likely to be so caught up in whatever she was doing that she wouldn't hear Simone's screams.

Pulling the car into the garage, he was so preoccupied with thoughts of what he would get up to with Simone, that he didn't notice the figure waiting for him.

Before he had a chance to roll the window back up someone pressed a gun to his temple.

"No, no," said a voice. "Leave the car engine on."

Shocked, he turned his head to confirm that the face matched the voice. "*You*? It's you? *You're* the killer?"

"Uh huh," Isabella nodded, her face filled with a huge grin. It was the first time he could recall seeing the girl smile.

"Are you insane?" Logan demanded.

"Probably," Isabella nodded agreeably.

"You killed them all?"

"Yep. Brooke, and Lewis and Samantha, Gloria, and Lincoln."

"Brooke was your mother. You killed your own mother."

"I know," the smile was still on her face, making her look near psychotic.

"Why?" he asked, hoping to keep her talking long enough to get her gun.

"Because they all deserved to die," she said simply. "You all do. And that's enough chitchatting." She tossed him a role of duct tape. "Use this to secure Simone to the seat." When he didn't move fast enough, she shoved the gun harder against his temple. "Tick tock, this place is crawling with security, which means we have a time limit. Not usually how I like to do things, but we must work within the parameters we are given."

Reluctantly, Logan took the duct tape and turned to his wife, wishing for the first time in their marriage that she wasn't so pathetically weak and had been able to help him fight back. Logan wanted to make a move. Try to get away. But he could see the pure insanity brimming in Isabella's eyes. She would most definitely shoot him. And Logan had a feeling that she would make sure his suffering was maximized. Defeated, he prepared the tape. Simone didn't open her eyes to look at him as he wound the duct tape across her chest and around her seat, pinning her in place.

"Your turn," Isabella singsonged. "Cross your arms across your chest please." Taking the tape with one hand, her other kept the gun pointed squarely at his head, and awkwardly wrapped layer after layer of tape around his body and the car seat until he was pinned in place, his arms trapped against his chest. Then she ripped off a piece and slapped it over his mouth.

"Now it's sleepy time," Isabella closed the garage door, and put on an oxygen mask. "Any last words? Nope? Well good, because I wouldn't believe a single lying word that fell out of your mouth."

As carbon monoxide from the running car began to fill the small garage, and he realized that death was about to come crashing down upon him, Logan started to panic. He struggled wildly against the tape, even though he knew it was fruitless. He tried to force a scream past the tape, but nothing more than a squeaking moan emerged.

Then as his body grew sleepy, his struggles slowly ceased. Beside him, Simone's head drooped limply down to rest against her bound chest.

He realized then that he had been wrong.

There had been someone else. Someone other than his wife who had known just what a terrible person he really was.

The last thing he saw before his eyes fluttered closed was Isabella waving good-bye to him.

AUGUST 18TH

"Here we are, sir. Home," Edmund announced.

"About time," Logan snapped from the back seat where he had been taking a nap.

Sofia wished she could nap. She was exhausted. Hadn't slept more than a few fitful minutes at a time in the last twenty-four hours. She was angry with Ryan. And angry with herself for being angry at Ryan when he was doing nothing more than his job. But even though she knew she was being unfair she couldn't seem to let go of her anger. "Father," she reprimanded. "It's not Edmund's fault that the police arrested you."

"No, it's not Edmund's fault," her father agreed snidely. "It's yours."

"Mine?" She turned in her seat to stare incredulously at him. "How is it my fault?"

"You're the one who got them suspicious of me in the first place. Carrying on about how you think Isabella is mine and Brooke's daughter. Telling them about this manuscript that Brooke supposedly wrote. Telling them that Gloria thought I was responsible for her son's death."

"What?" It had never occurred to her that Logan III's death had been anything other than the accident it had been described to her. "I never told them that. I never even knew Gloria thought you killed him."

"Well, then who told them?"

All three pondered this in silence then pronounced together, "Alan Payne."

135

"What do you know about Alan Payne?" her father raised an eyebrow and looked at her suspiciously.

"He was having an affair with Gloria," she replied.

"How did you know?"

"Isabella told me," Sofia explained. "If Gloria suspected you, she must have told him."

"That Isabella sees too much," Logan muttered.

"How did you convince the police that you didn't kill Brooke?" Sofia asked, probably for the twentieth time. "You know I could just ask Detective Xander or Detective Hood," she wheedled.

"I gave them my alibi," he said through gritted teeth

She waited for her father to say more, and when he didn't, she wiggled around in her seat once more to shoot him a disapproving frown. "You were with a woman."

The judge's glower confirmed that indeed he had been.

"Who?" For some reason, it was important to her to know who her father had been with when this nightmare began. "Who?" she repeated when he didn't reply.

"Mary-Anne," he answered tightly.

"Mary-Anne Letcher?" Sure it couldn't be. Her father wouldn't do that to her.

"So what if it was?" her father shot back with a sullen growl.

Hot tears burned the backs of her eyes. "How could you? She was one of my best friends. You promised you wouldn't do my friends anymore, after last time." She had been fifteen when she'd walked into her bedroom one day to find her father and her friend going at it on her bed.

"Mary-Anne was hot," her father shrugged unapologetically. "Well, whatever, I just want to go inside, have a hot shower, some sleep in my own bed, and forget that all of this ever happened." The judge climbed from the car and began to stalk toward the front door.

"Forget this ever happened until another one of us ends up

dead," Sofia uttered wearily, dragging herself from the car and swiping at the tears trickling down her cheeks.

"I'm not going to let anyone hurt you, Sofia," Edmund took her arm to steady her. "And neither is Detective Xander," he added gently.

"Don't, Edmund," she warned her friend, not in the least in the mood to hear another lecture about how unfair she was being to Ryan.

"I think you should talk to him," Edmund insisted as he helped her up the front steps. "At least hear him out."

"I don't want to," Sofia objected. All she wanted was some good, uninterrupted sleep that wasn't haunted by nightmares, and from which she wouldn't awaken to learn of another dead family member.

"Then you're not going to like this," his gaze shifted to something behind her.

Following her friend's gaze, Sofia turned to see Ryan parking his car beside Edmund's. He climbed out and paused, watching her carefully.

Groaning, Sofia pulled her arm free from Edmund's grip and headed as quickly as she could for the door. Footsteps pounded behind her, and then Ryan was grabbing her shoulder and spinning her around. His bright blue eyes were like magnets, drawing her own gray eyes to his, his so sad that she had to look away.

"I just want to talk," he implored.

"I don't want to talk to you right now."

Hope lit up his face, "So you *will* talk to me later?"

"I didn't say that," Sofia hated for people to put words in her mouth.

"Sofia, please . . ." he began to beg.

Not in the mood to listen, "You arrested my *father*, Ryan. You can't expect me not to be upset about that. And you lied to me. You promised that you would stay with me, but when I woke up from a nightmare you were gone . . ."

"I'm sorry," Ryan interrupted, staring at her so pitifully that she almost screamed.

"Stop saying that to me," she exploded. "I don't want you to be sorry, I want you to be gone. I don't need another person in my life who wants to make decisions for me. I am *more* than capable of making my own choices." She waved him quiet when he opened his mouth to defend himself, "No, no, I can guess what you're going to say. I've been through a lot, I'm not well, you didn't want to wake me because I needed the sleep. I've heard it all before, Ryan. I thought you were different. I told you how much I hate it when people treat me like that. I thought you understood. But you don't. You were just pretending. And I don't need another liar in my life." With that, she began to storm toward the front door, wishing that it wasn't so far away. She was so tired, her head was spinning, her chest aching, her eyes watering, all she wanted was to lie down quietly.

"Sofia, just talk to him," Edmund caught up to her and grabbed her arm, holding her in place.

Yanking free, "No."

"Stop being stubborn," Edmund reached for her again.

Dodging out of reach, Sofia almost lost her balance, her wobbly legs buckling. Ryan caught her before she hit the ground. For a moment, pressed against his chest, she felt her heart melt. Sofia didn't want to be mad at him, she wanted to let his strong arms make her feel safe. But that didn't change the fact that he had lied to her and manipulated her.

Wearily, she extricated herself from his grip. "You want to do something for me, Ryan, then just find this killer before I end up like the rest of my family." This time neither of the men followed her as she headed for the house.

"I'll talk to her," Edmund assured Ryan.

"I'm only making things worse for her," Ryan protested.

"No, you're good for her," Edmund contradicted. "Something

else is bothering her. I'll get to the bottom of it."

Blocking out their voices, Sofia hated for people to discuss her like she wasn't there, but right now she was too tired to bother about it. She wanted to hold her tears in until she was inside, away from Ryan's prying eyes, but as she reached the door she froze. Her father stood there. Calmly watching her. Had probably stood there calmly watching the entire exchange between herself and Ryan. Bursting into tears, she rushed as quickly as she could for the stairs, leaning heavily against the banister to help drag herself up.

Pausing halfway up the stairs when she heard Ryan's voice, "I need to see her."

"No. Absolutely not," her father told him.

"Please, Judge Everette."

Twisting, Sofia saw the judge blocking the doorway so Ryan couldn't enter. As angry as she was with her father, at this moment she was glad that he was there, stopping Ryan from following her.

"She's sick, she's stressed, and the last thing she needs right now is the man who arrested her father stalking her. Now get off my property and leave my daughter alone."

Leaving her father to deal with Ryan, Sofia dropped to her knees, too exhausted to remain on her feet any longer, and crawled the rest of the way up the stairs. Reaching the second floor, and with no energy left, she lay her head down against the carpet and curled herself into a tight ball, letting her tears flow freely.

A hand grasping her shoulder made her jump.

"Sofia? Are you okay?"

Bushing away tears, Sofia opened her eyes to see Isabella crouching beside her. The sight of her baby sister, the only member of her family that she trusted, that she knew actually cared about her, that actually loved her, made her sobs start all over again.

"What's wrong?" Isabella asked, but Sofia was crying too hard to answer.

Allowing her sister to wrap an arm around her shoulders and lift her to her feet, Sofia barely made it to her old bedroom, where Isabella turned down the covers and helped her lie down. "I just want this nightmare to be over," she whispered, sleep already had her eyes falling closed.

"Soon, it will be. I promise."

Sofia had time to wonder how her sister could be so sure before her drained mind and body gave out and she drifted off to sleep.

* * * * *

10:30 A.M.

"You're almost late. Again."

"But I'm not," Ryan snapped at his partner. Lifting his wrist to show her his watch, "In fact I'm right *on* time."

She sighed, "How did it go?" Paige asked.

"Not well," Ryan replied, glaring at her.

"She still won't talk to you?"

"No," he said through gritted teeth. He was angry. Furious, might be a better word. Ryan had wanted to yell at Sofia that she was being unreasonable. Unfair. She wasn't close with her father. In fact, he was pretty sure she only loved him in a 'he's my father so I have to' sort of way. She couldn't be this upset about the judge being arrested. And even if she was, it was hardly his fault. He was only doing his job. He had wanted to yell at Sofia that she wasn't being fair, but he hadn't. He'd held it in. Bitten his tongue.

He hadn't been able to speak openly with her, and that was bothering him. He did believe that Sofia would get over her anger at him. She was in shock which, given everything she was going through right now, was completely understandable. But if he and

Sofia were going to have a real relationship, then they would have to be honest with each other. He wanted a real relationship. One like his parents had. One like his younger brother had. He wanted the real thing. And he thought he might have found it with Sofia. But if he couldn't bring himself to talk openly with her then they would never be able to have it. Sofia was right. He *was* afraid of her. Afraid of hurting her. And he knew why. He was going to have to finally deal with what had happened with Katrina so he could move forward.

"She'll get over it, just give her a little time for all of this to sink in," Paige comforted.

He shook his head, "No, I don't think she will. I made her cry." The picture of Sofia fleeing him for her front door, barely able to stand, crying hysterically, was haunting him.

Paige gave his shoulder a reassuring pat. "She really will get over it. Right now the best thing you can do for her is catch this guy."

"Sofia said that," he murmured.

"She's right, this is your priority right now, you have the whole rest of your life to fix things up with Sofia."

"Ryan, Paige."

They turned as one toward Belinda, who was waving at them from the door of the conference room. Ryan trudged past the messy desks that cluttered the dingy space, as he walked through the door his gaze was drawn immediately to the photos lining the top of the bulletin board. Sofia's mother, brothers, sisters-in-law. All dead. Sobering, he couldn't let Sofia end up like the rest of her family.

"Okay," Belinda began wearily, dropping down into a seat at the table. "Anything from last night's crime scene?"

Shrugging fitfully, "The usual," Stephanie replied. "I'm sure the only fingerprints we've collected are from the Everette family and employees. Other than that, nothing."

"Carbon monoxide poisoning cause of death?" Belinda

directed the rhetorical question to Frankie.

"Yeah," she nodded tiredly, they had all been working around the clock on this case, the killer was relentless, taking another victim with each passing night, and the strain was beginning to wear them all down.

"I thought cars are meant to be built to make suicide by carbon monoxide poisoning difficult?" Belinda asked tersely.

"They are," Frankie agreed. "But unluckily for Logan and Simone Everette they drive a classic car. Older cars don't have all the emission controls that newer cars are made with these days."

"Well, talking of luck," Paige's brown brows were raised in disbelief. "Logan couldn't have been luckier that the security guard turned up when he did."

Logan had been barely alive when the guard patrolling the Everette estate had found him tied with duct tape to his car seat. He had been rushed to the hospital, and when Ryan and Paige had talked with his doctors, they'd been told that Logan would have had only minutes left to live if he hadn't been found. Ryan didn't like Sofia's oldest brother, so he didn't really think it was lucky Logan had survived. Unless of course he was able to identify the killer for them. So far his condition had not been stable and they had been unable to speak with him.

"All right," Belinda rubbed at her dark eyes. "So where are we on a suspect? The judge is out?"

"His alibi checked out," Paige made a face. "Although watching the recording of what he'd been up to was not fun."

Ryan couldn't help but laugh at his partner's expression. Suffice it to say, watching hours of footage of the seventy-two-year-old judge and his twenty-eight-year-old girlfriend dressed up in a range of costumes as they had round after round of wild sex had not been a fun viewing experience.

"The judge was definitely otherwise occupied while Brooke Mariano was killed, so he didn't do it. And he was here in our police station when Simone died. Although," Ryan pondered, "I guess it doesn't necessarily count out the fact that he could have hired someone to do it. Or that he committed the other murders."

"I don't think he hired someone," Paige considered. "Brooke's murder was too personal. Plus, the baby. I don't think a hit man would take the baby in that manner."

"Maybe he saw an opportunity with the baby and took it to sell on the black market," Belinda suggested.

"Then why cut it out of Brooke while she was still alive? That was too personal for a stranger," Paige reminded him.

"Granted," Belinda acknowledged. The lieutenant was about to say more when her phone began to ring. Waving them all silent she answered. "Yes," Belinda snapped. Eyes growing wide. "When?" Listening to the response. "And no one saw anything?" A deep frown developed on her face as she heard the answer. "Ridiculous. Absolutely ridiculous," she growled. "All right, I'll send someone over to run the crime scene . . ."

Ryan's blood ran cold at the word crime scene. Surely there couldn't be another murder already. So far the killer had stuck to his schedule of a kill a night. But perhaps he was getting desperate. Perhaps he felt as though the police were closing in on him.

"What happened?" he demanded the second Belinda hung up her phone.

"Relax," Belinda shot him a knowing glance. "Nothing happened to Sofia. She's fine. Her security detail is checking in regularly. It's Logan, the son," she added, "he disappeared."

"From the hospital?" Paige looked surprised.

"Yep."

"And no one saw anything?" Paige asked

"Nope."

"How do you disappear from a crowded hospital without anyone noticing?" Paige was sounding as frustrated as Belinda looked.

"Exactly," Belinda nodded fiercely. "Stephanie, can you head over there? I don't think you'll find anything, but I want you to check anyway."

"Sure," Stephanie dragged herself to her feet. "I'm going to call my kid first. I haven't seen Cindy in days."

"Given that he's disappeared do we think Logan could be the killer?" Belinda surveyed them all from tired eyes.

"Both Logans were suspects from the beginning," Paige reminded her.

"If Brooke had already run a paternity test and told Logan Junior he wasn't the father, I guess he could have freaked out and killed her, then taken the baby to punish his father," Ryan suggested.

"Could Logan have faked his attempted murder, Frankie?" Belinda asked the medical examiner.

"Mmm," Frankie considered this, brown eyes thoughtful. "I would say yes, he could have restrained Simone, then turned on the engine, closed the garage door, and put himself in the car. It would have been risky. If the security guard had been delayed, even a couple of minutes, then he could have died. But I'm not sure he could have put the tape on himself the way he was found. It's hard to tell, though. The guard who found him wasn't concerned with preserving evidence when he cut off the tape, just in getting Logan out and into the fresh air as quickly as possible. We'll run some tests with the tape and see if it would be possible and get back to you."

"All right, so, summarize what we know about Logan Everette IV," Belinda commanded.

"Well, from all accounts he doesn't seem too intelligent," Paige began. "He doesn't seem to be held in very high esteem by his family. He has been pretty open about his affairs, and didn't seem to care if his wife knew or not."

"Alan Payne didn't like Logan," Ryan added. "Said he was cruel for cruel's sake."

"He was at the estate at the time of all the murders, and he was there the night Sofia was shot," Paige continued.

"Motives for the family murders?"

"Maybe he wanted to take over the empire," Ryan suggested, refusing to think about watching Sofia fall to the floor as a bullet plowed into her chest. "The family own a lot of real estate and a chain of hotels, plus a couple of finance companies. Maybe he got sick of sitting in second, thought he'd get rid of his father and siblings so he had no rivals. Or maybe he just hated them. There's something chillingly cold about him, I wouldn't put anything past him."

"What about Sofia's dreams?" Paige shot him an apologetically quizzical glance.

He was confused then, "What about them?"

"Don't you think they could be relevant?"

"Why? She has nightmares about her father arguing with lots of women. That's not related to her brother."

"Actually," Paige corrected gently. "She said she sleepwalked, and wasn't sure if the things she saw were dreams or real. We assumed that the women were who her father was having affairs with. What if they were women Logan Junior was having affairs with? Everyone seems to agree he's not very smart; what if it was their father cleaning up Logan's messes that Sofia saw?"

"That's a lot of what ifs," Ryan said uncertainly. If Sofia really had seen something pertinent to what was happening now, then it put her at even greater risk. It also meant she would have to confront some things that she clearly had buried deeply. Ryan wasn't sure she was up to it right now.

"I was also thinking," Paige continued, "what if Logan Junior is really Isabella's father? Sofia only said she saw Brooke giving birth and her father in the room. That doesn't make the judge the father. If Brooke and Logan were Isabella's parents and the judge covered it up because Brooke was so young at the time, and now the judge goes and gets Brooke pregnant, it could have pushed Logan Junior over the edge. Set all this in motion."

"That's all just conjecture," Ryan protested.

"Agreed," Paige nodded calmly. "But we need a direction to move in and this could be it."

"Okay, lets investigate your conjecture," Belinda said, dragging her hands across her face. "Set up an interview with Sofia, see if you can push her to remember what she saw."

"That might be a problem," Ryan cleared his throat. He continued when Belinda arched an irritable eyebrow in his direction. "Right now we aren't really Sofia's favorite people. I'm not sure she'll want to talk with us. And if we're pushing her to confront things she buried since she was a child, then she needs to trust us. At the moment she doesn't."

"Then you better make nice with her. Dismissed, people." Belinda stood and headed for the door. "I want this case closed while there are still *some* members of the Everette family left alive. And don't forget, once they're all dead, this killer could disappear forever and we'll never be able to find him."

* * * * *

4:42 P.M.

"Honey, I don't really understand why you're making such a big deal about this." Edmund was staring at her, his hazel eyes confused.

Shrugging fitfully, Sofia was feeling better after her nap but she was still too tired to concentrate. She was still tucked up in bed, right where she had been since Isabella had helped her there after her argument with Ryan. Sofia wasn't sure how long she had been asleep but apparently Edmund had stayed with her, waiting until she awakened to grill her once again about Ryan. Resting her aching head against the pillows, Sofia pulled her quilt tighter around herself. Despite the warm weather, she was chilly.

"What's going on with you?" Edmund sat on the edge of her

bed and hooked a finger under her chin, tilting her head so she was looking at him.

"I don't know." She closed her eyes so she didn't have to look at her friend's face, she hated lying to him, but she was too tired to properly sort out what she was feeling right now.

"I think you do know," Edmund persisted. "Talk to me, Sofia. I just want to help you. We both do," he added, including Isabella.

"You can trust us," Isabella added. "We both love and care about you."

"Given how you feel about your father, you can't be this upset over that," Edmund continued.

"They *arrested* him," Sofia reminded him, her eyes still firmly closed.

"I know, honey, but you yourself were scared that he could be the killer, so you can't be that upset, or surprised, that he was arrested," he reminded her.

"He's still my father," she retorted.

"Fair enough, but..."

"But nothing," she cut him off. "Aren't I allowed to be upset that my father was arrested for murder?"

"Of course you are," Edmund soothed. "I just don't think it's the reason you're so angry with Ryan."

"He lied to me." Tears were stinging the backs of her eyes but Sofia was fighting them.

"Okay," Edmund sounded pleased that they were making progress, "what did he lie about?"

"He promised that he'd be there with me, that he'd keep me safe," her voice began to tremble, she wouldn't be able to hold her tears in for much longer. "But he was gone. When I woke up, he was gone. He left me alone so he could arrest my father."

"Open your eyes," Edmund instructed softly. "Please," he added when she didn't.

Slowly opening her eyes, she expected to see a sharp reprimand in her best friend's eyes, but instead they were watching her sadly.

"He hurt you," Edmund murmured, brushing a hand across her forehead and tucking her wild red hair behind her ear. "I'm sorry. I hate it when you get hurt. But you know that Ryan was just doing his job."

"But I needed him, Edmund, and he wasn't there, even though he promised he would be." Sofia hated how vulnerable she sounded. "How can I trust him after that?" her bottom lip wobbled and she chewed on it, stubbornly holding back her tears.

"I think you can trust him, Sofia," Isabella announced quietly, in her serious way. "I like him."

Turning to her little sister, "But I need someone who I can count on indefinitely. What if I need him again and he's not there?" she whimpered.

"Honey, you know that no one can *always* be there," Edmund reminded her. "You also know that Ryan would do his best to give you whatever you need."

"I guess," she nodded reluctantly.

Narrowing his eyes at her. "You're afraid," Edmund pronounced.

Nodding again, slowly this time.

"Of what, honey?"

Staring at her hands in her lap, twisting them together until Edmund gently pulled them apart, keeping a grip on them when they started to stray toward each other again.

"What are you scared of, Sofia?" he repeated gently.

She finally lifted her eyes to meet Edmund's. "That I really like him. That it might actually go somewhere."

"Why are you scared of that?" he asked, confused. "For as long as I can remember you've been longing to have a family of your own. You've always been looking for your Mr. Right, and now that you think you may have found him, you're backing off? Why?"

A couple of tears escaped and slid down her cheeks, where she angrily brushed them away. "Because it doesn't change anything."

"What do you mean?" Both Edmund and Isabella still looked puzzled.

"I'm still dying," she whispered.

"Oh, honey. You don't know that," Edmund said sadly.

"Well, I'm not getting any better," she reminded him. "And it's been months now."

"That does *not* mean that you are dying," Edmund reprimanded sharply.

"What if I let things happen with Ryan and then I get worse? That doesn't seem fair."

"Isn't that up to Ryan to decide? You don't like people making decisions for you, he probably doesn't either," Edmund pointed out.

"I asked him," her voice was still wobbling. "If he could deal with it. I said if he couldn't handle getting involved with me and then me dying, then he should just walk away now."

"And what did he say?" Edmund prodded when she paused.

"He said he believed that I was going to get better," remembering how his confidence had ignited her own.

"You liked that," Edmund smiled. "He made you feel safe."

Hesitantly, she nodded. "I lied to him, too."

"How did you lie?" Edmund pushed.

"I told him that I believed that he was going to find this killer, but . . ." she trailed off, a sob about to break free.

"But now you're not so sure," Edmund finished for her, fear flashed across his face and Sofia knew he was scared too that the police wouldn't be able to catch the killer before her whole family was dead.

"I *want* to believe him," she was crying now. "I believed him when I said it, but now, now I don't know. Now I'm scared that it's already too late."

"It's not too late, Sofia," Isabella assured her firmly.

Weeping uncontrollably now, she clung to Edmund as he put his arms around her. "Why can't I stop crying?" she mumbled against his shoulder.

"Because you're in the middle of a nightmare," he reminded her, tightening his hold.

"I don't want to cry anymore, I don't want to be scared anymore, I don't want to be sick anymore," she sobbed.

"Shh," Edmund rubbed her back soothingly. "I'm pretty concerned about you right now, so I'm going to give you some sleeping pills, all right? You need a full night's sleep, and you should be safe enough here with your security detail and your father's security guards. If you're not doing any better by tomorrow, then I'm going to take you to the hospital."

Too worn out to protest, Sofia took the sleeping pills Isabella gave her and swallowed them, then allowed Edmund to settle her down in the bed. "Stay with me, please," she begged, not wanting to fall asleep on her own.

"Of course," Edmund took her hand with one of his, and with his other began to stroke her hair.

Sofia hoped that she hadn't been lying. That her confidence in Ryan had been well placed. All that was left now was her, Isabella, Logan and their father. And another night was ticking ever closer.

* * * * *

10:52 P.M.

Isabella hated what this was doing to her sister.

Perched on the bed beside Sofia, who was still fast asleep, she was stroking her sister's thick red hair and wondering whether she'd taken things too far.

Not with her murderous plan.

That was exactly what her horrible family deserved. They were always pretending to be so perfect. So righteous. People to be looked up to and admired. But Isabella knew the truth. About all of them. They were monsters. Cruel and vicious monsters, without a conscience between them. Even those who had not participated had perpetuated the crimes by keeping their mouths shut. Which meant all of them deserved their just punishment. Death.

Except Sofia.

Isabella was glad she wasn't going to kill her sister. But she was worried that she might end up causing Sofia's death unintentionally. She was concerned that she'd gone too far with the mushrooms. She'd just needed to get her big sister out of the way for a little while. Sofia was the only member of their family who ever paid any attention to her, so when Isabella was planning all of this, she had to make sure that Sofia wouldn't find out. She hadn't really wanted to hurt her sister, just incapacitate her for a while, so poisoning had seemed like the perfect answer. With Sofia constantly sick she hadn't had the time or energy to pay much attention to what Isabella was up to.

She had done her research, chosen a mushroom that wasn't supposed to be lethal. However, now she was concerned that she'd got it wrong. Or maybe she was just giving Sofia too much. She had picked the Tricholoma pardinum because the gastrointestinal symptoms of nausea, dizziness and vomiting seemed a good way to keep Sofia occupied without making her too seriously ill. The fact that the vomiting left her dehydrated and wary of eating, helped to keep her weak and drained and barely able to leave her house, which meant Isabella was free to plan her killing spree.

It hadn't been hard to get Sofia to eat the mushrooms. They both smelled and tasted nice, and Isabella always prepared them in a vegetable soup. They also took only a short time for their toxins to start affecting the body of the person who ate them. Symptoms could appear in as little as fifteen minutes after ingestion, which was helpful if Isabella needed to distract Sofia quickly. It also took four to six days to completely recover, which meant Sofia was out of commission even if Isabella couldn't get to her every day.

Now, however, Sofia appeared to be falling apart. Months of poisoning, of vomiting and dizziness and overwhelming tiredness, had taken their toll. Isabella would have to be careful not to feed her too many more mushrooms. Still, that shouldn't be a problem; she had almost finished what she'd started.

Upset as she was about her sister, she couldn't be more pleased with how things had turned out with Logan IV.

It had been a risk.

A calculated one.

But in the end, it had paid off perfectly.

Isabella hadn't wanted Logan dead. Yet. So she had watched the security guards her father had hired, learned their routine, and then timed her kill to the second. Leaving just enough time to kill off Simone but leave Logan clinging to life for the guard to find.

Killing Simone and Samantha just had to be done. And, Isabella comforted herself, they could have opened their mouths at any time. Told what was going on in this house. Done something to stop it. But they hadn't. And now their silence meant that they were complicit, and so they too had to die.

Having Logan weakened would also be beneficial for later. Although she was tall, and solidly built, and she spent hours working out, Logan was still bigger and stronger than her. So anything she could do to give herself the advantage was definitely worth taking the time to do. And having Logan weakened with carbon monoxide would certainly give her the advantage when the time came.

Speaking of advantages, Isabella had another idea.

So far, the police had not suspected her. They had no reason to. But there weren't many of them left now. They knew Sofia wasn't the killer. And the judge had now been cleared. That only left Logan IV and herself. Since Logan had disappeared from the hospital, he had become their number one suspect, but that didn't mean they couldn't move on to her.

Unless she made herself a victim.

She was a little limited in what she could do to herself. A stab wound or gunshot were too serious; she wouldn't be able to recover fast enough to finish her plan. A drowning would be too hard because it was so up close and personal, which had made Gloria's kill so much fun. A drug overdose was too risky; again, it could knock her out for too long.

Maybe she could go with suffocation.

Perhaps tie a plastic bag around her head.

That should work. She'd tie the bag around her head and then use some rope to secure her hands behind her back. She knew the guard's routine, so she'd place herself somewhere where they would be sure to find her.

She was getting excited. This would be fun. And there wasn't a lot that excited Isabella Everette. In fact, she could think of only one thing. Murder.

In her sleep, Sofia began to whimper. Her sister's brow creased in concern, and Isabella wished she could take all Sofia's worry and pain away. Gently smoothing her sister's forehead, soon this would all be over and then finally they could both be happy. Once their horrible family was disposed of, they could move forward. Sofia would be free to patch things up with Ryan and make a life with him. And she would be free to live and do as she pleased.

Brushing a kiss to Sofia's cheek, Isabella quietly crept from the room. She'd have to hurry. The guards swept the kitchen at half past eleven. If she was quick, she could get herself set up there, ready to be found.

Maybe she should leave the door out to the gardens open. Then the police would think that her attacker had simply fled when they heard the guards approaching. Which would explain why she survived.

Heading straight for the kitchen, Isabella quickly located some rope and a bag, then took a moment to choose the most appropriate spot in the large kitchen. A ten seater table was down one end, behind which French doors opened out onto the garden.

The other three walls were covered in benches and cupboards; a large island took up most of the middle of the room.

It was late. In her statement to the police, she would tell them that she had been unable to sleep and come downstairs for a bottle of water and a snack when she had been grabbed from behind. So near the refrigerator was the ideal place.

Collecting a plate on her way, she opened one of the doors, then took a bottle of water from the fridge, and a peach—her favorite fruit. Dropping all three on the floor, Isabella lay down beside them. Putting the bag over her head, she used a piece of the rope to tie it tightly around her neck. Then taking slow, deep breaths, so as not to use up her small air supply until she was done, she put her arms behind her back and struggled to tie her wrists together.

When they were well enough secured, she settled back and waited.

Wondering as she did whether Logan was correct and she was insane.

* * * * *

11:28 P.M.

Sofia hated the basement.

Why was she down here anyway?

Shouldn't she be in bed? Her nanny had tucked her in earlier.

She must have been sleepwalking again.

Why did she always end up down in the basement whenever she sleepwalked?

She hated it down here.

The basement was huge. It must have been almost the same size as the house. But it was dark. Too dark. And Sofia was scared of the dark. Her nanny always left the night-light on so her room wouldn't be too dark. But that made shadows. She was almost as scared of shadows as she was of the dark.

She crossed the basement on tippy-toes.

Heading for the light.

Just as she did every night.

And just like every other night she wasn't sure if she was dreaming or awake.

Tucking her braids behind her ears and lifting her long white nightgown so it didn't drag along the rough concrete floor, she kept heading for the light.

She could hear voices.

Arguing.

They were always arguing, but she could never make out the words.

She stopped as she always did at the door, peering through.

Bright light splashed shadows across the other room and she shivered.

Bad things happened down here. She was sure of it.

Inside the room there were figures.

Two of them.

Arms waving wildly as they argued.

On the floor there were sticks. Lots of sticks.

She took a step inside the room.

A hand clamped around her shoulder.

Startled, she turned.

"You're dreaming, Sofia," her father told her.

As he picked her up, she looked over his shoulder one last time.

There was red.

Lots of red.

Sofia knew the red was blood.

Then she was screaming.

And screaming.

And screaming.

Sofia woke up with a start. She was tangled in the covers,

breathing harshly and sweating.

She hated that dream.

It had plagued her for as long as she could remember. And just like when she was a child, she was never sure if it was real or all a dream.

She was alone in the room.

Edmund must have gone home, and Isabella must have gone to get some sleep herself. Sofia hated waking up alone. Which was why Ryan promising that he'd be with her when she awoke, screaming and scared, and then leaving her, had upset her so much.

But Edmund and Isabella were right. She could trust Ryan and she had been being unfair to him. She would have to make that right.

Right now, however, she was hot and thirsty and even a little hungry. She needed something to eat and drink. And then some more sleep. Hopefully this time minus the nightmares. If she could get enough sleep, then maybe she could avoid the hospital tomorrow. Edmund would be as good as his word. If he didn't think she was coping, he would take her straight to the hospital first thing in the morning, and make her stay there until she was better. Which could be never.

Standing slowly, testing her legs, Sofia was pleased when, despite a small wobble, they held. Taking her time, she wound her way through hallway after hallway, passing empty bedroom after empty bedroom, on her way to the kitchen. As a child she had always wondered why a house needed so many bedrooms. The house had a total of one hundred and two, and yet she had never been allowed to have her friends come and sleep over.

Sofia had been upset about that for a time, around her thirteenth birthday. She had screamed and sulked and whined and cried and begged. But it had done no good. Her father had told her that she would never be allowed to have any friend spend the night here, so she may as well stop asking. Always the good girl, she *had* stopped asking, but had continued to resent her father for it. Gloria, too. Her mother should have understood how important it was to a teenage girl to have sleepovers with her friends. A real mother would have understood. That Gloria didn't care enough to stand up for her only served to remind a young Sofia just how little the woman loved her.

Still, now wasn't the time to be worrying about old grievances.

Gloria was gone now. And so were two of her brothers. And her sisters-in-law. Plus, she'd almost lost her other brother. Not to mention that someone had tried to kill her, too.

She stopped to take a break. Propping her back up against the wall, Sofia took a few deep breaths, as deep as she could manage with her broken ribs anyway. She needed to get away from here, before it was too late. In the morning she would get Isabella, and ask Edmund to take them both far, far away from this place. Then when things had calmed down she would come back and sort things out with Ryan.

Her heart was telling her to fix things with Ryan first. But what good would it do to make things right with him only to end up dead? No, right now her priority had to be getting herself and her baby sister someplace safe.

Forging onwards, she let out a small sigh of relief when she finally reached the kitchen. She wished that she'd asked Edmund to take her back to her own place earlier. The only reason she'd stayed was because of Isabella. She'd asked, begged, her sister to come home with her but Isabella had refused to leave the estate. So Sofia had stayed, hoping that the officers assigned to watch her and her father's security people were enough to keep her alive until tomorrow.

Something was wrong.

Sofia could tell as soon as she entered the kitchen.

A breeze was blowing.

There shouldn't be any breeze inside at this time of night.

Glancing over, she saw that someone had left one of the doors open. Her chest tightened and a knot formed in the pit of her stomach.

"Hello?" she called tentatively.

There was no answer.

She knew that she should stop. Call for help. Call for the officers watching her. Call Ryan or Edmund.

But she didn't.

It was like her feet were possessed. Almost against her will, they walked her through the kitchen door. Scanning the shadows, remembering her dream, searching for anything that moved. Seeing nothing, her feet continued to walk her across the room. Around the island and finally she froze.

On the floor lay a figure.

The figure had a bag over its head.

The figure wasn't just anyone.

It was Isabella.

Her baby sister.

Dead.

Screaming, she flung herself down beside Isabella, grabbing at her frantically. Her shaking hands unable to do anything useful.

Then gentle hands were on her, tugging her to her feet.

She was still screaming. Struggling frantically against whoever was holding her. Trying desperately to get free. To get back to her sister.

"Shh, it's all right, Ms. Everette," a calm voice soothed. "It's me, Officer Parks."

Officer Parks, one of the officers guarding her. She remembered him. He was nice, sweet, had a new little baby at home. Sofia tried to calm herself with these facts. But she couldn't. All she could focus on was her sister's lifeless body.

"It's all right, Ms. Everette," Officer Parks repeated. "She's alive. Are you hearing me? Your sister is still alive. Try to calm down, you're going to hurt yourself."

Abruptly, she went still. She would have crumpled to the floor if Officer Parks wasn't holding her with an arm wrapped firmly across her waist.

"I'll call for an ambulance," she heard Officer Sand announce, but his voice was faraway.

"Better make it two," Officer Parks added.

She wondered briefly why they needed two ambulances.

Then she fainted dead away in Officer Parks' arms.

AUGUST 19TH

12:13 A.M.

He rushed through the hospital halls in a blind panic.

Ryan hadn't taken a proper breath since Officer Parks had called to tell him there had been another murder attempt at the Everette estate, and that both Isabella and Sofia were being brought to the hospital by ambulance. It had taken the young officer a couple of attempts to finally convince him that Sofia was okay. That she had only fainted. That they were only bringing her to the hospital as a precaution because of her current medical condition.

He halted as he rounded a corner and saw her.

Sofia was sitting in a chair. Elbows propped up on her knees, head resting on her hands, her hair falling in thick red waves obscuring her face.

Officers Parks and Sand were standing guard, a few feet away from her to give her some privacy. Officer Parks glanced his way and waved, gesturing to his partner before coming over to him.

"Detective Xander, you didn't have to come, she's okay, they both are," the young Officer explained.

"I know, I just had to see her with my own eyes," Ryan could feel his cheeks heating in embarrassment.

The officer nodded understandingly, "Yeah, I get it."

"She's really okay?"

"Doctor said she's fine, that she can go home whenever she wants. She just passed out, which, given everything that's going on is perfectly understandable."

Heart clenching, Ryan had to glance at Sofia to convince

himself she really was all right. "She found Isabella?"

"Uh huh. We heard her screaming, came running in, she was pretty hysterical, I had to pull her off the sister. She was crying and fighting me, didn't stop until I told her that her sister was still alive. Then it was like she just mentally checked out. Went limp and fainted in my arms."

"How is Isabella?"

"She's fine, too. Doctors want to keep an eye on her for a couple more hours, and then she can go home too. You can take her statement anytime you want."

Exactly what Paige was on her way here to do. For the moment all Ryan could do was stare at Sofia and pray that she wasn't going to be next on the killer's list. She'd already survived one attempt; there were no guarantees she'd survive the next one. "Did you see anyone else on the estate?" he asked, trying to focus on his job and not the rock of fear in his stomach.

"Just the private security guys. And the judge," Officer Parks eyes darkened.

"What?" Ryan raised a questioning brow.

"We woke him up before we rode here in the ambulance with Ms. Everette, told him what had happened, asked him if he wanted to come with his daughters to the hospital. He said no. Said he was tired and didn't want to get out of bed. That he needed a good night's sleep. Said the girls would be fine without him."

"I hate that guy," Ryan muttered.

"Yeah, he's a real piece of work," Officer Parks agreed. "It's almost a shame he turned out not to be the killer."

"All right, I'm going to leave...

"You don't want to talk to her first?" Officer Parks looked confused.

"No. Don't let her out of your sight," he cautioned. "And if she wants to go home, please don't take her back to the estate. Take her to her house, or her friend Edmund Kendall's."

"Will do," Officer Parks nodded, then headed back to join his partner.

Ryan was about to turn to leave when Sofia suddenly lifted her head, her silver eyes brimmed with tears as she studied him. He didn't move, and Sofia tentatively rose to her feet.

Unsure whether he moved, or she moved, or they both moved. But the next thing Ryan knew Sofia was throwing herself into his arms, and he was holding her so tightly he was sure he must be hurting her.

He pressed her face against his chest as she cried. "I'm sorry," she mumbled through her tears.

"I'm sorry," he cradled her head in his hand, and drank in the feel of holding her again. Keeping her wrapped up in his arms until her tears finally eased to a few hiccupping gulps, Ryan gently guided her back to the chair she'd been sitting in, and eased her back down into it. Crouching beside her so he could look up into her face. "Are you okay?"

She nodded, but her eyes were haunted.

Brushing away a lock of hair that was stuck to her wet cheeks. "Oh, baby, I'm so sorry. I'm so sorry that I made all of this worse for you." Ryan felt sick that he had added to her pain at the worst possible time.

Shaking her head. "I'm sorry. I pushed you away because I was scared. I'm sorry, Ryan. I acted like a spoiled brat. I was unfair to you. You were just doing your job, I understand that."

He was a little alarmed by how weak she sounded. "No, cupcake, you have nothing to be sorry about. I didn't handle things well. I should have woken you and explained the situation. I shouldn't have made decisions for you, I know you don't like that, I won't make that mistake again."

A small smile lit her face. "So, you forgive me?"

"Only if you forgive me," he smiled back, and cupped her face in his hand, gently stroking her cheekbone with his thumb.

"Can you take me home, Ryan?" she asked as she tilted her

face further into his hand.

"The estate is going to be crawling with CSU and officers," he reminded her, avoiding saying that he never wanted her to set foot on that property again.

"No, I meant my home," she corrected.

He was concerned by the dark smudges under her eyes, and her virtually colorless face. "Maybe you should spend the night here," he suggested. "Let the doctors make sure you're really okay."

He expected her to protest, but instead she nodded wearily, "I am a little tired," she acknowledged. "Maybe staying here isn't so bad an idea." Then her bottom lip began to tremble, and fresh tears filled her eyes. "I was so scared, Ryan. I thought she was dead."

"But she's okay," he reassured her. "Because of you. Did you see anyone?"

Not to be placated, Sofia continued, "But what if I had been just a couple of minutes slower getting to the kitchen? Isabella would be dead right now."

Applying gentle pressure to her back, he rubbed small circles, trying to get her to focus. "Honey, did you see anything?"

"Just Isabella. Lying there. I almost lost her. Another member of my family was almost gone. And Isabella, she's the only member of my family that I know actually loves me," she blinked, sending the tears spilling down her pale cheeks.

His heart was breaking for her. "Oh, cupcake," he pulled her into his arms and let her cry it out.

When her tears were spent, she rested against him. "I always wanted to find my biological mother," she murmured against his shoulder. "Maybe now would be a good time."

"If that's what you want, then I'll help you," rubbing her back to help calm her.

"I always wondered what she was like," voice faraway, detaching herself from a reality she couldn't deal with right now.

"I wondered if my mom was like Brooke. A young teenage girl, alone and looking for a better life, seduced by the judge, then pressured into giving me up. I always believed that she really wanted me, but that the judge took advantage of her. Do you think that's what happened?" she looked up at him with all the fragile vulnerability of a small child.

"Maybe, cupcake." If that was what she needed to believe right now, then he wasn't going to burst her bubble by bringing up any other possibilities. "Sweetheart, look at me for a moment," he waited until she lifted her head. "I need you to focus, can you do that for me?"

Struggling to sit herself back up properly in her chair, she nodded.

He took her hands, "How do you know that Isabella is Brooke and your father's daughter?"

Brow crinkling in confusion, "I already told you. I saw Brooke giving birth to her, my father was there."

"That doesn't mean he's the father," he said gently.

He could see the possibility had never occurred to her. "I . . . I guess," Sofia stammered. "But Isabella looks just like him. If not him, then who?"

"Isabella isn't the only who looks like your father," he waited for her to connect the dots for herself.

Ryan could tell the exact moment when it clicked because her face seemed to somehow pale further. "One of my brothers," she murmured. Then met his gaze, hers stricken, "Logan?"

He nodded, "Could that be a possibility?"

She was shaking now. "I guess. He was sleeping with her recently so I guess he could have been back then, too." Eyes going vacant, "You think he's the killer," she mumbled tonelessly.

Squeezing her hands to bring her back into the moment, Ryan asked, "Do you think Logan could be the killer?"

"I was scared of him when I was little," her voice had dropped to a mere whisper and he had to strain to hear her.

His gut tightened, "Why?"

She didn't answer. Didn't even appear to have heard him.

Taking her shoulder, he gave her a firm but gentle shake. "Why were you scared of him, Sofia?"

Her eyes still unfocused, she answered, "He would yell at me. Over anything. Even small things like me leaving my coat on the floor or my toys lying about. I . . . I tried to avoid him as best I could."

"Sofia? Did Logan ever hurt you, or . . ." forcing himself to say the words, "or touch you inappropriately?"

She flinched as though he'd slapped her. "No. No," she repeated, her cloudy eyes finally clearing. "No, he just yelled, but it was enough to scare me. He's out there somewhere, isn't he? He ran away from the hospital, so he's out there somewhere, and he's still trying to kill us."

Letting out a relieved breath, although Ryan still suspected there was more to it than she was admitting. "Shh," he attempted a smile, but hated the fear that laced her voice, he didn't want Sofia to be afraid ever again. "I don't want you to worry about your brother right now. I'm not going to be leaving your side anytime soon, and Officer Parks and Officer Sand are right here, too. You're safe."

Sofia looked empty, she leaned forward so she could wrap her arms around his waist, and rest her head against his shoulder. "Tell me about your family," she pleaded.

He settled her against his chest. "We were a pretty normal family. My parents were great, happily married, and fabulous role models for us..."

"That's nice," she whispered. "You were lucky."

"Yeah," he agreed, wishing that he'd always seen it that way and not taken his parents for granted most of his life. "I have two brothers," he continued. "One older, Jack; he's a detective too. And one younger, Mark; the only one of us boys who's married. I have four little nephews and nieces. One of whom has had a tough time with leukemia lately . . ."

Sofia made a distressed noise at that, no doubt thinking about her own illness.

"But thankfully, he's doing okay now," he assured her. "That's about it. We're just your typical family. Sometimes we fight, argue, bicker, but we all know that we love each other and are lucky to have one another." She was virtually asleep now, head nestled against his neck, her warm breath whooshing across his collarbone.

"How is she?" Paige suddenly materialized beside him.

"Wiped out," he replied. "How's Isabella?"

"Wiped out," Paige answered. "She see anything?"

"No, what about Isabella? She see anything?"

"Nope," Paige shook her head. "Said he came up behind her and grabbed her; she never heard him and she never got a look at him. She staying here tonight?"

"Yes."

"You staying with her?"

"Yes." Raising a challenging eyebrow, daring his partner to disagree.

Paige merely smiled. "Good. I'll call you in the morning. Try to get some rest because we have to talk with her about her dreams tomorrow...uh I mean today." With a backwards wave, Paige disappeared down the corridor.

Ryan knew that was not going to be an easy conversation, and he was worried Sofia wasn't physically or emotionally up to delving into a past she had convinced herself was nothing but dreams. Unfortunately, he knew it had to be done.

Gathering Sofia up into his arms. "Okay, sweetheart, let's go find you a bed."

"You're not going anywhere, are you?" she raised her head to ask, uncertainty in her silver eyes and Ryan hated that he had put it there by breaking his promise last time.

"No, Sofia, I'm not going to be going anywhere, I promise," he assured her, hoping she could believe it, as he headed for the nurses' station to ask for a room for Sofia, and a doctor to come and check her out.

She must have believed him because she nodded once, closed her eyes, and let herself sink deeper down into his arms.

"You have absolutely nothing to worry about. I'll be right by your bed while you sleep, and Officers Parks and Sand will be right outside your room. All you have to do is get some sleep and build your strength back up. I'm going to take care of you. I'm always going to be here to take care of you."

* * * * *

6:40 A.M.

Hazy.

Everything was hazy.

His eyesight, his hearing, his mind.

He wasn't sure where he was. Or how he had gotten here.

He wasn't sure of anything.

He tried to focus on the last thing he remembered.

But he couldn't.

This was a nightmare.

Logan IV drew in a deep breath and focused his mind. He would just take things one step at a time. First things first, he needed to open his eyes. Once they were open he'd be able to see where he was and perhaps that would jumpstart his memory.

Concentrating all his energy on his eyes, he tried to pry them open but couldn't manage it. He wondered why it was that he couldn't even open his eyes. Maybe he was sick. Had conjunctivitis or something and that was why he was having trouble with this usual trivial task. Attempting to lift a hand to wipe his eyes, he was alarmed when it didn't move. And there was something rough and scratchy around his wrist.

Panic shot through him, enough to pop his eyes wide open. And Logan found himself in a small room. Maybe ten feet by ten feet, illuminated by a single globe dangling from the ceiling, the only furniture in the room was a wooden table, and a bed that he appeared to be tied to. His wrists and ankles were secured to the bed with ropes.

He was also naked.

Horror mingled with terror mingled with unspeakable fear ran through his veins and he began to scream. Logan screamed and screamed and screamed until his throat was so hoarse that even breathing hurt. Then he struggled wildly against the ropes that bound him. He twisted his fingers to try and claw at the ropes, yanking on his arms and legs to try and pull them free. He lurched his middle off the bed as though that would loosen the ropes.

At last he fell back against the mattress, drained. Wrists and ankles rubbed bare, throat aching. The fear inside him seemed to be a living being, weighing him down as though it were a physical weight on his chest, smothering him.

Then the tears came.

He sobbed huge, gut wrenching sobs. Tears streamed down his face, and his nose was stuffed up. Logan felt like he was choking but couldn't seem to stop crying. He bawled for what seemed like hours, unable to stop, until his exhausted body gave out and all that was left were a few sniffles.

"What a crybaby," a voice announced.

He could hardly see through his blurry, tear-filled eyes, but still Logan's head turned in the direction of the voice. A shadowy figure loomed above him. Blinking to try and clear his eyes, the figure slowly morphed into something recognizable.

"You," he muttered, voice croaky from all his yelling.

"Yep, me," Isabella agreed sociably.

Gradually, his memory began to return.

He and Simone had been returning from a charity event. He'd parked the car in the garage when someone had pointed a gun at him. Isabella. She'd made him tie up Simone and then wound tape around and around him until he was trapped in his seat. Then she'd left the car engine running until both he and Simone passed out.

Logan had thought he was going to die.

But someone had found him.

He vaguely remembered a strong man dragging him from the car. The relief of fresh air blowing on his face. Drinking in breath after breath. Realizing just what a precious thing it was to be able to breathe.

He remembered the whirl of sirens and the swirl of blue and red lights that had left him feeling dizzy. Paramedics had given him oxygen and driven him to the hospital. That was the last thing he could recall.

Somehow Isabella had managed to get him out of the hospital and to . . . here. Wherever here was.

"How did I get here?" he wheezed.

Gray eyes glowing with a manic gleam. "I brought you here. I impersonated a nurse at the hospital. It wasn't hard," she explained, tone frighteningly conversational. "I just faked an ID, dressed like everyone else, and pretended I was supposed to be there. Then I simply loaded you in a wheelchair and walked you right out the door. No one even blinked in my direction. Pretty lax hospital security," she chuckled. "Or maybe I'm just awesome. Then I threw you in the back of a van and drove you here."

"Where is here?" Logan wanted to hurl insults at Isabella and unload his anger but was refraining because she was clearly unbalanced.

"A safe little hidey-hole," Isabella grinned.

"Which safe little hidey-hole?" he demanded. If she'd taken him back to the estate and tucked him away in one of the many secret rooms, then surely someone would find him. The house was big, but the place was always buzzing with staff. Optimism dimming slightly, that was assuming that there were still family members left to employ staff. Last he knew there was only his father and Sofia left. And Sofia didn't even live on the estate anymore. And his father was in jail.

"One in the attic," she smiled.

At least they were still on the estate and she hadn't spirited him away to some unknown location. Even if there was no family or staff here there had to be police and crime scene techs. "Someone will hear me, then," he smiled back smugly.

"I don't think so," Isabella shook her head, sending her red hair flying around her face.

"Why?" he asked, his confidence dimming, he had been screaming for hours and no one had come.

She clapped her hands, "I soundproofed up here."

"You got someone in to soundproof?" That seemed unlikely. His father monitored who came in and out of the estate religiously, and he would have noticed if Isabella had brought in workers to soundproof the attic.

"No, I did it myself," she answered.

The scariest thing about all of this was just how much time and effort Isabella had put into planning this. To go to the trouble of soundproofing the attic meant she had intended to hide him away up here. Which meant she had always intended to abduct him from the hospital. Which meant she had never intended to kill him with carbon monoxide in the garage. Which meant she had planned it down to the exact second so that he would be found still alive. Which meant she was far more evil than he had ever given her credit for.

Perhaps even more evil than he was.

She had been completely cold and calculating about wiping out their family.

She had never intended any of them to survive.

She was systematically wiping them out one by one.

And who would ever suspect the quiet, shy, serious teenager?

Her plan was genius.

She was an evil genius.

But why? Why kill them all?

"I don't understand, Isabella." He studied her face, trying to read in it the answers he sought. "I don't understand why you're doing all of this."

"I think you do," the malevolent smile left her face, replaced by a malicious snarl.

Was it possible Isabella really did know what he'd done? If she did, how had she found out? He had been careful. Covered his tracks. Isabella couldn't know.

"You don't know anything," he challenged, trying to make himself look as threatening as a naked man tied to a bed could look.

"I know every horrible thing you ever did," she contradicted, her snarl softened back into a smile.

"If you really do know, then why kill the others? If you know then you also know that father and Gloria, and Lewis and Lincoln, and Simone and Samantha, had nothing to do with it. Neither did Brooke Mariano. And you shot at Sofia, I doubt she's ever done anything in her life to deserve being murdered." Logan had to admit that Sofia was a bit of a freak in their family. Somehow, despite all the odds being stacked against her, she didn't seem to have a selfish or mean or vindictive bone in her body. She always wanted to do the right thing, even when it hurt her. And for some reason Logan couldn't fathom, she seemed to truly enjoy helping others.

"They knew, Logan. You know they did. All of them. They know what you did, or at least that you were up to something. And they didn't do anything to stop you. Are you telling me that doesn't warrant death?" She was watching him quizzically now, honestly seeming to want to hear his answer.

If he were a better person, he probably would have tried to bargain for his surviving family members' lives. As best he knew both his father and Sofia were still alive. But Logan didn't care about them. Only himself. Perhaps he could bond with Isabella over violence. It seemed like his best option of getting out of here. "You knew, Isabella," he said quietly, as calmly as his pounding heart would allow. "And you didn't go to the police? You knew. Why didn't you do something?"

"I did do something. I am doing something. I'm doing this. I'm making sure this family's evil ends here."

Before Logan had a chance to say more, Isabella slammed something into his head and the world exploded into a fireball of pain, and then nothing.

* * * * *

9:08 A.M.

"I thought you didn't want me to come back here," Sofia was peering at them warily from the back seat of his car.

"You didn't tell her?" Paige asked as he pulled the car to a stop in front of the Everette family home.

"Tell me what?" Sofia demanded.

Sighing, Ryan hadn't wanted to tell Sofia right away that they were taking her back to her family's estate to visit the basement and get to the bottom of exactly what she knew about her family's long buried secrets. "We need to talk to you about your dreams," he told her, not telling her yet that they were going to be doing that in the basement.

"They're just dreams," she protested.

"I don't think you really believe that," Paige contradicted gently. "I think it's just what you told yourself because you couldn't deal with what you saw."

Shaking her head adamantly. "No. That's what he always said. That I was just dreaming. And then he'd take me back to bed."

"Who's he?" Ryan asked, twisting in his seat to see her properly.

"My father," she answered quietly, pushing open her door to climb out.

Hurrying to help her, Ryan took her elbow and began to guide her toward the house. Her feet slowed the closer to the front door they got, and she leaned heavily on him, her breath was catching in little gasps. "Are you okay?" he tipped her face up and examined it carefully.

"I don't want to go back in there," she whimpered.

"And I don't want you to. I hate that I have to bring you back here. But I think we both know that they aren't dreams. They're memories, and if those memories can save your life, then we have to find out what you know. I'm going to be right beside you the whole time." Taking her face in his hands, Ryan pressed a kiss to her forehead. Then, ignoring the fact that it was completely inappropriate given that she was a witness, and that his partner was standing right behind them, he brushed his lips against hers. He intended it to be quick and light and nonthreatening, but Sofia deepened the kiss, raising her hands to his face to keep him there when he would have pulled away.

"Thank you," she whispered when she eventually broke contact. "I needed that. All right, let's get this over with."

Determinedly, she started for the door. Ryan cast a glance at Paige, who rolled her eyes, before they both followed her. "We'll avoid the kitchen," he murmured in Sofia's ear as he caught up to her.

She uttered a small sigh of relief. "Thank you." Looking up at him, "Thank you for knowing what I need without me having to say it."

Her smile dimmed as she walked through the front door, and he grasped her arm as she went toward the front sitting room. "Sofia, wait, we have to do this in the basement."

All color drained from her face. Concerned she was going to pass out, Ryan grabbed for her, but she backed away. "I'm not going down there," she looked at him as if he were crazy.

"Cupcake, you have to . . ."

"No," she pressed her hands to her ears, blocking out his voice. "No, no, no, no, no. I am *not* going back down there. I can't, I can't, I can't, I can't, I can't," she babbled hysterically.

Taking her by the shoulders, Ryan shook her. "Sofia, snap out of it. You *can* do it. You can."

"Please," she begged. "Please don't make me do this. I'll tell you. I'll tell you what I dream, just please don't make me go down there."

"If there was another way . . ." he began, wishing for an excuse, any excuse, not to have to inflict this on her. This was hell, even if it was for her own good.

Her eyes filled with panicked desperation as they implored him to save her. "Please, Ryan. Please. Don't make me."

Sobbing, she threw herself into his arms. Clinging to him, her small hands curled into fists as they clutched at his shirt, burying her face against his chest. Ryan had only felt this helpless once before. The night his fiancée had died. He hadn't known what to do that night, and he didn't know what to do now. All he did know was that he couldn't force the hysterical woman in his arms to go down to the basement that terrified her. Looking helplessly to his partner, he silently asked her to help.

"I hate playing the bad guy," Paige muttered, but nonetheless she came to his rescue. Taking hold of Sofia's chin, she forcibly lifted her face, leaning in so they were eye to eye. "Sofia, I need you to snap out of it. You need to focus. Ryan isn't going to push you on this because he's fallen for you. And as much as I think you're a really sweet person, I have not fallen for you. So we *are* going to do this. It could save your life. Your sister's, too. You don't want anything else to happen to Isabella, do you?"

Slowly, Sofia shook her head.

"Okay then, well unless you come with us to the basement and tell us what you saw happen down there, then the killer could come back and finish what he started. You don't want that to happen, do you?"

Guilt flashed across Sofia's face, and for a moment Ryan hated his partner for putting it there, and yet at the same time he was eternally grateful that Paige was able to do what he couldn't.

"Good girl. Let's get going then, get this over with," Paige took Sofia's arms and gently, but firmly, extracted her from his grip.

Sofia allowed Paige to tug her from his arms and toward the stairs to the basement, but the look Sofia shot him was stricken. He took her hand, "I'm coming with you, squeeze as hard as you need to."

She did, digging her nails into his hand so tightly she drew blood. "Sorry," she murmured when he winced, but didn't loosen her grip.

"You're fine," he assured her, even though she looked about as far away from fine as it was possible to look.

At the top of the basement stairs she froze, her terrified eyes darting up to his. "I don't think I can do this."

"You *can* do this," Paige said firmly before he had a chance to answer.

But as Paige opened the door exposing the staircase and the dark basement below, Sofia turned green. "I'm going to be sick." Yanking herself free from their holds, she bolted, as fast as her wobbly legs would allow her, for the nearest bathroom. A moment later they could hear her throwing up. Then the toilet flushed and water ran for several minutes.

Ryan was about to go into the bathroom to check on her when the door opened. Sofia stood there, face dismal, trembling, looking like she was about to face the executioner. Ryan's heart broke. "Are you okay?" He blotted at her sweat-streaked face with his handkerchief.

"No, I'm not okay. But Paige isn't going to let me go until I go to the basement, so let's just get it over with." With a steely determination that left his heart beating wildly with pride, she stomped back to the basement stairs, faltering a little as she reached them. She held out her hand, and he grasped it firmly. "I hate the stairs. In my dreams, or whatever they are, I'm always already down them. I never know how I get there, because any time I tried to go down when I was awake I always froze at the top."

"This time you aren't going down alone," he reminded her.

Taking a deep breath, she tentatively reached out a foot and placed it on the first step. Seeing how hard this was for her, Ryan wanted to lift her into his arms and carry her down, but he knew this was important. Sofia needed to feel like she was in control if she was going to let them pry her dream out of her.

Ever so slowly, she brought her other foot down to join the first. And that was step number one conquered.

"You're doing great," he assured her.

Grateful, she smiled at him, and with him on one side of her and Paige on the other, she haltingly made her way down to the bottom. Letting out a relieved breath, Sofia sunk down to the floor, tucking her knees up to her chest, and for a moment they let her be, allowing her to gather herself.

"It's big down here," Paige commented, circling around the large space.

"Not much stored here," he added, one eye on Sofia as he scanned the basement. The huge room was virtually empty, a few boxes of Christmas decorations sat in the far corner, some skis and snowboards in the adjacent one, and that was it.

"I wonder what went on down here," Paige pondered. "It's so dark and dismal, I can't see anyone wanting to come down here. And there are so many rooms in this house, so it's not like this is the only place to have any privacy."

"Your answers are sitting over there," he inclined his head at Sofia.

"You're right, and she's had enough time to adjust to being down here again," Paige pronounced. Crouching at Sofia's side,

Paige took the other woman's face and tilted it up. "Okay, Sofia, you said in your dreams that they always started down here, what's the first thing you remember?"

Glancing at him for support, Ryan knelt beside her and took her hand. "I'm here."

"I'd always wonder why I was here," Sofia began, her eyes had taken on a vacant, distant glint.

"No going into a trance on me, Sofia," Paige warned. "What next?"

Sofia's eyes cleared a little, "I'd think about how much I hated it down here. I was afraid of the dark, and it was always dark down here. Except for the other room."

Exchanging glances with Paige, there didn't appear to be another room down here. "What other room?" Ryan asked her.

"I'd walk toward it," Sofia continued as though he hadn't spoken. "On tippy-toes. I didn't want anyone to hear me."

"Cupcake, what other room?" he pressed.

"There were voices arguing," she continued, lost in her recollections. "Two people. I'd stop at the door to look in. Their arms were waving about as they argued. I could never understand what they were saying, though."

"Sofia," Ryan made his voice softly commanding and tapped lightly at her cheeks. "What other room?"

"It was the room where bad things happened," she whispered in a little girl voice.

He let that go for the moment, she wasn't quite ready to confront what she'd seen happen in the room. "What happened next in your dreams?" he asked instead.

"My father would grab my shoulder. I'd jump, scared. Then he'd tell me that I was just dreaming," she finished flatly.

Ryan glanced at Paige to see if she'd picked up on the same thing he had. "Your father was behind you?" he confirmed.

Sofia nodded glumly.

"And you didn't see anyone come past you out of the room?"

Paige inquired.

She shook her head, not yet catching on to the significance of that.

"If your father came from behind you, and he didn't leave the room while you were there, then it couldn't have been him who was arguing with someone," Paige summarized.

Shocked, "Then who...who was in the room?" Sofia stammered. "Logan?"

"That would be my guess," Ryan agreed, glancing at his partner, who nodded that she had come to the same conclusion.

"Can I go home now?" Sofia asked so pitifully it had tears stinging the back of his eyes.

"Not yet, honey," he stroked her hair. "What happens next in your dream?"

"My father picks me up, but I look over his shoulder..."

"What do you see, Sofia?" Paige asked gently.

Her dazed look returns, "I see red."

"What does that mean, Sofia?" Paige pressed, taking one of Sofia's hands and squeezing, trying to get her to focus.

"It's so red," was all Sofia could mumble.

Understanding dawned on Ryan, "Is the red blood, cupcake?"

She bobbed her head up and down.

"Do you know whose blood it is?" Paige continued. If Ryan hadn't known better, he would think his partner was cold and uncaring, the way she kept pushing Sofia relentlessly. But they'd worked together for years now, and they were good friends, Ryan knew Paige wasn't enjoying this, just doing it because it had to be done.

"No," Sofia replied, sounding impossibly childlike.

However, they both caught something in her voice. "Did you ever go down there during the day?" Ryan asked.

"Even in the daytime it was dark down there," she whispered as an answer. "I don't like the dark."

"Come on, Sofia," Paige shook her. "I need you to focus just a little while longer."

"You're doing great," Ryan encouraged. "Did you ever come down here during the day, when you were sure you were awake?" he asked again. "You said that you could never make yourself walk down the stairs when you weren't dreaming, so if you tried to come down, did you ever make it?"

"I wasn't allowed down here," she replied.

"Sofia, that's not an answer," he pushed carefully, extremely aware that if they pushed too hard then they could end up pushing her right over the edge. "Did you come down here one day?"

Scared silver eyes that seemed too big for her thin, pale face, looked back at him. "I came down one time," she admitted.

"Was anyone down here?" Paige's eyes lighted. Sofia was slowly leading them in a roundabout way to what had really gone on down here.

"I was home sick from school," she squeezed her eyes closed as she spoke. "The nanny was off during the day. I was supposed to be in bed," she was speaking quickly now, breathless. "But I was hungry. I went down to the kitchen. The door to the basement was open. I stopped. I didn't want to go down, but my feet started walking down the stairs anyway. The light was on. In the room. Just like it was in my dreams . . ."

Taking her shoulders, Ryan shook her, "Breathe, cupcake, you have to keep breathing."

Drawing in a shaky breath, "I...I...walked toward the light. There was a bed. On it was a girl. She looked only a little older than me. She...she was tied up."

Sofia was looking so distressed, it was taking every ounce of Ryan's strength to keep from picking her up and spiriting her out of this house forever. Still, he knew she needed to tell. Not just so they could find the killer, but for her own sake. Whatever she had seen clearly still haunted her to this day. "Was someone in there with the girl, Sofia?" he asked quietly.

Jerking a nod. "He's on top of her. She's screaming, trying to get away, but she can't because of the ropes. He's laughing. Telling her he likes it when she struggles. He's ... he's raping her ..." Tears seeped out the corners of her eyes, which were still squeezed tightly shut.

Brushing the tears away. "Can you see his face? Can you see who's raping the girl?" he asked.

"I don't know," she cried. "I don't know."

"Sofia," fighting to keep his voice calm when what he wanted to do was scream that Sofia had been drawn into all of this, "open your eyes for me." Her eyelids obediently fluttered open. "Try to concentrate on the man's face."

"I'm so tired," she groaned quietly, pressing a hand to her head.

"You have a headache," Ryan murmured, taking her face in his hands and massaging her temples with his thumbs. She moaned softly, and after a minute, he could feel her start to relax. As much as he wanted to know who in her family had been raping women in this house, he was concerned enough about Sofia's emotional well-being to take things slowly. "Okay, cupcake, now look at me." Her pupils shifted, but her eyes looked straight through him. "*At* me, Sofia," he repeated, increasing the pressure on her temples. Her eyes moved again, seeing him now. "All right, now think."

Concentrating, "It's...it's Logan," she answered miserably. "Oh my gosh," her voice grew panicked. "I thought it was my father arguing with women, but it wasn't. It was Logan and his victims. Begging him for their lives. All these years I thought it was arguing, but it was murder. I saw him killing them. My father must have known. He was there. He knew what Logan was doing. He probably helped him cover it up. Oh my gosh, oh my gosh." Sofia scrunched her eyes closed once more and began to rock herself backwards and forwards.

Fighting tears of his own, a glance at Paige confirmed she too had tears standing in her brown eyes. What a horrible thing for a child to have witnessed. No wonder Sofia had blocked it out. And to know that her father was involved. Even if it was only helping Logan cover it up, it still made him complicit in the crimes. Ryan had known as soon as she'd said her father was down there that he was involved somehow, but it had taken Sofia's frazzled mind longer to come to the same conclusion. "Come here, baby," he took her in his arms. "I'm so sorry you had to see that. I wish I could take that out of your mind, make it like it never happened."

She burrowed against him, clutching tightly, frantically, at him, but then she suddenly pushed away, frenetic. "There were sticks on the ground."

"What?" Paige asked, puzzled.

"I thought they were sticks but they weren't, they were grave markers. He buried them down here." She began to hyperventilate, "I can't breathe, Ryan. I can't breathe."

"Shh," he soothed. "Yes, you can. Open your eyes, honey," he waited until they struggled open. "There you go, good girl, just rest your head here," he pressed it down against his shoulder, cradling it with one hand. With his other he rubbed comforting circles on her back to help calm her. "I want you to breathe slowly with me, in and out, we'll do it together." After a couple of minutes, Sofia grew quiet, snuggled against his chest, and he wondered if her exhausted mind had given out and she had drifted off to sleep.

"Sweetie, I hate to do this to you," Paige looked truly distressed. "But we need to know where the room is. Can you show us?"

Wearily, Sofia lifted her head, "I want to go home now," she pleaded.

"I know you do, sweetie," Paige patted her shoulder. "And this is the last thing I need from you. Can you show us where the room is?"

"Yes," Sofia leaned heavily against him as he wrapped an arm around her waist and practically lifted her to her feet. "This way." She led them to the wall farthest from the stairs, but she didn't look to the wall; instead, her gaze dropped to the floor. "Down there."

"Down here?" Paige repeated.

"There's a trapdoor and a tunnel," Sofia looked completely drained, barely able to remain upright.

Concerned she'd drop to the floor when he released his grip on her to search for the trapdoor Ryan asked, "Sofia, do you want to sit?"

"I'll be okay," she murmured, but her eyes had gone vacant again. She had just about reached her limit of what she could handle.

Tentatively, he removed his arm from around her waist, ready to catch her if she fell, but somehow she managed to stay standing. Joining Paige, they quickly located the trapdoor. Pulling it open, Ryan noted that the hinges didn't creak. Someone had been taking good care of it, so it had most likely been used recently. About to drop down into the tunnel below, he cast a worried glance Sofia's way. He didn't think she was up to seeing this room again, but he wasn't sure that Paige wouldn't want to ask her more questions.

"Leave her there," Paige nodded understandingly. "If we have more questions we can ask them later; I think she's done enough for now."

Grateful, he joined his partner in the tunnel. It was narrow, but not so narrow that they weren't able to walk side by side. It wasn't too long either, only about ten feet, then there were three steps and they were in another large room. Just as Sofia had stated, there was a large bed on one side, and at least thirty grave markers taking up most of the room. Around the bed, the floor was stained a dark red. Blood. They both began to pace the room, searching for anything useful.

A sharp gasp had them both spinning around.

Sofia stood at the top of the steps. A trembling hand held over her mouth.

"What are you doing in here?" he asked, dismayed.

"I was scared on my own," she whispered, her eyes riveted to the graves. "Ryan, what if...what if...my biological mother was one of Logan's victims? What if she's buried here?"

"There's no reason to think that, cupcake," he assured her.

Swaying unsteadily, "Ryan, I think I'm going to pass out," she murmured.

Springing toward her, he hoped to catch her before she collapsed, but he was too far away. Her knees hit the concrete floor with a horrible thud, but he managed to reach her in time to get a hand under her head before it cracked into the floor. A concussion was the last thing she needed right now. Sofia was shaking, still clinging to consciousness, although barely. Shrugging out of his jacket, he wrapped her up in it, then scooped her into his arms. "I'm going to take her out of here," he informed Paige. "She's totally exhausted, physically and mentally."

"I'm sorry, Ryan," Paige said quietly. "I didn't enjoy any of that. I didn't mean to push her so hard that she fainted. I didn't want to upset her; I was just doing what I had to so we can save her life."

"I know, Paige," he assured his partner. "You got out of her what I wouldn't have been able to. The only way she was giving that up was if we pried it out of her."

Leaving Paige to search the basement, he carried Sofia back through the tunnel and out into the other side, then up the steps, calling for CSU as he went.

Stephanie met him at the top of the stairs, her hazel eyes going immediately to Sofia. "Is she okay?"

"No," Ryan answered, "she's not. She just relived the worst thing she's ever seen."

"Poor baby," Stephanie clucked sympathetically. "And how are you?" she eyed him shrewdly.

"Worn out," he replied. He hadn't slept last night, even before he'd gotten the call about Sofia. He'd been lying in bed, awake, trying to figure out a way to get things back on track with her. Then at the hospital he'd sat beside her bed, holding her hand, and watched her sleep. "This killer is relentless. Another victim every night. He doesn't leave us time to catch up, let alone get ahead of him."

"But he's failed three times now," Stephanie reminded him. "Or two, I guess, if the killer is Logan. You'll get him."

In his arms, Sofia stirred. "I don't want to go in the basement again," she mumbled tiredly.

"You don't have to, cupcake," he assured her. "Just rest now."

"What can I do for her?" Stephanie asked, gently stroking Sofia's hair.

"You can get your team to go over every inch of that basement with a fine-tooth comb and find me something to nail Logan Everette IV to the wall."

* * * * *

4:21 P.M.

This could be disastrous.

It could ruin everything.

Isabella was watching the hubbub from a shadowy corner. So far no one had noticed her, which was lucky considering the number of people swarming throughout the house.

At the moment most of the attention seemed to be on Sofia. Her sister was lying on a settee, covered in blankets, in the middle of the library. She appeared to be asleep but every so often Ryan would go to her, perch on the sofa beside her, and ask her questions. Isabella couldn't hear what they were saying, but she'd seen the door to the basement open earlier so she had a pretty good idea.

Sofia was well protected. Two officers were standing nearby, Ryan and his partner came to check on her what seemed like every few minutes, and there were crime scene techs everywhere. They needn't have worried, though. Isabella was not a threat to her sister's safety.

As she continued to watch unseen, Ryan returned to the room, crouched beside the sofa and gently ran a hand through Sofia's hair. At his touch, her sister's large silver eyes fluttered open to gaze adoringly up at him, and she pulled a hand out from under the blankets to take his and hold it to her cheek. Whatever Ryan said to her was obviously upsetting because Sofia began to cry, and Ryan took her in his arms and held her.

Tears stung the backs of Isabella's eyes as she watched how tender Ryan was with Sofia. She wished that one day she could find someone who would look at her the way Ryan did at Sofia.

She was glad that she wasn't going to kill her sister.

There was no reason to. Despite the fact that Sofia knew more about what Logan had done than most of the rest of the family, Sofia hadn't known that she knew. Had probably blocked it out. She'd only been a child when she'd stumbled upon the horrors going on in the family basement, so it was completely understandable that she would bury the memories away, convince herself they were just dreams.

Besides, now that Sofia had unlocked those memories, she had told the police. She was doing what she could to put a stop to Logan's crimes, despite the obvious toll it was taking on her.

Unlike the others.

The judge and Gloria had known what Logan was doing, so had Simone. Lewis and Lincoln had known, too, although maybe not all the details. And yet not a single one of them had lifted a finger to stop him. They had let innocent young girls be tortured and murdered under their roof and ignored it. Isabella couldn't comprehend how they could do that. In keeping their mouths shut, they were complicit in the crimes and just as guilty as Logan.

So Isabella had come up with this plan.

She had always known that Logan was evil, but it had been Sofia's dreams that had given her the first insight into just what a monster he really was. After listening to Sofia talk in her sleep about the terrifying things she'd seen in the basement, Isabella had begun to investigate. She'd set up cameras and microphones down there and managed to get tangible proof of what Logan was up to. That was when she knew she had to act. If the others wouldn't take care of Logan, then she would. She would take care of all of them.

Still, having this place crawling with police was worrying. They now knew that Logan had been kidnapping, raping and killing women, then burying their bodies in the basement.

That *could* end up being a good thing. It would keep the focus of their investigation firmly on Logan. Which should mean they would have no need to look elsewhere. They would just assume Logan was wiping out his family because they knew what he had been doing.

The flip side was that Isabella didn't know just how much Sofia would remember. Her sister might know more than she thought, something that could divert the police's attention away from Logan. She was going to have to get Sofia alone at some point and find out the specifics of what was going on.

She was so close now. There was only the judge left to kill. And then Logan would be lucky last. Then she would disappear forever. She was so close to finishing that it would be devastating for anything to happen that would derail her plan.

Isabella wasn't going to let that happen.

She'd go check on Logan, whom she was positive the police would never stumble upon, even if they searched the entire house. Next, she'd take out the judge once the estate quieted down for the night. Then she'd go and speak with her sister and make sure that Logan was still the number one suspect.

Right now she still had her options open as to how to end

things. She could kill Logan and make it look like suicide, like he'd killed himself because the police were closing in on him. Or she could kill him and hide the body, make it look like he had fled the country. Or she could kill him openly, take all the credit, say that he had come back to try and kill her again, and she had killed him first in self-defense.

However, the police might somehow get suspicious of her or they might lose interest in Logan and move on to someone else, maybe revive their theory that it was someone with a grudge against the family. Whatever they thought, if Logan was no longer a suspect, then Isabella would have to make him look like another victim, then make herself disappear.

First things first; she'd go back to Logan.

She slipped unnoticed up the stairs and back to the attic. Inside the hidden room Logan was still unconscious. Perhaps she had gone a little overboard earlier. But he had made her mad when he'd said that she hadn't done anything to stop him either. She *had* done something. She'd done what needed to be done. And it was working.

Taking a glass of ice water, she threw it over his face. "Wakey, wakey, Logan," she sing-songed.

He groaned.

Impatient now, Isabella slapped at his cheeks. "Come on, Logan, wake up now. I don't have all day; I have things to do."

Another groan, but his eyes fluttered open, struggling to focus on her. "I was hoping you were just a nightmare," he muttered weakly.

"Well too bad for you," she snarled, "because I'm real. Probably all too real for you." She studied him closely, wondering whether he would finally own the truth after all these years.

Brow furrowed, "What do you mean? I wish you'd stop talking in riddles."

"Still can't say it out loud?" she mocked. "Want me to help? I'm your daughter."

Shock flashed across his face. "How... how did you find out?"

Shrugging, "I got curious as to who our mothers were, did some DNA testing. Imagine my surprise to find out that the judge isn't my father, but you are. You and Brooke," she spat out the woman's name. "Your father's mistress. Disgusting."

"It wasn't like that," Logan stammered.

"What I don't understand," Isabella plowed on, ignoring Logan, "is why she was different than your other victims. Was it because she was too old? I mean, you liked girls, right? Young women my age. You lured them here, probably with the promise of money, and then you tied them up in the basement, raped them repeatedly, and then made them beg you for their lives. But Brooke, my mother, you let her live. Why?"

"Because he told me to," Logan answered simply.

"The judge?"

"Who else?" Logan snapped.

"Always gotta do what daddy tells you to?" she mocked.

"He said Brooke knew too much. That she was too smart. That too many people knew she was obsessed with our family. That killing her would draw attention to me, to us. He said if I was going to kill, then it had to be girls who no one would ever link to me. So that's what I did," Logan's face grew dreamy, as he presumably reminisced about the time he'd spent with his victims. Then his face grew sharp, "With them, it was the only time I was ever in control."

"Boohoo to you," she scoffed. "Your daddy was controlling, so you had to kill women. I don't care why you did it, I only care about making you stop. Which I have. You won't ever kill another girl again."

"But you," he met her eye and held her gaze, "you will. You think you can stop after I'm dead? You think you won't ever be tempted to kill again? You're even more delusional than I thought. Don't forget, I'm your father."

"We are not the same," Isabella returned confidently.

"I'm a killer and your mother used you to get rich, sold you to my father. You think murder and selfishness aren't in your genes?" his tone was condescending now.

Rage bubbled inside her. She wasn't going to be ridiculed by the father who had never acknowledged her. Before she even knew what she was doing, her hand had whipped out and slapped his face. "Brooke begged, you know. Begged for her life. Offered me money. That's how stupid she was. Offered *me* money, when the only money she had came from blackmailing the judge."

"She didn't know what I was doing, Isabella," Logan grew serious. "Why did you kill her?"

"Because she deserved it," Isabella spat out. "She dumped me like I was garbage."

"See," Logan raised a pointed red brow. "It was personal. You killed her because you wanted to. She's your mother and you murdered her, not because of me and what I did, but because you didn't like her."

"Brooke Mariano was *not* my mother," she ranted. "She was nothing more than the woman who gave birth to me."

"She was pregnant," Logan was reproachful now.

"The baby wasn't yours," she informed him. "The police said it was the judge's; that's why they arrested him for her murder."

"Still to kill a pregnant woman..."

"You actually care," Isabella was shocked, hadn't thought her biological father was capable of loving or even caring about someone else. "You actually liked her."

"We were a lot alike. If the judge had let me, I would have married Brooke."

"Then you could have murdered together," she said snidely. "The police know. They know everything. They found your room in the basement. That's why they now think *you're* the killer. So I can do whatever I want without having to worry about them suspecting me. I get to finish off the judge, then take care of you, and disappear forever, and no one will be any the wiser."

So far Logan had remained fairly calm, probably thinking he could somehow bond with her and convince her to let him go, but when she took a menacing step toward him, fear flashed through his eyes.

"You don't have to kill me, Isabella," his voice was laced with terror. "We can run away together. Father and daughter, together at last. Please, please don't kill me. I'm begging you, please," tears began to seep out, tumbling down his cheeks.

"Begging, just like your victims," she grinned, enjoying her father's horror. "You know it's not really me you should be worried about, but Sofia."

"Why?" he managed to choke out past a sob.

"Because Sofia knows things. Even *if* the police found us before I kill you, you'll only be going straight off to jail."

"How... how does Sofia know?"

"Because she was your first."

$$* \quad * \quad * \quad * \quad *$$

10:58 P.M.

He was enjoying the cool night air.

It had been a long week. A long, unpleasant week.

These last few days had been the worst.

Being arrested, taken to a police station, going through booking like a common criminal. It had been humiliating, and Judge Logan Everette was furious about it. Having to disclose what he had been doing while Brooke Mariano was killed had been the most mortifying of all. Knowing that people had seen him and Mary-Anne in their most intimate of moments was simply appalling.

All he'd wanted upon leaving the police station was the peace and quiet of being left alone in his own home, and even that had been denied him. His house had been crawling with police

191

officers and crime scene techs basically the entire time. The killer had invaded his estate once again to make an attempt on Isabella's life. The girl had survived, apparently because Sofia had interrupted the killer, and some pathetically inept young officers had woken him up to inquire whether he wanted to accompany his daughters to the hospital. Of course he had not. His girls were used to taking care of themselves.

Then Sofia must have remembered what she'd seen in the basement as a child because her cop boyfriend and his partner had taken her down there, following which, once again, the house had been filled to the brim with what seemed like half the police department. Looking back, Logan supposed it had always been inevitable that eventually the truth would come out. Perhaps he should have handled things differently back then.

Now it seemed that even if he managed to survive this brutal killer's scheme to annihilate his family, his life was ruined anyway. No longer would he be a respected and feared judge. Now he would forever be the man whose family had been murdered. The man whose son was a violent psychopath. The man who had been questioned for murder.

Logan was wondering whether his life was even worth living.

Everything he'd worked so hard to control had all fallen apart.

He had always prided himself on knowing his wife and his children so well. Knowing the way their minds worked and what they were likely to do in any situation, so that he knew how to best manipulate them. And despite what they sometimes thought, there was very little he didn't know about each and every member of his family.

Gloria, his weak and pathetic wife, Logan was not at all sad about her death. He had picked her for those very qualities. He needed a wife who wasn't going to be independent, who was going to be able to be pressured into complying with his every whim. It hadn't taken him long to squash a young Gloria's spirit. Until the suicide attempt that led to her affair and subsequent pregnancy. Despite what he'd told the detectives, he had indeed engineered Gloria's young son's demise. It hadn't been hard to coerce the young maid into complying with his plan, a scandalous romp in the bedroom where he had snapped some photos of her naked and the girl had been so terrified that he'd show them to her devoutly religious family that she had been putty in his hands. He hadn't wanted to kill the child, but it had become evident that Gloria was never going to be interested in procuring him an heir while she had a child of her own. Needless to say, he was surprised that she had managed to figure out he was behind the little boy's death.

Isabella, that girl was an odd one. She was quiet and shy and studious. She never said much, but she was always watching everything with those somber gray eyes. He probably should have paid more attention to her. She always seemed to be at the right place at the right time to see and overhear things she shouldn't. If he was honest, he had probably neglected putting the time and energy into her that he had the others, because she wasn't his. Although he was starting to think that was a mistake. If both he and the girl survived, then he would keep much closer tabs on her in the future.

Sofia, the only member of the family that he hadn't had to worry about. The girl was a relentless do-gooder. Working tirelessly for charities, helping those less fortunate whenever she could, honestly loving and caring for others. She hadn't even cared when he'd threatened to cut her off financially. If he hadn't known for a fact that she was an Everette, then he would never have believed it. The only thing she had ever done to truly frustrate him was refusing to marry Edmund Kendall. And this taking up with a police detective was out of the question. Again, if both of them survived this killing spree, then he was going to have to put an end to this infatuation with the policeman and marry her off to a suitable young man as soon as possible.

Lincoln, the gambler. For some reason his youngest son

seemed to think that he was unaware of his huge gambling debts. If it wasn't for him, then Lincoln would be missing a few fingers or limbs or possibly even his life. Whenever Lincoln racked up debts too high he could never manage to pay them off, then he would step in, and wipe out some of the debt so Lincoln's loan sharks didn't come after him. He should have pushed harder to marry that one off, too. A bit of responsibility to tie him down would have been good for Lincoln. Should have nipped the affair with Brooke in the bud, too. Now that he knew Brooke was writing a book about the family, he was pretty sure that Lincoln would have been the source of her insider information. Too bad the boy was dead, or he would have taught him a lesson for betraying his family in such a way.

Lewis, the pathetic one. Probably the most obedient of the children he had raised. The only one who had never really caused him any trouble. He was weak-willed; it never took much to pressure him into doing something. He had married the woman chosen for him, worked in the family businesses as a reliable, although unremarkable, employee. If all of his children had been as easy to manage as Lewis, he probably could have had another ten.

Logan Everette IV. His namesake. He should have suspected from the beginning that his firstborn was the killer. But it was one thing for his son to kill strangers—random girls. But to kill his own family, the thought had never occurred to him until it was too late. He should have taken care of that boy years ago when he first found out that he was a killer. Logan had been just a child. Only eight years old. He had walked in on the boy beating a cat with a hammer. The hammer swinging down on the cat's already lifeless body again and again and again. He had known then that the boy was trouble. He had tried to at least turn his son's murderous impulses in a direction that would bring the family the least amount of trouble. Still, he wouldn't allow the family name to be tarnished, so he had covered up Logan's crimes. If it wasn't for him, the police would have found out what Logan had been up to years ago.

Brooke Mariano, while she may not be a member of his family, she was certainly well entrenched in it. He was pleased that she was dead. And that she had suffered. She had caused him enormous amounts of aggravation and cost him hundreds of thousands of dollars. What was worse is that he could blame no one but himself for inflicting her on his family. At first she had seemed like all the other young bimbos he bedded. But she had been different. Smart and calculating. Then Logan had become interested in her, tried to make her one of his victims. He had stopped Logan from killing her, only to have her come back at them with demands for money in exchange for Logan's baby and her silence. Then she had come back years later, and unable to escape the allure of being in bed with her, he had once again begun an affair with her. As had Logan and Lincoln. And once again the witch had turned up pregnant and demanded more money for the baby and to keep his family's secrets. She had deserved what she had gotten.

What a mess of a family he had created. If he had known all the pain and trouble his children were going to cause him, he may not have been as enthusiastic to have heirs as he had been as a young man. Even as he thought it, though, he knew it could never have been so. Logan couldn't explain the burning desire inside him to produce children. It was like it took him over, it was all he could think about, all he could ...

Something whizzed past him. And then fire erupted in his shoulder and he clutched at it, his brain refusing to comprehend what was happening. Bringing his hand away from his shoulder, he was surprised to find it sticky with blood.

His own blood.

Someone was shooting at him.

Snapping back into the moment, he spun to face the direction the shot had been fired from, expecting to see Logan standing there, but instead it was …

"Isabella?"

"Surprise," she grinned at him.

"It was you?"

"Yep," she nodded agreeably.

"You killed them all?"

"Yes."

"You killed Brooke?"

"Uh huh."

"And Gloria?"

"Yep."

"Lincoln and Lewis?"

Looking at him impatiently, "We can keep going like this or you can just accept that I was telling the truth when I said I killed them all."

"Wh…why?" he stammered, still unable to process that his sixteen-year-old granddaughter was the killer.

"I think we both know the answer to that…grandfather," she replied snidely.

"You know," he said flatly, the reality that he wasn't as good at keeping things hidden as he thought he was sinking in. Isabella knew and Sofia knew, and Gloria, too, of course. Lewis and Lincoln had known only that their brother was a rapist, but he supposed that was enough. Simone knew it all too, although she was too afraid of what Logan would do to her if she ever told anyone.

"Of course I know, and thanks to Sofia, the police know now, too. They have proof, so you can't just go painting Sofia as sick and delusional," she raised a reproachful red eyebrow.

"You won't get away with it, Isabella," he warned, watching her carefully. She kept her gun trained on him, aimed at his head, but if he was able to distract her enough, he may still be able to make a run for it. They weren't all that far from the house, and if he could get close enough to scream, then one of the CSU techs or officers would be bound to hear him.

"I already have," she said smugly. "The police aren't even blinking in my direction because they think Logan is their guy. There's only you left to kill, and then Logan, and then I can disappear."

"Logan's still alive?" That his firstborn wasn't dead should make him happier, but he couldn't deny he would have been relieved to hear his son was finally gone.

"For the moment at least," she smirked.

"What about Brooke's baby?" he demanded. That child was his, and Isabella had no right to interfere with it. "What did you do with the baby?"

"That baby is better off without any of you," Isabella snapped.

Isabella's gaze grew unfocused for a second and the gun dipped slightly. Seizing what might be his only opportunity, Logan turned and started to run as fast as he could toward the house.

Letting out a frustrated growl, Isabella fired off a shot, but her aim was off and the bullet soared above his head. Continuing to run, dodging through the trees, he was making good progress, despite the fact he was losing blood quickly from the wound to his shoulder. Behind him he could hear Isabella puffing along. He may be seventy-two while Isabella was only sixteen, but she was only strong, not fit at all, while he had maintained his active lifestyle religiously over the years.

As she ran, Isabella continued to fire shots at him, most went long, but one flew by his neck so closely he could feel the bullet's heat. Her next shot was dead on target, piercing his leg and sending him flying to the ground. Blood was gushing from the wound, but he hardly noticed, using his good leg and arm to crawl on his stomach along the ground as fast as he could.

He had dragged himself maybe another twenty yards across the sticks and rocks, the house now in sight, when Isabella caught up to him, stomping a foot down on his injured leg.

Screaming in agony, Logan rolled onto his back, and tried to push Isabella's foot off his leg.

Batting his hands away, she giggled manically. "Kind of ironic, don't you think?"

Hardly hearing her words, his hands and face torn up by the crawl through the woods, the pain in his shoulder and leg overwhelming, the blood loss starting to make him weak.

"You were the one," she continued, "who insisted I learn to shoot, and now I'm going to kill you by shooting you." She laughed at what she obviously thought was a hilarious twist of fate.

As she pressed the gun to his forehead, Logan's last thought was that he was going to die unloved by all, even the children he had gone to such lengths to have.

AUGUST 20TH

2:26 A.M.

Sofia hadn't moved a muscle since he'd put her on the couch ten minutes ago.

She was starting to scare him.

After leaving the basement yesterday morning, Ryan had set her up in the library. Laid her down on a couch, covered her in blankets because she wouldn't stop shaking, and left her there to rest while CSU combed the basement. As Stephanie and her team searched the basement, he had kept a close eye on Sofia, checking on her regularly to make sure she was doing okay, or to ask for clarification on something.

When the crime scene guys had finally finished, he had taken Sofia with him back to the station while he and Paige updated Belinda on the case's progress. Now he had finally brought her back to her place for some proper rest, but she was just sitting there like she was stuck in a trance.

Each time he had had to wake her to ask her a question about Logan or the basement or things she remembered from the past, she had withdrawn further and further inside herself.

Now she sat there like an empty shell.

After she had asked him how many bodies they had found in the basement and he had told her there were thirty-two, she had completely shut down. Ryan hadn't wanted to answer her when she asked, but she had looked so wearily distraught as she begged him to tell her. And he felt like she deserved the answer after all the emotional upheaval she had gone through telling them what she remembered, so he had reluctantly complied.

Now he was wishing he hadn't.

Ryan wanted to pull her back into the moment, but he wasn't sure how to do it. "Sofia?" he sat beside her. "I made you some tea," he pushed the steaming cup into her hands.

She didn't move.

"Sofia." He took her chin and gave it a gentle shake. "Come on, cupcake."

Sofia blinked and slowly her eyes focused on him. "It's my fault," she whispered.

"What is?" he asked, confused.

"The girls," she murmured.

"What girls?"

"The ones Logan killed. If I'd said something earlier, then they would still be alive."

She was shaking so much Ryan quickly took the mug of tea from her hands before she could spill the boiling liquid over herself. "That's not true, Sofia," he told her forcefully. "It's not true at all."

"Yes it is," Sofia said, nodding. "Some of those girls have only been dead a few months. If I'd told earlier what I'd seen, then Logan would have been stopped."

Ryan regretted telling her that, too. He hadn't wanted to, but they had needed to know if Logan still used the basement. "No, baby," he soothed, concerned about the haunted gleam in her eyes, "that's not true. You didn't know that it was real. He convinced you it was just a dream, you had no reason to doubt that." He pulled her into a hug but she remained like stone in his arms.

"I killed them," her voice was scarily toneless.

He held her at arm's length, her guilt crushing not only her but him too. "No, cupcake. Logan killed them. You had *nothing* to do with it. Oh, baby, what do I say to convince you?"

Teardrops sat on her eyelashes; she blinked and they tumbled out and rolled slowly down her cheeks. "Just hold me, please."

Lifting her into his arms and settling her on his lap, she rested against him, nestling her head on his shoulder, crying silent tears. Ryan let her rest for a moment, and just enjoyed holding her. If he played his cards right, then this could be the way they spent every night. Cuddled together on the couch, minus the tears of course. Right now, though, he had to get her through this, alive and emotionally in one piece. "Sofia, you have to believe that it wasn't your fault," he said at last.

"I believe it in my head," she whispered. "I just feel so guilty."

"Because you're a good person," he kissed the top of her head.

"I have a horrible headache," she lifted a hand to press to her temple.

"I'm not surprised," Ryan stood, holding Sofia in his arms, then lay her down on the couch, propping her up against some pillows. "Drink some tea," he passed her the mug. "I'll be right back."

Going to the kitchen, he retrieved some painkillers and Sofia's medication, then rummaged through her cupboards until he found a cloth. Turning on the cold tap, he ran the cloth under the water, then collected the pills and returned to the lounge room. He paused at the door to simply look at Sofia. Even weak and worn out, she looked beautiful. Her long red hair pillowed out around her face, silky and shining red and gold as it caught the light. Her complexion was milky white, her skin looked so soft, her lips so full, that Ryan couldn't wait to take her face in his hands and kiss her until the worried lines in her forehead smoothed away.

Sofia shot him a watery smile when she saw him watching her. "Hey."

"Hey, yourself," he crossed over to her and sat on the edge of the couch. "Feeling any better?"

"Not really," she admitted.

"This should help," he placed her medications in her hand, she swallowed them quickly with a mouthful of tea. "Close your eyes and try to relax," he placed the cold cloth over her forehead, then moved behind her and began to massage her shoulders. It took several minutes, but eventually she started to loosen up, the tension easing off her. Returning to sit beside her, he removed the cloth, "Feeling better now?"

Her large silver eyes stared up at him, then suddenly filled with tears and she began to cry again. Holding her close against his chest, Ryan rubbed her back, unsure what to say to help her, so instead he just held her. Realistically, there was nothing he could say to make any of this better, but before she had just wanted to be in his arms, and that he could do. He could make sure that she knew that she had a place where she could feel safe and secure when her world was a swirling mist of chaos.

"I'm sorry, Ryan," she said at last, her voice muffled against his chest.

"For what?" he pulled her back so he could see her and with his thumb brushed away the last of her tears.

"I really like you. I mean I *really* like you, and I *really* want this to work, but you must think I'm the biggest mess."

"I don't think that, cupcake," he assured her.

"I thought after the basement I was emotionally drained, but somehow there's still more tears inside me," she continued miserably. "I don't want to be a quivering mess anymore. I don't want to be weak and pathetic and a ... a mess."

"You're not a mess," he told her.

She raised a disbelieving eyebrow at him.

"Okay," he agreed with a smile. "You are a mess, but anyone would be in your situation. Honey," he grew serious, "you're sick, you're grieving, and you're scared for your life. It's completely normal to be a mess, but you are not weak and pathetic. You've told me everything you think I needed to know, even when your father was threatening you. You're strong and brave and amazing." Once again, he picked her up and settled her in his lap, taking a deep breath and readying himself. "You accused me of being afraid of you, well I am." She stiffened in his arms and tried to pull away, but he held her firmly. "Just not in the way you think."

She eyed him warily, "Then why are you scared of me?"

Deciding to just say it and get it over with, like ripping off a Band-Aid. "I was engaged. Three years ago. Her name was Katrina. She committed suicide."

Her face fell, "Ryan, I'm sorry. That's awful. But why would that make you afraid …" Her eyes grew wide, then looked both disappointed and frustrated, "I am *not* suicidal, I would never even think …"

He cut her off, "No, Sofia," he soothed. "I don't think that you're suicidal. With Katrina, I knew that she was depressed, I knew that she wasn't doing so good, but I thought that I could handle it. I thought that I knew what to say to her to help her, but I didn't. I tried. I did and said everything I could, everything I thought I should. It wasn't enough, though. She swallowed an entire bottle of sleeping pills."

"And you think it's your fault," her gentle fingers wiped away his tears.

"I was her fiancé, and I couldn't give her what she needed." Ryan's guilt over Katrina's suicide had been severe. Still was. He had truly believed that he could be enough to help her. He had tried. Over and over again. Trying to say and do all the right things. And still it hadn't been enough.

It was meant to be the happiest time of their lives. Planning their wedding and their lives together. Ryan had thought that Katrina was getting better. So coming home that night to find her dressed in her wedding dress and passed out on their bed had been a horrifying shock. She had sounded off on the phone when he'd called her before leaving work. He had asked if anything was wrong but she had denied it. Still, he hadn't been convinced, so he had assured her he would be home soon and he was there for her if she needed to talk. When he had arrived home she had still been alive. He had been too late by just a couple of minutes. She had died in his arms. He had performed CPR but it hadn't done any good. She was already gone.

Following her death, Ryan's self-confidence had been shaken. Not only had he lost the woman he'd loved but he had blamed himself. He had felt if he'd only known what to say to Katrina to help her, then she would still be alive. So he no longer trusted that he could say the right thing to anyone. And he hadn't been in a relationship since. The only place he had still felt in control had been at work, so his job had become his life.

"That's why you were worried about saying the wrong thing to me," her eyes were full of sympathy and understanding.

"It's a sensitive issue for me. Katrina was vulnerable, and you're vulnerable. I loved her, and I'm falling in love with you. I want you to know that you can count on me, trust me, rely on me to lift you up when you're feeling down. I didn't do that for Katrina; I let her down, because I couldn't give her what she needed. I haven't been able to date yet, because I didn't trust myself with others. I had grown up seeing the way my parents supported each other, and my younger brother and his wife supported each other through their son's illness, and I thought it was me. I thought there was something wrong with me, so I decided that I wasn't going to get married, I didn't want to…" He paused to mentally search for the word he was looking for, "inflict myself on anyone. But from the moment I saw you, I knew you were different. I want to be everything that you deserve."

"That's sweet," she smiled and lifted a hand to his face, running her fingers softly through his hair. "But I don't need you to be anything other than what you already are. You're a great guy, thoughtful and caring and sensitive. Any woman would be lucky to have you," she brought his face down to hers and kissed him, long and soft and deep. "I'm lucky to have you. And you have to know that your fiancée didn't commit suicide because of anything you did or didn't say to her—she was sick, it wasn't your fault."

Remembering what she'd said earlier about feeling responsible for her brother's actions, he understood because he felt the same way about Katrina. "I understand it in my head, I just feel so guilty."

"I get that," she snuggled herself closer against him, nestling her head in the crook of his neck. "I think we both have some guilt issues to work through."

He tightened his arms around her, "We can help each other."

"I'd like that," her voice had gone faint, she needed sleep.

"All right, let's go to bed and get some rest. Today is going to be another long . . ." he broke off as his phone began to ring. Picking it up, he saw Paige's name on the screen, concerned about what she was going to tell him, he gently slid Sofia off his lap. "It's Paige," he told her, "so I gotta take it."

He crossed to the other side of the room. "What's up?"

"Are you alone or is Sofia with you?" Paige asked.

Casting a glance at Sofia, who had curled herself up into a little ball on the couch, he replied, "I'm with Sofia. Why?"

"I have bad news," Paige sighed.

A sinking feeling took residence in his stomach. "Who's dead? Isabella or the judge?"

"The judge," Paige replied.

At least that was the better of the two options. He turned his back and lowered his voice so Sofia wouldn't hear what was going on. "How? Wasn't he at the estate? That place is crawling with cops and crime scene, how did Logan get in and kill him? Didn't someone see something?"

"Shot. Yes, he was at the estate. I don't know how Logan got in. And no, no one saw anything," Paige answered his list of questions.

Shaking his head, this nightmare just kept getting worse and worse. "Okay, I better go tell her, I'll see you later."

"You two going to be okay tonight?"

"Officers outside and I have my gun," he assured his partner.

"We'll be fine." Hanging up the phone, he turned back to Sofia. She was still curled up in the corner of the settee, hands pressed together, her cheek resting on them, mouth open in a small o. Even in sleep she looked worried. She looked so fragile, so vulnerable, but Ryan knew that Sofia was strong. Perhaps the strongest person he'd ever met. He wasn't sure he'd be able to deal with believing he was dying. Or seeing his family slaughtered one by one.

Kneeling beside her, he swept his fingers across her lips, wanting to kiss away all her troubles.

"Tell me what?" she opened one eye to peer at him.

"I thought you were asleep," he took her hands, absently rubbing his thumbs across her knuckles.

"I couldn't sleep. Tell me what?" she repeated, prying open her other eye.

"I have bad news," he stalled.

She grew paler, "Isabella or my father?"

Hating what he had to say, he answered, "Your father. I'm sorry, cupcake."

For a long moment Sofia didn't move. Just sat staring blankly at him, and Ryan started to worry that she was going into shock. Increasing the pressure on her hands, about to speak when she suddenly burst into tears and wrapped her arms around his neck, clinging to him tightly.

"Shh," he comforted. "It's going to be okay. Shh, shh, baby, shh."

"He didn't even like me, and I know he was a bad person, that he covered up Logan's crimes, but I still loved him," she sobbed against his chest.

"Of course you loved him, he was still your father," Ryan reassured her, kissing away her tears. "Shh, baby, please don't cry anymore." When she didn't stop, he kissed her again, on the mouth this time, soft and gentle. At first she didn't respond, but then she kissed him back, a small sigh escaping her lips when he eventually broke contact.

He eased her back so he could see her face, "It's not wrong to love him, Sofia. You know that, right?"

Nodding slowly, he could literally see the last of her energy draining away. "I feel faint," she whispered.

With a hand supporting her head, Ryan laid her back down to rest against the pillows. "When did you last eat?"

Letting her eyes fall closed. "I'm not sure, I don't remember."

"Well I've been with you for the last twenty-four hours and I haven't seen you consume a single thing. You need to eat."

"Isabella made soup," she murmured tiredly. "It's in the fridge."

"All right, I'll get you some; you just stay here and try to rest." Leaving her there, he went to the kitchen and dished up two bowls of soup, heated them in the microwave, then took them both back to the lounge room and set them on the coffee table in front of the couch. "Here you go," he passed Sofia a bowl.

She clutched it with one hand, the other lifting a spoon to her mouth, but her hands shook so much that she sloshed the soup.

"Here, I got it," setting aside his own bowl, he gently took the spoon from her, filled it again, then brought it to her lips.

"I'm sorry," she mumbled after she swallowed the mouthful. Her eyes dipped, embarrassed.

"For what?" hooking a finger under her chin, tipping her face up so she was looking at him again. "You don't need to be sorry for needing help, you haven't eaten in a day, no wonder you're feeling weak." Ryan fed her several more mouthfuls; she'd finished about half the bowl before her eyes got so heavy she could hardly hold them open. "You ready for bed?"

"Let's just stay here," she reached for his hands and tugged him toward her.

Stretching out on the couch beside her, she snuggled against him, a moment later her breathing evened out as she drifted off to sleep. Exhaustion had his own eyes closing, he hadn't eaten any of the soup but he wasn't really hungry anyway, just tired, he was almost asleep when Sofia jerked up.

"What's wrong?" Ryan asked, instantly wide awake.

"I'm going to be sick," Sofia tried to stand, but her knees buckled.

Catching her as she fell, he murmured, "I got you." He quickly picked her up and carried her to the downstairs bathroom, setting her down in front of the toilet and holding back her hair as she threw up. Sofia was sick again and again, until at last she slumped down to the floor, barely conscious.

"Baby, what's wrong with you?" Ryan said to himself as he wet a cloth and wiped at Sofia's sweat-streaked face. He had told her that he believed that the doctors would find out what was wrong with her, and he had believed it at the time. But now he wasn't so sure.

Now he was worried that even if they caught Logan before he tried to kill Sofia again, he was going to lose her anyway.

And that he could not accept.

He already had one woman he loved die; he wasn't going to let it happen again.

* * * * *

9:47 A.M.

Ryan hoped he'd find something helpful here.

He wanted to run a DNA test to prove that Isabella was Logan's daughter. They needed to start building a case against Logan that wasn't just circumstantial, and he was hoping this could help.

When he had left for the Everette estate, he'd left Sofia with Paige. This time he'd done things the right way. Woken Sofia up, told her what he was planning on doing, and that Paige was going to pick her up and take her to the station. That was the safest place he could think of for her. Logan was almost done. There were only Sofia and Isabella left alive. But in the police station, surrounded by cops, with his partner keeping a watchful eye on her, she would be safe. Ryan hadn't told Sofia yet but he intended to keep her there until Logan was found.

Parking in front of the mansion, things looked quiet. Crime scene had finished with the house, and since Isabella was with Sofia at the station, it should be empty.

It shouldn't take him long to retrieve something from Isabella's room. He would have asked the girl for her hairbrush or toothbrush, but he hadn't wanted to tell her what they were thinking until they had proof. Isabella was already going through enough, and it wasn't worth turning her world upside down if they were wrong.

He headed straight for the fifth floor, Isabella's floor. There were so many twisting hallways up here, so many bedrooms and bathrooms, that even with Sofia's directions it took him several minutes to locate Isabella's room.

The room was virtually empty, but for a bed, a wardrobe, and a dresser. The only other things in the room were bookshelves. They lined two full walls and were stuffed to the brim with hundreds of books. Ryan perused the titles; there was fiction and non-fiction, a range of genres, and every topic one could think of.

Isabella was a strange girl. So quiet and serious. Ryan hadn't seen her smile once, given the current circumstances that was understandable but he got the feeling it wasn't unusual. He guessed a lot more went on inside Isabella's head than anyone realized. When this was over, he was going to suggest to Sofia that they get Isabella to talk to a psychiatrist. With everything that had happened she was bound to be traumatized, especially if it turned out that Logan was her father and that he had killed her family and her biological mother.

He was going to make sure Sofia got some counseling, too. Ryan didn't like her blaming herself for her brother's actions.

Right now, though, they had to end this.

In the bathroom, he collected Isabella's toothbrush and was about to drop it into an evidence bag when it slipped and clattered to the floor. As he stooped to pick it up, he noticed something tucked away on the bottom shelf of the cabinet. Curious, he bent to get a closer look.

Shocked when he saw what it was, Ryan pulled it out. Confirming that he'd been right. They were DNA test kits.

What would Isabella need with DNA test kits?

And whose DNA was she testing?

Her own?

Maybe Sofia was wrong; maybe Isabella *did* know that Brooke was her mother. Perhaps even that Logan was her father.

A tiny spark of suspicion ignited inside him.

Why would Isabella even think to do a DNA test on herself? And why wouldn't she tell someone what she had found? Confront the judge and Gloria for lying to her?

He wondered what else Isabella was hiding in her room.

Starting his search, nothing else turned up in the bathroom, so he moved on to the bedroom. There weren't many places to look. He checked under the bed and mattress, nothing. Then the dresser, again nothing. The wardrobe, too, was empty. He eyed the bookshelves. There were a lot of them and even more books. To go through them all would take hours. For now, he'd just do a brief check, maybe see if there was anything hidden behind the books.

Quickly, be began to rifle through the shelves, tearing books off the shelves, until he came to an abrupt stop halfway through the second wall. There was a small door.

Eagerly, he slipped on gloves, then yanked it open. Inside there were several discs and a book. Taking them out, his blood ran cold.

The book was about mushrooms.

Poisonous mushrooms.

Sofia's mysterious illness.

Isabella had been poisoning Sofia.

A wave of anger so strong his vision turned red rushed through him, and he nearly slammed his fist through the wall.

He fought through the rage, breathing deeply until his eyesight cleared. He needed to remain calm. If Isabella, and not Logan, was behind all of this, then she would pay. He would make sure of it. *No one* would mess with Sofia and get away with it.

Grabbing the discs, he went looking for the nearest DVD player. Ryan had a sinking feeling that whatever was on these tapes was going to be proof of Isabella's guilt. And as much as he wanted to find this killer and end this, he knew it would break Sofia's heart to find out that the only member of her family that she trusted was a murderer. She had come to terms with Logan being the killer, but not Isabella.

Recalling that there had been a large TV screen and DVD player in the library, he made his way back downstairs. Popping in a disc, his heart stopped when an image of Sofia, asleep in her bed, filled the screen. He breathed through another wave of fury. Isabella had been secretly filming Sofia as she slept. Invading her privacy in a place where she should have been safe.

On the screen, Sofia tossed and turned in her bed, then her voice suddenly filled the room. As Ryan listened to Sofia talk in her sleep, he realized that Isabella knew everything. When her mind was relaxed in sleep, Sofia had revealed everything she had buried deep in her subconscious.

Switching to another disc, this one also revealed a sleeping Sofia. Going to the third, a shot of the basement filled the screen this time.

The secret room.

Just as it had been when Sofia showed it to them. The grave markers on the floor. The bed over in the corner. Only this time the bed wasn't empty.

This time the bed was occupied by a girl.

A naked girl.

She couldn't have been more than sixteen.

She had long red hair and pale white skin.

As he watched, Logan entered the room. Ryan couldn't hear what he was saying, but it looked as though he was taunting the girl. Logan took off his pants and climbed on top of her and Ryan had to avert his eyes; he couldn't watch Logan rape the girl.

When he looked back, the girl was off the bed and standing before Logan. He had a knife in his hand and was stabbing her over and over again. Her arms were waving wildly, attempting, albeit pointlessly, to fight him off. Eventually, her body folded and she dropped to the floor. Logan didn't stop. Stabbing her at least a dozen more times before he finally stood over the now dead girl, both of them drenched in blood.

Isabella had known what Logan was doing, and she hadn't said anything to anyone. Apparently, she had decided instead to take matters into her own hands. Decided that she had to kill their entire family and frame Logan.

But that wasn't what was making Ryan shake with terror.

It was the fact that the girl he had just watched Logan kill looked exactly like Sofia.

Sofia had said that Logan had never touched her.

However, she had buried her memories of what she had seen him doing, so it was completely plausible that she had buried this too.

Sofia was very likely one of Logan's victims.

* * * * *

11:56 A.M.

"Cause of death on Judge Everette?" Belinda asked Frankie.

"The shot to the head," Frankie replied. "He was shot two other times, once in the shoulder and once in the leg, before the fatal wound to the head."

Paige was watching Ryan as the ME elaborated in more detail about the wounds Logan Everette II had received just prior to death. Her partner had been subdued, almost withdrawn, since he had returned from the Everette estate. Paige didn't think that he could be worried about Sofia's safety. From the second she'd collected Sofia this morning, she'd kept a close eye on her. She'd chattered away with her in the car to try and keep her a little distracted from what she was going through. Once she'd gotten Sofia safely to the station, she had set her up at Ryan's desk so she could keep watch over her while she worked.

She hadn't just kept such a close eye on Sofia for Ryan's sake, because she knew it would kill him if anything happened to her, but she was genuinely concerned about Sofia's safety. Logan was almost done. There were only Sofia and Isabella left now. And he had to know that the police were closing in on him. That would probably make him desperate. And desperate people did desperate things. The more desperate a killer was, the more dangerous they were.

Something was going on with Ryan, and as soon as they finished this meeting, Paige intended to grill him on it.

She tuned back in to the conversation.

"Looks like the killer chased him through the woods," Frankie was saying. "Shoulder wound first, then the leg wound. Dirt under his fingernails and on his clothes, looks like he dragged himself through the woods heading for the house, cut up his hands and face in the process. Then the killer caught up to him and killed him."

"Suffering and death again," Paige muttered.

"Yep," Frankie nodded. "Just like the others."

"All right," Belinda said wearily, "any leads on where Logan may be hiding out?"

"We checked out all the properties and businesses that the Everettes own; so far, nothing," Paige answered. "But the guy is beyond rich, so I'm sure he has plenty of money to hole himself up somewhere until this all blows over."

"Only he isn't holed up somewhere," Belinda snapped. "He's still out there killing. He's killed his father and tried to kill Isabella."

Something flashed across Ryan's face at the mention of Isabella. Paige was about to question him on it when Belinda continued.

"Where's Stephanie?"

"Here she is," Stephanie bustled through the door backwards, a large stack of folders and papers in her arms.

"Where have you been?" Belinda demanded as she stood to take Stephanie's armload of files.

"Talking with Sofia," she replied before taking a seat. "You know she's out there going through missing persons files to see if she can identify any of the women she saw in her basement."

"We know," Paige told her. When they'd gotten to the station, Sofia had been desperate to do something to keep her mind occupied, specifically something to help with their investigation, so Paige had asked her to see if she recognized any of her brother's victims. "She's already identified two."

"She's amazing," Stephanie smiled. "Under the same circumstances, I don't think I'd have the strength to do it."

"Ryan, you've been unusually quiet," Belinda observed.

"Yeah, what's up with you?" Paige demanded, shooting him a concerned frown, she'd expected him to spring back to life at the mention of Sofia's name. "You've been in a weird mood since you got back from the estate. What did you find there?"

Instead of answering, Ryan looked to Stephanie, "Did you find them?"

Apologetic, Stephanie responded, "Yeah, sorry."

"Find what?" Paige looked from one to the other.

Her partner ignored her, "Fingerprints?"

"Yes," Stephanie nodded.

"Hers?" Ryan asked.

"Yes."

"You didn't tell Sofia, did you? When you were talking to her just now?" Ryan's blue eyes were piercing as they stared at Stephanie.

"Relax," she soothed. "No, I didn't tell her. I assumed you wanted to be the one to break it to her."

"Do you two want to let us in on your conversation?" Belinda frowned, frustrated.

"It's your theory," Stephanie said to Ryan.

Sighing and dragging his hands down his face. "I don't think the killer is Logan; I think it's Isabella."

Paige felt her mouth drop open in shock. Belinda and Frankie were staring at Ryan too. "You think what now?" Paige asked, wondering how he had jumped from Logan, who they already knew for a fact was a killer, to Isabella, the quiet and serious teenager.

"Because of what I found at the estate."

"Which was?" Belinda tapped her watch impatiently.

"DNA test kits, a book on poisonous mushrooms, and some DVDs," Ryan summarized.

"Sofia's been poisoned with mushrooms, that's why she's been so sick," Paige shook her head in disbelief. "The soup?" Ryan had called her an hour ago to tell her not to let Sofia eat any soup. Paige had assumed it was just because Sofia had been unwell overnight, but it seemed she was wrong.

Ryan nodded, "I'm assuming so. Sofia said that Isabella makes her soup, and last night after I gave her some, she started throwing up. I found the DNA kits in Isabella's bathroom, and the book and DVDs hidden in a secret compartment behind her books."

"What was on the DVDs?" Frankie asked.

"Footage of Sofia sleeping," Ryan replied tightly.

Her partner was furious, but trying to contain it, Paige realized.

That was why he had been so odd ever since he had returned from the Everettes. That Isabella had been deliberately making Sofia ill and filming her while she slept was killing him. "Sofia was talking in her sleep? About what she'd seen her brother doing in the basement?" she asked.

"Yes," he replied, voice still tight. If Ryan held himself any tighter together, he was going to explode.

"Maybe Logan was just hiding stuff in her room, since she would be our least likely suspect," Paige suggested.

"No," Ryan shook his head adamantly. "She put the cameras in Sofia's room."

"Isabella's fingerprints are on them," Stephanie confirmed. "She set them up, she watched the DVDs, she knows what Logan did."

"That doesn't make her the killer," Paige wasn't yet convinced that Isabella had done all of this.

"Then why poison Sofia?" Ryan demanded angrily. "If she's capable of that, then she's capable of the rest of it."

Paige was unable to argue with that. It showed premeditation. She had to research how to poison Sofia, choose something that would give the desired results, then source it. If she could do that, then it wasn't a stretch for her to have planned and executed everything else. "Let's interview her," Paige proposed. "She's right outside with Sofia."

"Uh, no she's not," Stephanie shook her head. "When I came in, it was just Sofia out there."

Ryan looked panicked. "Isabella's gone? Sofia is all that's left. Isabella will be coming after her next. She does not leave this building."

"Try to calm down," Paige said soothingly. "Sofia is safe, and she's going to remain that way. No one's letting her walk out of this building on her own. All right, so Isabella knows what Logan does, and she's been poisoning Sofia. What about the attack on her? Any chance she could have faked that, Stephanie?"

"Yes," Stephanie considered. "If she timed it properly. The knot on the rope around her neck was in front, so she could easily have tied it herself. And the rope around her wrists could have been tied by her too, it would have been difficult, but not impossible. And after reviewing the attack on Logan, I don't think he could have done it to himself. He had both arms crossed over his chest, he couldn't have taped himself up that way."

"But Logan *did* kill the women in the basement?" Belinda confirmed.

"Sofia remembers seeing him down there, and he's on Isabella's DVDs raping and killing a girl," Ryan replied.

"I know it's early, but any forensics from the basement, Stephanie?" Belinda asked.

"It's going to take a while to test the blood on the floor," she answered. "A lot of it's probably degraded, and we're assuming there were a number of donors. Plenty of hair and fibers and fingerprints. Yes, we found Logan's fingerprints down there," she added, anticipating Belinda's question. "Fingerprints and hairs on the bed, too. It'll take a while to go through them all. But we may get lucky and get DNA on some of the hairs, we may be able to identify more of his victims."

"The bodies, Frankie," Belinda turned her attention to the medical examiner.

"Preliminary ages on some of the bodies date them back maybe fifteen years," she explained. "Ages of the victims appear to be mid-teens, same age as the girl on the video."

"Same ages as the two girls Sofia identified," Paige added.

"All right, so Logan definitely killed the young women in the basement. Any chance maybe he and Isabella are in on these murders together?" Belinda pondered. "Isabella finds out that Logan is her father, they bond, and the two of them decide to take out the rest of the family. Then maybe Isabella turns on Logan, maybe once she finds out what he's been doing in the basement."

"I guess the major thing we need to consider is what we know about Isabella," Paige mused. "So, she poisoned her sister, which means she's potentially capable of doing this, but we never looked at her too closely as she was never really a suspect. We need to find out opinions of her from people who know her."

Shaking his head, "It's no good talking to Sofia," Ryan warned. "She's not ready to hear this yet, let's see what we come up with before we tell her."

"Well the gardener, Mr. Hannigan, doesn't like her, but Isabella was the one who outed his and Brooke's affair," Paige noted.

"And Mr. Payne the ex-head of security doesn't like her either, she outed his affair with Gloria," Ryan continued. "He also said that she has eyes in the back of her head and notices everything that goes on. That would certainly seem to fit in with our theory of her figuring out what Logan had been doing and engineering this plan."

"But both of those men had reason not to like her," Paige reminded him. "We need someone neutral."

"Edmund," Ryan pulled out his phone, already dialing the number. "It's Ryan," he announced as soon as Edmund answered. "I'm putting you on speakerphone."

"Did something happen with Sofia?" Edmund demanded.

"She's fine. She's here at the station, it's the safest place for her right now. We need to ask you some questions. Paige is here with me and our boss, Belinda, medical examiner, Frankie, and Stephanie from crime scene."

"What do you want to ask me?" Edmund's tone had gone wary.

"Tell us about Isabella," Ryan requested.

"Why?" Edmund's voice had grown from wary to suspicious.

"What's she like?" Ryan asked, instead of answering.

"First, tell me why you're asking," Edmund insisted.

"Edmund," Ryan began.

"No," Edmund interrupted. "If you want answers, then you

answer me first. Why are you asking about Isabella? Do you think she's involved?"

Ryan sighed, "She's been poisoning Sofia," he told him.

"She's been *what*?" Edmund exploded.

"Try to stay calm," Paige soothed. They needed him focused, not in a blind panic. "Ryan found a book on poisonous mushrooms, so we're assuming that's why Sofia's been sick."

"Isabella had the book?" Edmund sounded incredulous.

"Yes, she did," Paige told him.

"We need you to tell us everything you can about Isabella," Ryan pleaded.

Edmund drew a deep, shuddering breath. "I always thought Isabella was weird. She was too quiet, like she was studying everyone all the time. She moves quietly, too; I can't tell you how many times I turned around and found her there when I'd never even heard her enter a room. It was creepy. And she seemed to know *everything* that was going on in that estate. I guess because she was so good at sneaking."

"Had you ever known her to be violent?" Ryan asked.

"Well..." Edmund's hesitation couldn't have been more obvious had he been trying.

"What?" Ryan perked up.

"She still throws tantrums. Like toddler tantrums," Edmund elaborated. "She screams and stomps her feet, and cries and hits and kicks."

"That doesn't mean she's violent," Ryan looked disappointed.

"And..." Again, Edmund hesitated.

"And what?" Ryan snapped. He was quickly losing his patience.

"I don't think Sofia would like me saying."

"Well, I don't care. This could save her life, so just tell us," Ryan growled.

"All right," Edmund begun reluctantly. "A few months ago, there was an incident at her school, and she was expelled."

"What happened, Edmund?" Paige asked gently, before Ryan could bark at him again.

"She beat up four kids. At once. Two of them were boys. It wasn't the first such incident. There was another, when Isabella was about ten, the school didn't expel her then since it was the first time, but they did insist on anger management."

"Doesn't seem like it worked," Ryan muttered.

They had enough out of Edmund for now. At the moment, they needed to work on tracking down both Isabella and Logan Everette. "All right, Edmund, thanks for all your help," Paige told him.

"I'm on my way there now; don't any of you let Sofia out of your sight."

Once Edmund had hung up, Paige studied her partner. Other than her husband, Ryan was the one man that she understood completely. They were close, good friends, not just work colleagues. She knew the way his mind worked, and right now something else was bothering him. "What else is on your mind?"

Ryan looked troubled. "The girl on the DVD, she looked like Sofia."

Catching on to where her partner was heading, Paige responded, "So do both of the victims Sofia identified."

"Frankie said that the bodies dated back approximately fifteen years, which would make Sofia in her early or mid-teens at the time. The same age as the young women Logan was killing."

"You're scared Sofia was one of his victims," Paige noted.

"I'm terrified that Logan hurt her." Ryan was pale, his blue eyes wide with fear. "She kept dreaming of the basement. She knew what happened down there. She was scared of Logan. She could have been his first victim."

* * * * *

2:09 P.M.

Ryan stood and watched Sofia.

She was sitting at his desk, pouring through old missing persons files, her head propped up on her hand. She looked tired, and an arrow of rage toward Isabella shot through him. It was Isabella's fault that Sofia had been so unwell, that she had been scared for her life not knowing what was wrong with her or if she'd ever recover. Still, the one bright spot in all of this was that now Sofia could get better. Once she stopped eating the poisoned soup, she should start to heal. As soon as they had Isabella in custody, he'd take her to her doctor to make sure that Isabella's psychotic games hadn't done her permanent damage.

Still, despite the fact that she had been up sick most of the night and looked exhausted, she continued to go through file after file of missing teenage girls dating back fifteen years, to see if she could identify any more of them. Ryan couldn't be more proud of her. She was totally amazing.

As if she could feel his eyes on her, Sofia turned her head, a smile lighting her pale face. Returning her smile, he crossed the room and knelt beside her chair. "How're you doing?"

"I'm okay," she assured him, but a giant yawn almost split her face in two.

"You need a break," he took her hands and tried to pull her to her feet but she resisted.

"I want to keep going through these first," she insisted.

Tucking her hair behind her ear, he murmured, "I know you want to help, but you're not going to do anyone, least of all yourself, any good if you push yourself so hard you end up passing out."

Wavering, Sofia couldn't hide the weariness lacing her silver eyes, no matter how much she wanted to. "Maybe just a little break," she reluctantly agreed.

He picked her up before she could protest. "Let's go someplace quiet," Ryan wanted her alone so he could tell her about her sister.

"You don't need to carry me, Ryan; I can walk," she told him, but she sank down into his arms and rested her head on his shoulder.

Taking her into an empty conference room, he set her down in a chair and went to get her some water. When he returned, she had crossed her arms on the table and put her head on them. Wondering briefly if she'd gone to sleep, but she lifted her head when she heard the door close. Passing her the water, he asked, "Do you want to try something to eat?"

The expression on her face implied he had just suggested she jump out of an airplane without a parachute. "I'm not hungry."

Letting that go for the moment, they'd sort out her health issues once they sorted out finding Isabella and Logan. "We need to talk," he told her, pulling out the chair beside hers and taking a seat.

She raised an eyebrow in anticipation, and when he didn't continue, her brow furrowed in a small frown. "Now is not the time to be afraid of me," she warned. "This isn't about hurting me or upsetting me or saying the wrong thing; this is about finding out who's trying to kill me."

Ryan knew she was right, but that didn't make asking her what he was about to any easier. "Okay, I have to ask you some difficult questions."

Steeling herself, she said, "I'm ready."

"Cupcake, do you think it's possible that Logan might have hurt you when you were younger?" he asked gently.

Mouth dropping open, she stared at him in shock, then her eyes took on a vacant gleam.

Now Ryan was wishing that he'd said yes earlier when Paige had offered to come with him when he had this conversation with Sofia. Resisting the urge to wrap her up in his arms, she'd told him that she was okay with him doing what needed to be done and not coddling her, so he was going to have to believe that.

"Come on, Sofia," he kept his voice stern. "No zoning out, I need you one hundred percent, okay?"

Eyes focusing, she jerked her head in a minute nod.

"Did Logan ever do anything to hurt you?"

"I already told you no," she answered, frustrated.

"I know you did, but I wasn't convinced at the time, and now knowing that Logan picks victims that look just like you . . ."

"I...I didn't realize that before," Sofia paled, her scared eyes searching his face. "Do you really think Logan did something to me? I...I don't remember it."

"You didn't remember what you saw in the basement, either," he reminded her gently. "Is it possible he could have done something to you?"

"No. Absolutely not. I would know if Logan had molested me. He wouldn't do that. He's my brother. That would be..." she trailed off, seemingly unable to think of a suitable way to finish that sentence. "If...if he did, then why didn't he kill me like he killed all the others?"

"Maybe your father wouldn't let him," Ryan wished this was the worst thing they had to talk about today. "There's something else we need to discuss."

With traumatized, weary eyes, she looked up at him. "What?"

"It's about Isabella."

Panic lit her face. "Is she okay? Did something happen to her?"

"No, she's fine," he assured her.

Paling further, her hands clutched at his. "Did Logan hurt her? Is she one of his victims?"

"Your hands are like ice," he sandwiched them between his own and began to rub them. "Why didn't you tell someone you were so cold?" he admonished.

"Ryan, did Logan molest Isabella?" she begged.

"No, honey," he responded, positive at least that Logan had never laid a hand on Isabella. "Logan never touched her."

Visibly relaxing, Sofia asked, "Then what do you need to tell me about Isabella?"

"I don't think that it's Logan who killed your family members; I think it was Isabella." Ryan held his breath as he waited anxiously for her reaction.

Staring blankly at him, she forced her lips into a small smile, "That's a joke, right? You're trying to make me laugh because you feel bad about asking me if Logan ever hurt me."

"I'm so sorry, cupcake, I know how much you love her, but I have proof that Isabella knew about Logan and," he continued gently, "I have proof that Isabella has been poisoning you."

"Wh…what?" she stammered.

"You're not dying, and you are going to get better. Isabella has been poisoning you with mushrooms, in the soup she keeps bringing you." Ryan had to fight to keep his voice calm, his hatred toward Isabella burned every time he thought of how Sofia's supposed illness had robbed her of months of her life, and of how scared she had been thinking she was never going to get better.

"I don't believe you," Sofia eyed him defiantly. "Isabella would never do that. She'd never make me sick on purpose and let me think that I was dying."

"I found a book on poisonous mushrooms hidden in her room. And last night after you ate some of Isabella's soup, you got sick," he watched doubt flicker through her eyes for the first time. "The book wasn't the only thing I found in her room. There were also DVDs. DVDs of you. She put cameras in your room," pausing to let his words sink in. "To film you while you were sleeping, because she somehow figured out that you knew something about Logan. That's how she found out what he'd been doing in the basement."

"No," Sofia shook her head vigorously, sending her wavy red hair swinging wildly around her face. "I don't believe you."

"I'm sorry, Sofia, but it's true."

"But Logan killed all those women," she reminded him.

"Yeah, he did, but that doesn't mean he's responsible for *these* murders," he pointed out.

"You thought the killer was my father and you were wrong; you're wrong about Isabella too. You don't know her. I do, and she would never, *never*, kill anyone," Sofia protested desperately. Ryan could see he was getting to her.

He decided not to tell her that Edmund had told them about Isabella's anger issues. "I know you don't want to hear this but..."

"Have you forgotten that someone tried to kill Isabella?" Sofia demanded.

"Remember our crime scene tech, Stephanie?"

Reluctantly, Sofia nodded.

"She said that it would have been easy enough for Isabella to fake the attempt on her life. All she had to do was time it correctly."

"Stop it. I don't want to hear this anymore," Sofia pressed her hands to her ears. "I don't want to hear any more of your lies. I'm not listening to you anymore."

Gently, he wrapped his hands around her wrists and tugged her hands away. "I need you to tell me where Isabella might go if she felt scared or trapped."

"Trapped?" she echoed. "You're really going to arrest her when you find her?"

"Yes," Ryan answered honestly. "She was here with you earlier, but she's gone now. Did she tell you where she was going?"

A small shake of her head.

"Do you know any place where she may go to hide out?"

Another little head shake.

"Think, Sofia," he hooked a finger under her chin and tilted her face up to his so they were eye to eye. "If you know where she might be, you have to tell me; you're not protecting her by keeping quiet. She's dangerous. To you and to others, maybe even herself."

Hurt flashed through her silver eyes making them seem grayer.

"You think I'd lie to you?"

"No, I don't," Ryan told her firmly. "I think you're in shock and not thinking clearly right now. And she's your sister. You want to believe the best of her. That's your job. My job is to find Isabella before she hurts anyone else. Now, do you know where she might be?"

"No, I don't," Sofia snapped. She stood on shaky legs, angrily shoving away his hands when he moved to help her. "I don't want to see you right now, Ryan," she growled. "Or any of your friends, so don't send anyone to babysit me, I just need to be alone."

With that, Sofia stormed from the room, heading straight for the bathroom. Ryan watched her go, oddly at peace with how things had gone. He had hated upsetting Sofia further, but she had assured him that she was okay with him doing his job, even if it hurt her at the time. He had known this was going to be a shock for her, and her anger and need to be alone were both perfectly understandable. So, for the moment, he was going to leave her be and go and find her sister and brother.

* * * * *

4:27 P.M.

Everything felt so surreal.

Sofia didn't feel like she had managed to hold a coherent thought since she had found Isabella lying on the kitchen floor with a bag over her head.

Strike that, Sofia corrected herself, she didn't think she had managed to hold a coherent thought since this whole nightmare started.

She was still trying to process the whole basement thing. Even though she knew she had really been in the basement with Ryan and Paige, the whole thing felt like it had happened to someone else. Like it was someone else who had sat down there and recalled seeing their own brother rape and murder teenage girls.

Tears pricked her eyes and she angrily brushed them away; she didn't have time to cry now. Ryan would soon be on to her if he wasn't already.

After she had stormed out on Ryan, she'd gone to the bathroom, thrown up again, then cleaned herself up and tried to calm herself down. She was so angry. Although, not really at Ryan. He was just trying to do his job. She knew that. He had been wrong before, when he'd accused her father, and he was wrong this time, too. Isabella wasn't a killer. Sofia would know if her own sister was capable of such a thing.

She knew that Isabella had some problems.

Her sister was spoiled. Liked to have her own way. Sometimes threw tantrums if she didn't get it.

It was worse than that, though, she reluctantly admitted.

Isabella had a violent temper when she was pushed to her limits. It was like she lost control of herself and did things she'd never normally do.

The first time Isabella had exploded, she had been ten. Another little girl at her school had been teasing Isabella relentlessly because she was so tall. Isabella had punched her in the face and knocked out three of her teeth. Sofia had been the one to push for anger management and counseling for Isabella. Hoping it would help.

It hadn't.

Last year she had beaten up four kids at her school. Isabella had given one girl a concussion, another a broken nose, a boy a fractured cheekbone, and pushed another down a flight of stairs. What had led to Isabella attacking those kids had been bad. Not that that excused Isabella's violent behavior.

Again, Sofia had pushed for anger management and counseling, desperately hoping they could help her sister.

Still, just because Isabella had attacked some kids at her school didn't mean she was capable of premeditated, cold-blooded murder.

Or did it?

Sofia couldn't accept that Isabella would kill Lewis and Lincoln and Gloria and their father. She wouldn't do that. She couldn't. She wouldn't.

And yet Ryan had managed to spark the tiniest glimmer of doubt inside her.

He seemed to have a way of getting to her.

At the hospital after Isabella was attacked, her heart hadn't stopped hammering, fear hadn't stopped swirling inside her, until she had locked eyes with Ryan. Those bright blue eyes of his seemed to have a soothing effect on her. And then in the basement, when Paige had been prying out of her what she remembered seeing down there, it had only been Ryan's calming presence that had kept her sane.

Sofia trusted him, even more so since he had opened up to her about what he'd gone through with his fiancée's suicide. She intended to call him as soon as she had a chance to talk to Isabella alone.

Ryan was going to be mad when he found out that she had fled the police station.

Sofia knew that it wasn't the smartest idea. There was still a killer after her and she was safe at the station surrounded by cops. But she needed to talk to her sister before Ryan and his team found her. And so she had stayed in the bathroom, biding her time. Mostly she had been left alone. Paige had popped in once to check on her. But other than that, she had waited until everyone was busy and then made her escape.

When the taxi driver pulled up outside her family's estate, Sofia quickly paid him and headed inside. Against her better judgment, she found herself drawn toward the basement. Standing in the open doorway at the top of the stairs, she stood staring down into the dark. Now that she had remembered what she'd seen happen down there as a child it seemed that she couldn't make the images leave her mind.

She couldn't forget what Ryan has asked her either.

Was she one of Logan's victims?

She didn't remember it. But then, again, Ryan was right; she'd forgotten about the basement too.

It had never dawned on her when she'd identified two of the girls she had seen in the basement that they both looked like her. But Ryan was right about that as well. They *did* bear a striking similarity to her.

It had been Paige's idea to get her to go through old missing person's files. When Paige had taken her to the station, Sofia had felt lost and useless, she had needed to do something. She didn't just want to be some victim that had to be babysat. So she had begged Paige for something to do to help.

It had been a shock to actually see a face she recognized staring up at her from one of the files. It had made everything seem so much more real.

And it *was* real.

All of it.

Maybe if Ryan ever managed to find Logan, she would get the answer to whether or not he ever touched her.

Or maybe she'd never know.

She'd have to learn to live with that. Sofia hoped Ryan could, too.

Now, however, was not the time to be worrying about that. Now she needed to find Isabella and find out just how involved in all of this her sister was.

Earlier, when Paige had come to check on her in the bathroom at the station, Sofia had asked where Ryan had found this so-called evidence against Isabella. Paige had said he'd found it in Isabella's bedroom, so that seemed like a good place to start.

On the way up to the top floor, Sofia checked out all of the house's hidden rooms and hidey-holes that she could remember.

As a child she had loved to play in them, even though she'd had no one to play with. Her brothers had been ten, twelve, and fourteen years older than her, too old to want to play with their baby sister. And she had been twelve when Isabella came along. Since friends had never been allowed to visit her here, she had spent many hours alone, roaming the huge house.

Now, in hindsight, she guessed that was because her father couldn't risk Logan raping and killing one of her friends. That would have led to questions he didn't want anyone asking.

Finding nothing in any of the secret rooms, Sofia went to her sister's room. Tentatively, she walked to the bookshelves. This was where Isabella's hidden compartment supposedly was. If the hidden compartment didn't really exist, then this silliness about her sister being the killer could be over.

But as she looked, the small secret door was there. Right where Paige had said it would be.

If this hidden space existed, then Ryan really had found his proof here.

And if Ryan really had found proof that Isabella was the killer, then the proof must really exist.

And if the proof really existed, then maybe Isabella really was the killer.

And if Isabella really was the killer, then she had left the safety of the police station to come walking right into the lair of the person who wanted her dead.

Maybe she should call Ryan now, tell him where she was and ask him to come and get her. Pulling out her iPhone, she scrolled through her contacts looking for Ryan's number, he'd entered all his contact details earlier. She had just found it and was about to press call when something stopped her. The hairs on the back of her neck stood up, and she had the creepy feeling that someone was watching her.

Sofia thought she heard something move behind her. But as she turned to see what it was, her head suddenly exploded with a pain so vicious that all she could do was gasp and then sink to the floor and fade away into unconsciousness.

* * * * *

5:33 P.M.

This was bad.

On so many levels.

Isabella let go of the block of wood she had just slammed into her sister's head and dropped down to her knees at Sofia's side, pressing her fingers quickly to her neck to check she hadn't hit her sister too hard. Thankfully, Sofia's pulse fluttered weakly beneath her fingertips. Still, her sister had a large gash on her temple where Isabella had hit her, and blood was quickly puddling on the carpet beneath her.

She hadn't wanted to knock Sofia unconscious, but what choice had she had?

Sofia wasn't supposed to be here. When Isabella had snuck out of the police station earlier, she had left her sister there, safe and sound. And yet Sofia was here. In her bedroom. Standing right in front of the small safe she had installed behind her bookshelves. The safe was open, but the book on mushrooms and the DVDs of Sofia sleeping and Logan in the basement were all gone. And since they didn't appear to be lying on the carpet beside Sofia, Isabella thought it was a safe assumption that Ryan had already been here and found her secret stash.

So, Ryan knew that she was the killer.

And if Ryan knew, then he'd told his partner and the rest of his team of cops.

It seemed Ryan had also told Sofia.

Groaning, this was a nightmare.

Now she was going to have to do something with Sofia. Hide her away someplace safe. She didn't have long though; as soon as

231

Ryan realized Sofia was gone, he was going to go all out to find her.

For the moment, at least, Isabella would deal with one problem at a time.

First things first—she had to get Sofia someplace where no one would find her. She'd take her up to the secret room in the attic where she had Logan stashed. Then once she'd killed Logan and was ready to flee, she'd leave Sofia somewhere safe, where Ryan was bound to find her. She would have dropped Sofia off someplace now, but finishing the plan was paramount. Isabella couldn't afford to let herself get distracted.

Gently, Isabella eased Sofia's limp body over her shoulder, then balancing herself with a hand on the bookshelves, she stood, swaying for a moment under her sister's weight. Once she had regained her balance, Isabella carried Sofia as quickly as she could up the stairs to the attic and inside the little secret room she'd built herself.

Setting her sister down in a chair, she quickly secured her with some ropes, and then examined the wound to her head. Sofia needed a doctor. That was clear. But Isabella was almost done. She just had to take Logan down to the basement and make it look like he committed suicide in his little torture chamber, and then she could take off. On her way, she could leave Sofia outside a hospital. That way someone would find her, take her inside, and she could get the medical attention she required. Then once Sofia regained consciousness, she would identify herself and Ryan could go to be with her.

It would be a risk delaying her departure. And a risk by going to such a public place as a hospital to drop Sofia off. However, it was a risk worth taking. Sofia had always been there for her. Always supported her and given her the benefit of the doubt. Even when the rest of the family wanted to disown her.

It hadn't been her fault.

Either time.

Those kids at her school had asked for it.

Treated her like she was nothing.

Teased her. Mocked her. Made her feel like she was worthless.

They had gotten what they deserved.

Just like her family had.

Isabella used to wonder why she had such a violent, burning rage inside her. Ever since she had found out that Logan was her father, and just what he spent his time doing, it had all made sense. Murder was in her genes.

Despite everything she had done, Sofia had always stood by her. Supported her. Even tried to get her help. Not that it had done any good. Isabella had known, even at ten, that she was different. And no amount of counseling and anger management was going to change that. But she had played along. Mainly for Sofia's sake. Sofia loved her and wanted her around. Sofia had stopped the judge from abandoning her. Not that Isabella cared about her family, but she *did* care about Sofia, and was glad that her sister had remained in her life.

Maybe, she could take Sofia with her.

Maybe they could have the life they never could have had as long as their family was around.

Maybe they could both finally be happy.

No, Isabella told herself. That would never work.

Sofia was good and sweet and kind and thoughtful, everything that Isabella wasn't. It wouldn't be fair to Sofia to make her live a life on the run from the police. And the police were on to her, so for the remainder of her life Isabella would have to live constantly looking over her shoulder. And she couldn't subject her sister to that.

So she would keep with her original plan.

And she'd have to hurry.

She didn't know how much Ryan actually knew or how much he could prove. And she didn't know how long Sofia had been gone from the police station and whether Ryan was already looking for her.

With gleeful anticipation, Isabella set about the final stage.

* * * * *

6:20 P.M.

Ryan felt like he couldn't breathe.

Another bad choice could lead to the death of another woman he loved.

He shouldn't have left Sofia alone, only he hadn't realized she intended to flee the station, presumably to go looking for her sister. He had done as she'd asked and given her space, respected her need for privacy as she digested what he'd told her. However, instead of taking the time to calm down or think things through, Sofia had apparently decided instead to use the time to stupidly go running off on her own to search for her sister.

Growling angrily, Ryan was beyond frustrated at Sofia. It was unbelievably irresponsible of her to leave the safety of the station to go straight into the arms of someone who wanted her dead.

And yet as furious as he was, it didn't even make a dent in his fear.

Snatching at his phone when it began to ring, Ryan almost knocked it onto the floor but managed to catch it before it slid off his desk. "Hello?"

"Detective Xander?"

Disappointment washed over him when it wasn't Sofia's voice that replied. "Yes?"

"You wanted confirmation of whether a Sofia Everette ordered a taxi through our company earlier today?"

"Yes," he answered, hope spiking.

"Our records show she took one from your station to the Everette estate at approximately four o'clock this afternoon."

"Thank you," Ryan snapped, then hung up. "I'm going to the

estate, Sofia took a cab there," he rambled to his partner, grabbing his keys and standing so quickly he almost knocked over his chair.

"You're not going anywhere," Belinda announced from behind him. "I'll send someone to go and check it out, but you are not going anywhere near that house. You are involved with Sofia Everette. You can't be objective, and I won't have you running off and confronting Isabella and doing something we'll all regret."

When Ryan opened his mouth to protest that he was perfectly capable of handling himself around Isabella, Belinda's eyes dropped to his desk. Ryan followed his boss' gaze and saw several pens he'd subconsciously snapped in half. Reluctantly agreeing he may not be in control of himself enough right now, he plopped back down into his seat and checked his anger.

"It is not your job to find Sofia," Belinda reminded him. "It's your job to find Isabella, so let's do that."

"I found out some more about the incident that got Isabella expelled," Paige announced.

"Well, do you plan to share?" Ryan raised an impatient blond brow.

Ignoring his outburst, "It was five months ago," Paige continued. "Isabella claimed that four kids from her school, two boys and two girls, accosted her with a gun, forced her into a secluded storage shed at their school. Once they had her inside they made her take off all her clothes, then tied her up and sexually assaulted her for hours. When they were done, they simply left her there, still tied up. Apparently it took her almost twelve hours to work herself free of the ropes. No one noticed that she was missing. Not any of her teachers, not her parents, no one."

"She tell what happened?" Ryan asked, surprised and horrified by what Isabella had been through, but it did not give her the right to do what she had done.

"Yes," Paige nodded. "She told the principal of her school, some teachers, and her father. But the kids denied anything had happened. Isabella had a reputation for being weird and a loner with no friends. The kids said she had consensual sex with one of the boys, then got embarrassed when she found out he wasn't interested in her but just after some fun, so she made the whole thing up. Her wrists and ankles were cut up from the ropes, but the kids said that Isabella wanted it rough and that the ropes were her idea. The shed was regularly used by the school's teenage lovebirds, so there were plenty of DNA contributions. With no proof that anything illegal had happened, no further action was taken."

"Until Isabella decided to enact her own revenge and beat up the kids who assaulted her," Belinda added.

Paige nodded, "Sounds like it could have been the stressor that set all of this in motion. Isabella was assaulted, speaks out but no one believes her, so when she finds out what has been going on in her house she decides no one's going to believe her again, so she deals with things her own way. Punishes her family members because she thinks they knew what Logan was doing to all those young girls and didn't speak up. I spoke with Edmund again."

Sofia's best friend had completely lost it earlier when he had arrived at the station, expecting to find Sofia safe and surrounded by cops, only to learn instead that she was gone and none of them knew where. Ryan had been genuinely concerned that Edmund might pass out from the shock, the man had been practically hyperventilating. Eventually Paige had managed to calm him down, apparently enough to get some helpful information out of him.

"He says," Paige continued, "after the incident at her school, Isabella stayed with Sofia for a while. That's probably how she found out what Sofia knew, heard her talking in her sleep, and decided to bug the room to get the whole story."

"If Sofia's gone looking for her, she's going to kill her. Sofia was the one who knew it all, so she's probably the one Isabella wants dead most of all." Ryan felt so helpless, it was like he was being crushed.

"I'm not so sure about that," Paige disagreed, shaking her head slowly.

"What do you mean?" he asked, narrowing his eyes at his partner.

"Sofia knew all along," Belinda reminded Paige. "Not that I'm blaming her," Belinda added when she caught sight of the glare Ryan had aimed in her direction. "Her father had her convinced that it was nothing more than a bad dream, but still she knew, and Isabella is far from rational, so I'm doubting that she'll make the distinction."

"But she had her chance at Sofia, any number of them," Paige contradicted. "Isabella could have gone with a head shot at the charity benefit. She knew that Sofia was wearing a Kevlar vest, but she still went for the heart."

"She's been poisoning Sofia," Ryan argued.

"In small doses," Paige argued back. "Just enough to make her sick. She could have given her enough in one swoop to kill her off."

"Then why poison her at all?" Belinda looked baffled.

She shrugged, "Maybe to keep Sofia out of the way," Paige suggested. "Sofia was the only one who paid her any attention. If she was planning a diabolical murder scheme, then she would want to make sure she didn't tip anyone off. When I was speaking with Edmund earlier, he said that after the incident at the school, the judge wanted to send Isabella away. Off to some secluded estate he owns in England. Basically, he wanted to lock her up there, make sure she couldn't cause his family any more embarrassment. Sofia was the one who talked him out of it. I think Isabella truly loves Sofia, I don't think she's going to hurt her."

"Even if that's true," and Ryan couldn't let himself believe it just yet, couldn't let himself get his hopes up only to have them horribly dashed. "If she's backed into a corner, she could do anything."

"Granted," Paige nodded. "All the more reason we have to do everything we can to keep her calm when we find her," his partner shot him a pointed look.

"Now, Ryan, don't get mad," Belinda cautioned.

Of course, when someone said that to you it made you immediately tense up, and Ryan was no exception. "What?" he asked tightly.

"Is there any chance Sofia could be involved in all of this?"

Expecting himself to explode when faced with such a question, instead Ryan went still, completely and utterly still. "What?" his voice as frosty as pure ice.

"Other than Isabella and Logan, Sofia is the only one left…"

"Isabella shot at her," Ryan inserted.

"Or like Paige said earlier, it was a safe shot. We'd think Sofia was in the line of fire, but really she was never in any real danger," Belinda pointed out.

"This is insane," Ryan stood and began to pace restlessly, trying to work off some of his nervous/furious energy. "She's been poisoned."

"In non-lethal doses," Belinda reminded him.

"She told us everything that she remembered from her childhood," Ryan countered.

"Which kept the focus on Logan and away from her and Isabella."

"She was here helping us look for Logan's victims," with every comeback of Belinda's, Ryan could feel his blood boiling hotter and hotter.

"Again, which kept the focus on Logan. Look, Ryan," Belinda stood in front of him and made him cease his pacing, "I'm not trying to upset you, but it's also not my job to placate you. What I know of Sofia I like, and I don't really think she's involved, but we can't discount her purely based on the fact that you're attracted to her. Even if she wasn't involved, that doesn't mean that she didn't leave here to go and tip off Isabella. She still loves her sister, and she knew exactly how to play you to get away. She knew you wouldn't say no to her when she said she needed time alone, and she used that time to leave here and go and look for her psychotic sister."

"This is ridiculous and a waste of my time," Ryan again grabbed his keys. "If you don't have something more constructive to talk about, then I'm going to go look for..." he broke off as his phone trilled. Pressing answer, "Detective Xander."

"Detective, I'm Officer Middenorf. We've been searching the Everette family estate..."

"Did you find her?" Ryan interrupted. "Did you find Sofia?"

"I'm afraid not," the officer cleared his throat nervously. "But we did find blood in one of the bedrooms, and a block of wood, looks like it has blood and hair on it. We also found Sofia Everette's phone. Your number was displayed on the screen, looks like she was going to call you, but she was attacked first."

Ryan heard the words but they sounded far away. He could hear the officer on the phone calling his name, but all he could do was stand, open-mouthed, and try to comprehend what he had just been told.

Blood.

A weapon.

Sofia's phone.

They were too late.

Isabella already had her.

Sofia was going to die.

"Ryan?" Paige poked his shoulder.

Blinking dazedly, Ryan said, "They found blood at the estate and a weapon and Sofia's phone. My number was on her screen; she was about to call me when she was attacked."

Belinda eased the phone from his hand, "This is Lieutenant Jersey," she told the officer at the Everette estate. "I'm sending CSU and more officers. I want that entire place searched. Top to bottom." She hung up and tossed the phone on the desk, "Try not to panic, Ryan, we don't know anything yet."

"I spoke with the ex-head of Everette security a little while ago," Paige announced.

Ryan shoved his hands in his pockets so the others wouldn't see them shaking and took a deep, calming breath. "You've been a busy little bee while I've been panicking," Ryan attempted a smile at his partner.

She smiled back encouragingly, "Alan Payne said that the Everette house has hidey-holes. Lots of hidey-holes. So many he wasn't even sure that he knew them all. But Isabella grew up in that house. She'd be likely to know them all, probably played in them when she was little."

"You think she's still in the house?" Ryan asked doubtfully. "She has a hostage now, possibly two if she has Logan. If she's there, it'd have to be in a room big enough for three people."

"Maybe four," Belinda pondered. "We never found Brooke's baby. Isabella could still have it."

"So the hidey-hole would have to be big and someplace out of the way. A crying newborn can be loud and Isabella wouldn't want any of her family, or any of us, hearing it," Ryan thought aloud.

"Alan was going to email me a floor plan of the Everette estate and highlight on it all of the secret rooms he knows about," Paige explained. "Hopefully we get lucky and Isabella's hiding out in one of them."

"And if she's not...?" Ryan was fighting the fear swelling inside him and losing the battle.

"Then we'll keep searching until we find them."

Ryan was trying, but failing, to take comfort in his partner's words. He had been at this job long enough to know that there was a good chance that Sofia, Logan, and Brooke's baby were already dead and Isabella was long gone.

TWO

* * * * *

Ever so slowly, Sofia began to crawl out of the darkness.

And very quickly, she wished she hadn't.

The aching in her head was so severe she couldn't register anything else. Sofia was used to headaches but this one was something else.

She was trying in vain to recall what she'd been doing right before this headache had struck.

Was she at home? At the family estate? Was Ryan with her? Edmund? Isabella?

Giving up trying to think, as it was too hard right now, Sofia was about to slide back into the darkness when something pressed against her neck.

A wave of panic coursed through her.

Where was she and what had happened?

"Sofia?"

The voice sounded as though it were a million miles away.

The pressure on her neck increased.

"Sofia?"

She tried to reply, failed, and teetered on the edge of the calm blackness swamping her mind.

"Come on, Sofia, you're scaring me."

The voice was more insistent this time and Sofia tried again to respond. Managed only a small moan.

"Sofia?" the voice now sounded excited. "Wake up. Please, wake up."

Drawing on every ounce of energy she possessed, Sofia fought the pain and tried to pry her eyes open.

Tried and failed.

However, the effort of trying had prodded her closer to waking up. And with greater consciousness came greater pain. Pain and the sensation that she was spinning wildly in circles.

Trying to concentrate on one thing at a time.

Managing the dizziness had to be number one.

Sofia could think through the pain but not through a swimming head.

"Sofia?"

This time a shake to the shoulder accompanied the voice and it jarred her closer to consciousness.

As she slowly became more aware, things started to seep through her dizzy, aching head. There was something scratchy around her wrists. It didn't feel as though she were lying down.

Something was wrong.

This time she concentrated harder, forced her eyes to obey her, and somehow managed to pry them open.

"Sofia?"

Isabella's face flashed before her eyes. Then blackness again. Then her sister's scared face once more, closer this time. And another flash of blackness. Her eyes must be fluttering. Struggling to remain open.

"Sofia? Can you hear me?"

"Isabella?" she managed to croak, startled by how weak she sounded.

"Thank goodness," Isabella let out a sigh of relief. "I thought I'd killed you."

Certain her spinning head had caused her to mishear, Sofia asked, "What?"

"I'm sorry. I didn't mean to hurt you so badly. I just didn't know what else to do," Isabella implored.

"What did you do to me?" Her eyes finally stayed open enough to take in her surroundings. She was right. She wasn't in a bed, either at a hospital or in her bedroom. Instead, she was in a small room. Maybe ten by ten at the largest. There was a bed in the corner, a wooden table, and the chair in which she sat. Her wheelchair. Her wrists were tied to the arms, her ankles to the legs.

Wave after wave of nausea buffeted her. She would have thrown up had there been anything in her system to expel. It wasn't just the head wound making her nauseous. It was the knowledge that Ryan had been right. It *was* Isabella. She had killed them all. And now she was going to finish what she'd started.

"It's true," the words fell from Sofia's lips without her realizing.

"I'm sorry," Isabella was crying. "I'm sorry. You have to believe me, I never wanted to hurt you. I didn't. I promise I didn't."

Isabella's voice was oddly little girly. In all these years, even when Isabella was a child, Sofia couldn't recall a single instant when her little sister had ever sounded like a little girl.

Head still swimming, Sofia squinted her eyes to try to focus better. "Have you really been poisoning me?"

"I'm sorry," that seemed to be her sister's new mantra. "I just needed you out of the way so I could do this."

Tears burned her eyes. "Why?" Sofia was desperate to understand how her little sister could murder so many people so easily.

"They're all evil; you know they are," Isabella's eyes were begging her to understand. "They deserved to die. They didn't tell what he was doing. They let him get away with it. They let him keep doing it. How many more women should I have let him kill?"

"But to do this?" Sofia was fighting off unconsciousness, wishing that she'd told Ryan where she was going, wishing that she had stayed at the police station where she would have been safe. Now if she let her eyes fall closed she may never open them again. Her insane sister might kill her.

As if reading her mind, "I'm not going to hurt you, Sofia," Isabella beseeched, looking offended.

"You already have," she reminded her sister. "You poisoned

me, you let me think I was dying, you knocked me unconscious, and now you have me tied up."

"Just while I finish, then I'll take you to the hospital before I leave. I love you, Sofia. Of all our family you're the *only* one I love. I'm not going to kill you, please believe me. I love you," Isabella repeated.

Shaking her head sadly, Sofia whispered, "I'm not even sure you know what love is."

"How can you say that?" Isabella demanded, looking crushed.

"You shot me," Sofia reminded her sister. If Isabella had forgotten, Sofia most certainly had not. She hadn't been able to draw a breath without pain since the bullet plowed into her chest.

"But I knew you were wearing a vest; that's why I went with a heart shot instead of a head shot," Isabella retorted.

"You used me," the pain of knowing her sister wasn't who she thought was almost as painful as her blinding headache. "You put cameras in my room and filmed me while I slept."

"It was an accident at first, but when I heard you talk in your sleep about Logan and the basement, I had to know more. When I found out, I had to do something. I had to stop him."

"Then why didn't you go to the police?"

"The police?" Isabella snorted a guffaw. "Last time I told something, no one believed me."

"I did," tears began to spill down her cheeks. "I believed you."

"I know you did," her sister was crying too. "That's why I had to protect you. Why I had to protect those girls. I had to stop him. I had to stop them all."

"But the way you did it," Sofia couldn't wipe the shocked horror off her face. "Cutting Brooke's baby from her womb while she was still alive. Stabbing Lewis and Samantha. Drowning Gloria. Strangling Lincoln. Carbon monoxide poisoning Logan and Simone. Shooting father. You hated them."

"You did, too," Isabella countered.

"They were our family and now they're gone." A thought

occurring to her. "What did you do with the baby? Brooke's baby?"

"You mean my baby sister?"

"You know Brooke was your mother?"

"Of course," Isabella scoffed, then serious, "she's fine. The baby is fine. She's right here," Isabella moved behind her and reappeared a moment later with a tiny infant wrapped in a blanket. "See, she's perfectly fine. I would never hurt her. I've been taking good care of her."

"Isabella, please," Sofia begged, "let me take the baby and drop us both off at the hospital. I don't feel so good." This couldn't be more true. Her body was already weakened from the poisonous mushrooms, and Isabella had probably given her a concussion from the blow to her head. She needed a doctor.

"I know," Isabella held the baby with one arm, with her other brushed a hand lovingly across Sofia's face. "Soon, I'll get you to the hospital…soon. I just have to finish this."

"Logan is still alive?" Ryan had said he'd escaped from the hospital, but apparently Isabella had abducted him instead.

"Not for long," Isabella assured her. "Not for long."

"He's our brother, Isabella. He did horrible things, deplorable things, things I can never erase from my mind. But he doesn't deserve to die like this. He deserves to go to jail, to face the families of the young women he killed. You can end this the right way." Sofia knew reasoning with her sister was most likely pointless, but Ryan would figure out where she'd gone, he'd find her, she just had to keep them all alive a little longer. "Take me and the baby to the hospital, take Logan to the police station. Or call Ryan, he'll know what to do. Please, Isabella, please don't kill our brother."

"Logan isn't your brother, or mine," Isabella bounced from foot to foot, and paced manically.

Confused and tired, her head ached and she longed to close her eyes and sleep. "What?"

"I did DNA tests on all of us," Isabella ceased her frantic pacing and flung her face up close. "Logan is my father, yours too."

Unable to process that. "I don't understand."

"Logan is our father," Isabella repeated.

"Then wh...who's my mother?" Sofia was starting to think she was still unconscious and this was all just her imagination gone into overdrive.

"Gloria. Gloria is your mother," Isabella replied.

Sofia was sure that couldn't be right. Gloria was her father's wife. Or if what Isabella had told her was true, her grandfather's wife. But Logan would have only been fourteen when she was born. Gloria would have been forty. There was no way. Isabella was delusional. "I...I...I don't...that can't..." Sofia stammered. "That can't be true."

"Well it is," Isabella stormed over to the bed in the corner. "Tell her. Tell her it's true. Come on, Daddy," she sneered, "tell your firstborn all about how she was conceived."

* * * * *

9:34 P.M.

"Tell her," Isabella was jabbing him. "Tell her it's true. Tell Sofia that you're her father, that Gloria was her mother."

Maybe it was the lingering effects of the carbon monoxide poisoning, maybe it was the effects of the blow to the head Isabella had given him earlier, or maybe it was just that he was stuck here with nothing else to do. Whatever the cause, Logan found he had grown very contemplative the last few hours.

Surprisingly, he was no longer afraid. Isabella was going to kill him, of that he had no doubt. And yet death no longer scared him. Maybe it was because deep down he knew it was what he deserved. He'd killed so many young girls. Thirty-two to be exact.

So it seemed only fitting that he die in a small, quiet prison. Alone. Stripped of all dignity. Just as they had.

"Tell her," Isabella screeched, stamping her feet impatiently. "Tell her right now."

Raising his head, Logan saw Sofia tied to her wheelchair. She looked abysmal. She was thinner than the last time he'd seen her, her face looked as though it hadn't an ounce of flesh on it, her pallor was a deathly white, and blood covered half her face, dripping down to splatter her neck and shoulder.

For the first time in his life, Logan felt a stab of concern for someone other than himself. He was grateful that his and Simone's daughters, Tina and Natasha, were safely away on the other side of the world with their maternal grandparents.

"Tell her, tell her, tell her," Isabella started to pummel him with her fists.

"It's okay, Isabella," Sofia's weak voice floated through the air. "I believe you. Just leave him alone."

"No, he has to . . ."

"All right," Logan interrupted. "I'll tell her; I'll tell her everything." Maybe it was time to confess. To unburden all the terrible deeds he had committed before he died.

Satisfied, Isabella nodded and then produced a pillow, which she propped beneath his head so that he could easily see both her and Sofia.

Again, a flicker of concern flashed through him as he studied Sofia. Her eyes were glassy and she appeared to be battling to remain awake. Meeting Isabella's insane gray eyes, he began, "I'll tell you everything and then you take her to the hospital, agreed?"

"Of course," Isabella nodded hastily. "Just tell her."

Looking back to Sofia, "It's true. I'm your father."

"No," she said, tears welling up in her eyes.

"Yes. I was only fourteen when you were born. The judge thought it would be better to pass you off as his daughter, things would be less messy that way," he added sardonically. The judge was always concerned with appearance. More often than not, it was *all* he cared about.

Shock and horror mingled in equal portions on Sofia's face. "Gloria?"

He nodded, "She was your mother. She was my first."

"Your first?" Sofia's voice had raised a couple of octaves, now bordering on hysterical. "You mean your first victim? I know what you were doing in the basement, Logan. I saw you. You were kidnapping teenage girls, tying them up and raping them, and then killing them. Is that what you did to Gloria? You raped her?"

"Yes, Sofia," Logan answered calmly.

"I...I...I don't belie...I can't und..." Sofia stammered. "Gloria? She was our father..." catching herself, "she was *your* father's wife, and you raped her? Why?" Her eyes begging him to make her understand, even though they both knew that nothing he could tell her could ever make her understand.

"I'm not like normal people; you know that, Sofia. I always enjoyed hurting things. Causing pain. It was a compulsion. But then animals, they just weren't enough anymore. I needed more. I needed control. And the judge was not big on letting us have freedom, you know that," Logan caught the pleading quality in his voice and controlled it. He didn't need Sofia's acknowledgment that life for them as kids under the judge's care had been tough. "One night I couldn't sleep, I was wandering the house and I saw Gloria. She was just standing in the yard, bathed in moonlight. Before I even knew what I was doing, I had dragged her out into the woods and ripped off her clothes. I needed to see her eyes. See the shock and horror and fear in them. I needed to hear her beg me to stop."

"Stop," Sofia begged now. "I don't want to hear anymore."

But Logan couldn't stop, "The judge found us. He went berserk. Even more so after Gloria turned up pregnant. He warned me to stop. Told me I would ruin the family's name if I got caught. But by then, I couldn't stop. Raping Gloria was like my first hit of an addictive drug. I was hooked. Over the next couple of years, there were maybe fifty girls. I started with ones I knew wouldn't tell. Prostitutes. Illegals. Drunk college girls. After a while, the thrill wore off. I didn't get the same rush from raping them. I needed more. I needed to kill. So I chose a girl, kidnapped her, and tied her up in the basement. When I'd had enough of raping her I made her beg me for her life and then I killed her. What a rush. It was so exhilarating. I'd never felt more alive. I killed thirty-two young women. And I loved every second of it."

Logan knew his eyes had gone glassy as he recalled the pure ecstasy he'd felt as he'd watched the blood drain from that girl. It was the single greatest moment of his life. Over time he'd learned how to refine the kill. Make it last as long as possible. Strike in just the right place with his knife so that his victims bled out slowly and he could watch, capturing the exact second in which the life left their bodies.

Sofia was crying in earnest now, tears mixing with the blood on her face and leaving little trails down her cheeks. "Please, stop," she sobbed. "Please. I don't want to listen to this."

Snapping out of his reverie, he said, "There's nothing more to tell." Catching Isabella in a firm stare, "Now I told you everything; it's time to take Sofia to the hospital."

Isabella was staring at him intently, "Tell me about Brooke," she demanded. "Did you rape her, too?"

"No. Brooke was into it. She even liked it rough. In a way, she was like me. At first I didn't know that she was doing the judge, too. That she was just after money." For a while, Brooke's betrayal had stung. But then the judge had arranged for him to marry Simone and he had found the perfect woman to vent his rage on in between girls. "She got herself a cool million dollars when she sold you to the judge."

"Arrgghhh," Isabella screamed, her hands pulling manically at her hair as she paced the length of the small room.

Realizing Sofia had grown quiet, Logan glanced at her, her head had lolled forward, her chin now resting against her chest, she'd passed out. "Isabella," he said forcefully. "Listen to me. Sofia needs medical attention now. I know that you love her, so do the right thing, get her help. You want to kill me, fine, I deserve it. But Sofia and that baby don't. They haven't done anything wrong. Take them someplace safe."

But when Isabella turned back to him, he saw in her eyes that something had changed. She had been crazy before, but now it was pure madness that consumed her. Launching at him in an uncontrolled fit of rage. "I hate you," Isabella screamed. "I hate you, I hate you, I hate you," repeating the words over and over and over again.

"Isabella," Sofia murmured feebly. "Stop. Please."

Unhearing, Isabella continued. Then abruptly she stopped, spun on her heel, marched to the table and returned with a knife. It gleamed in the light of the room's single globe.

"Isabella, no," Sofia yelled.

"It's okay, Sofia," Logan assured his oldest daughter. "It's what I deserve."

The knife hung above him.

Isabella's cold gray eyes stared down at him.

Sofia screamed.

The baby screamed.

The knife plunged down, piercing his chest.

The white hot pain was unbearable.

Then Isabella tugged the knife free and brought it down again. Over and over.

Stabbing him again and again until his chest was one wet, sticky mess.

Sofia screamed.

The baby screamed.

Isabella stabbed.

And Logan's life dripped out of him just as his victims' had.

* * * * *

11:41 P.M.

Almost done now.

Isabella repeated the mantra over and over to herself. It was the only thing keeping her going.

She was exhausted. She wasn't sure she'd slept properly since that incident with those horrible kids from her school.

A shiver of fear sliced through her and she struggled to control it.

Isabella hated to feel afraid. Hated to feel out of control.

Those hours in the shed had been the worst of her life.

A gun pointed at her.

Ropes securing her to the floor.

Naked.

Humiliated, scared, and alone.

Forced to lie there helplessly while those boys raped her and those girls just laughed.

What was worse was what came later.

Her family or teachers never knowing she was gone even though those kids had tortured her for almost three hours. It had taken her another twelve to finally free herself from her binds. And yet no one noticed that she hadn't turned up for classes or come home for dinner.

She had been naïve.

She had told what they'd done to her. Told her father, told her teachers, told anyone with ears. And no one had believed her. Those kids had lied. Made up stories about her. And everyone had bought it.

And then to add insult to injury, when she had tried to punish them herself she had been the one to get in trouble. Just because of what had happened with that other little girl when she was ten.

Just because she was different. Just because she didn't have friends. She was labeled a liar and a troublemaker. Labeled violent and unmanageable.

But she had gotten her revenge.

Those kids would think twice before trying something like that with anyone else.

And then she'd heard Sofia talking in her sleep.

About girls being hurt in their basement.

So she had to find out more. She had to do something to stop it. No one had helped her just like no one had helped those girls.

She had done the right thing. She was sure she had.

And now it was almost done.

Looking down at her feet, Logan lay there. His lifeless body slumped awkwardly, vacant eyes staring at nothing.

They were in the basement.

A fitting place for Logan to spend eternity.

Isabella had dragged him down here. Even though she was big and strong, the exertion had almost drained her. But it had to end here.

She glanced at her watch.

It would be tight, but she thought she could make it.

Once she lit the match and set the basement on fire she wouldn't have long to get herself, Sofia, and the baby out of the house before it was consumed with flames.

With a last look around this basement of horrors, Isabella took a moment to think of the girls whose lives had been lost here. Then she pulled the matches from her pocket, struck one, and threw it onto the floor.

The accelerant that she'd added earlier caught quicker than she had anticipated. Within seconds, the basement was filled with fire and smoke.

Hurrying up the stairs, all five flights of them, Isabella burst into her secret room in the attic and froze.

Sofia was gone.

TWO

Scrunching her eyes closed, she had to be wrong. She'd left Sofia tied up, there was no way her sister could have gotten free. However, when she opened her eyes the scene before her was still the same. The room was empty. Sofia was gone.

And then she remembered. Her sister had been unconscious. Worried, Isabella had untied her and laid her down on the floor. Concerned Sofia was going into shock, she had covered her with a blanket, and left her there, intending to come back for her once she disposed of Logan.

Panicking, this was a nightmare.

Sofia was weak and injured, she'd never make it out of the house on her own. But Isabella didn't have a lot of time. The house was already on fire. The police were already on to her. They'd been here earlier searching this place for any sign of them. Luckily, no one knew of the room she'd built herself, and the police had been unsuccessful in their search for her, Sofia, and Logan. However, they could return at any second. Isabella needed to collect her sisters and flee immediately.

Frantically, she spun and retracted her steps. Surely Sofia couldn't have gone far. Then she noticed a few drops of blood on the carpet. Taking a couple more steps and she found some more.

A trail.

Following it, then pausing, she decided she should take the baby with her, save herself another trip up to the attic once she found Sofia. Once she had retrieved the infant, she continued her search. Finally, she found her sister by the top of the last flight of stairs. Somehow Sofia had managed to drag herself down four flights of steps.

"Sofia."

Her sister froze. Turned slowly. Tears and blood streaked her pale face. "Let me go, please, Isabella."

"Of course," she nodded empathically. "But you're weak. Let me help you. I'll take you to my car, drive you to the hospital." Moving toward Sofia, intending to help her, but her sister shrunk away, taking a step backwards.

"Don't hurt me," Sofia begged.

Isabella was offended. "Do you really think I'd hurt you?"

"You killed Logan," her sister sobbed.

"He deserved it, you know he did, he told you he did," she protested.

"I just want to go home," Sofia pressed a hand to her head, swaying unsteadily.

"I'll take you home," Isabella promised. "But please, you're hurt, let me help you." Setting the baby down, with hands held out to indicate she wasn't a threat, Isabella started toward her sister.

But Sofia took a step backward, teetered at the top of the stairs, then lost her footing and fell.

With crash after sickening crash her sister plummeted down the stairs.

Heart hammering as hard and fast as if she'd just run a marathon, Isabella just stood. Frozen. Unable to move.

She was unsure how long she stood there. Then all of a sudden her reasoning took back over and she sprinted down to the first floor as quickly as she could.

She gasped as she stood beside Sofia. Her sister wasn't moving. One leg was twisted out awkwardly beneath her, one shoulder looked like it had popped out, she looked dead.

Dropping to her knees, Isabella pressed her fingertips to her sister's neck. Relieved beyond imagining to find a pulse, Sofia was alive but in bad shape.

To make matters worse, the first floor was starting to fill with smoke. The fire in the basement had to be a raging inferno by now.

"Sofia?" she called hopefully, resisting the urge to shake her sister, since she didn't know how severe Sofia's injuries were, she didn't want to risk making them worse.

"Sofia?" she called again when she got no answer.

Yanking out her phone, she dialed Ryan Xander's number.

He answered after the first ring, "Detective Xander."

"It's Isabella," she announced.

"Where's Sofia?" he growled. "If you hurt her …"

"Relax," she cut him off, she didn't have time for this now. "I would never intentionally hurt Sofia. I love her. I don't want her to die. But," hesitating slightly, "there was an accident …"

"What did you do to her?" he demanded.

Insulted, Isabella said, "I told you I would never hurt her. It was an accident. I swear it was just an accident."

"What happened to her?" Anger had him over-enunciating each word.

"She fell. Down some stairs." Tears were threatening to spill out. "She's hurt bad, Ryan. I tried to wake her up but I couldn't. I can't wake her up, Ryan. You have to get here quickly; you have to get her out. I set the place on fire, there's not a lot of time."

His breath had quickened. "Tell me where you are?"

"We're at the estate."

"You can't be," she could practically hear his frown. "We searched the place, they didn't find anyone."

"Yeah, well lucky for me there were no Everettes there with you to tell you all of the house's secret hiding places," she retorted. "I'm not lying. We're here at the house, and it's going to burn down around us if you don't hurry up and get here."

"I'm on my way," a pause, "and you better still be there when I get there."

Then he was gone.

To speed here as quickly as he could, Isabella hoped.

Sofia was badly injured. Even if she regained consciousness, there was no way her sister was getting herself out of this house. Isabella wanted to get her out, but she didn't have the time. She couldn't still be here when Ryan arrived. He'd arrest her. He'd never understand why she'd done all this.

"I'm sorry, Sofia," she pressed a kiss to her sister's forehead. "I pray Ryan gets here in time."

Sprinting back up the stairs, Isabella snatched up the baby, then hurried back to Sofia, checking one last time to make sure her sister was still alive.

The air was now thick with smoke.

Time was running out.

Trusting that Ryan would save her sister, Isabella took one last look back, then left to begin her new life.

AUGUST 21ST

1:18 A.M.

He was speeding to the Everette estate as fast as his car could manage.

Ryan had his lights and sirens going, but still there was a limit to the speed his car could reach. As much as he wanted to get to the estate as quickly as he could, he also wanted to get there in one piece. Sofia's life was at stake, so taking foolish risks was out of the question.

Thankfully, he had already been fairly close to the Everette house when Isabella had called. He had been debating with himself going there and re-searching the house. Not that he had really thought the officers who performed the search hadn't done so thoroughly, but he was desperate.

After hanging up on Isabella, Ryan had immediately called his partner. Explaining the situation to Paige, he had asked her to send backup and paramedics to the house.

He kept replaying his conversation with Isabella over in his head.

She had said that Sofia's fall was just an accident. Of that, he couldn't be sure. It was very possible that she had done it intentionally to keep Sofia from telling everything.

Isabella had also said that Sofia was badly hurt. Of that, he *could* be sure. Ryan didn't think that Isabella would have risked calling him unless Sofia's injuries were serious.

With that in mind, he was trying to prepare himself.

The combination of the mushroom poisoning, the fall down the stairs, and the smoke from the fire Isabella said she had lit, could mean that Sofia would already be dead by the time he found her.

He knew what it was like to find the woman he loved lying dead, and he had to be ready to experience that all over again.

The night of Katrina's suicide was forever etched into his mind.

It was a mid-fall evening. The temperature was cool but not cold. The leaves were changing into a mass of red and yellow and orange and gold, swirling merrily through the air, then resting on the ground to form a patchwork carpet of autumn beauty.

The wedding was approaching, set for Christmas Eve, and he had been searching for his Miss Right from the moment he hit eighteen. Ryan had always known that he wanted to marry. Even as a child, he had known that he was lucky to have parents who were as happy and in love as his were. His childhood had been a happy one, he and his brothers had been well loved, and he had longed to replicate his cherished home with a wife and children of his own.

A tiny tinge of apprehension had been alight in him that night.

Something was up with Katrina. He had sensed it on the phone. As was his custom, he had called to let her know he was leaving work and would be home soon. But his fiancée had been distant, preoccupied.

Still, he had been completely unprepared for what he found when he walked through the front door.

The house had been quiet. And dark. Usually when he arrived home, the smell of dinner came wafting from the kitchen to meet him at the front door. But that night there had been nothing.

Ryan had called out for Katrina, wondering whether she had gone to bed because she was unwell and that had been the reason for her distracted tone on the phone.

So he had sprinted up the stairs to their bedroom.

Where he found his fiancée.

But not curled up in bed, asleep.

She was dressed in her wedding dress, sprawled over the antique quilt her grandmother had made her when she was a little girl, which covered their bed. An empty bottle of sleeping pills lay beside her.

Ryan wasn't sure how long he had stood there, in shock, staring at the scene before him. In reality, he guessed it couldn't have been more than a second or two, but at the time it had felt like an eternity.

When at last he regained control of his body, he had all but thrown himself at his fiancée. His quaking fingers had searched her neck for a pulse. He had found one, but it was little more than a faint flutter.

He had screamed at her to wake up.

Yelled at her not to die.

Begged her not to leave him.

But in his arms she had taken her final breath.

Even though he knew he was fighting a losing battle, the bottle of pills had been full the day before, Ryan knew this because he was the one who had picked up her prescription. The bottle was now empty, and there was no way anyone could survive swallowing an entire bottle of sleeping pills. Still, he had dragged Katrina's body to the floor and begun to perform CPR. It was too late, though. She was already gone.

It had been a shock to him when paramedics arrived. He didn't remember calling them, although in fact he had. They had gently pulled him away from Katrina. Repeating patiently to him over and over again that they were sorry but his fiancée was dead.

Paige arrived shortly after. Then his family. They had all tried to help, to say and do the right thing, even though no one knew what that was. But Ryan had never felt so alone. So helpless.

And now there was every chance that history was going to repeat itself and he was going to walk into the Everette estate to once again discover the woman he loved lying there dead. He had been too late to save Katrina by mere minutes.

Ryan prayed that this time there'd be a different outcome.

Tires squealed as he stopped the car in front of the house, not bothering to turn off the engine as he beelined for the door. Smoke was already billowing from the building, and as he yanked open the door he could see spot fires sprouting up. It looked as though Isabella had set fire to the basement, the flames now spreading to consume the first floor. It wouldn't be long until the entire house was a raging inferno.

Retrieving a bottle of water from the trunk of his car, Ryan poured it over a handkerchief and then tied it around his face, hoping to filter some of the smoke. Entering the house, visibility was low, but it didn't take him long to locate Sofia.

He found her in a crumpled heap at the bottom of the stairs.

She wasn't moving.

Heart in his mouth, Ryan flung himself down beside her.

"Sofia?" Hand on her neck, feeling for a pulse, thankfully he found one. She didn't answer him. Her breathing was shallow and labored, whether from the smoke or an injury, he couldn't tell.

Beginning a systematic check for injures, her head and face were caked in blood. There appeared to be at least two different impact sites. There was a large gash on her left temple, and another on the back of her head that was the cause of a small pool of blood. There were also bruises forming on her face, including a large lump on her right cheekbone. One of her shoulders was dislocated. When he rested a hand on her chest it felt like she may have broken some more ribs in her fall. Her right leg was twisted out at an unnatural angle. He looked closer and a strangled gasp escaped his lips when he saw Sofia's leg was broken so badly the tip of the bone had come clear through the skin.

Muttering a curse under his breath, Ryan knew he needed to get Sofia out of the burning building, and yet moving her could cause further damage. There was no way to know whether she had injured her neck or spinal cord in her fall. Waiting for the paramedics was out of the question. Who knew how far away they were. If he didn't get her out now, then the whole house could come crumbling down around them.

Praying he wasn't doing more harm than good, Ryan ever so gently eased an arm beneath her knees, then his other around her shoulders, and carefully lifted her off the floor. Sofia hung limply in his arms as he carried her toward the door. The air was now so thick with smoke that visibility was down around zero. By memory he retraced his steps, hoping he wouldn't crash them into any walls or furniture.

At the door, he realized that he hadn't seen any sign of Isabella. He had forgotten about her, his focus had been on Sofia. There was no point going back to look for her. Fire had the walls cracking and gave the floor an almost springlike quality as it weakened the wooden floorboards. The estate was about to implode, and he wasn't going to risk going back inside it.

Instead, he carried Sofia what he hoped was a safe distance away from the inferno, then carefully laid her out on the lawn.

Breathless from both the smoke and fear, Ryan choked on the fresh air and erupted into a coughing fit. When it passed, his fingertips pressed to Sofia's neck to make sure she was still alive. Detecting a pulse, weak but there, he lay down beside her, exhausted, waiting for help to arrive.

* * * * *

2:00 A.M.

Something was burning.

That was the first conscious thought that registered in Sofia's mind.

Absently, she wondered what it might be.

Deciding to find out she tried to move her body, but pain tidal waved over her. White hot, burning agony. Enough to make her almost pass out again. Every single inch of her hurt. From the tips of her toes all the way up to her head.

She must have gasped aloud because someone suddenly loomed over her. Fingers pressed to her neck, in the distance someone called her name. Maybe Ryan? The pain was making her groggy, making it difficult for her to think.

Tapping on her cheek seemed to reverberate inside her aching head.

"Sofia? Please, please, open your eyes so I know that you're okay. Please, cupcake. Open your eyes for me. Come on, Sofia. Wake up. Please, wake up now."

Ryan's voice was so desperate that she tried to comply with his commands.

Scrounging up all her energy, she tried to force her uncooperative eyes open. She was surprised, and pleased, when they did.

It was indeed Ryan kneeling over her, and when he saw her eyes open relief radiated off him.

"Oh, thank goodness," he murmured. His fingers brushed at her face, their touch feathery soft as though he were afraid of hurting her. "You had me so scared, cupcake," he said, mustering up a small grin.

"What happened?" she tried to ask, it came out as little more than a croak.

"You had an accident," Ryan answered vaguely, clearly trying to hide something from her. "Don't worry about that right now. Just rest. Paramedics are on the way, we'll get you to the hospital, get you all fixed up."

Sofia wanted to do as he suggested. Wanted to let her eyes fall closed and unconsciousness take away her pain, but something was bothering her. Something she thought she should know but couldn't recall.

"Something's wrong," her voice sounded feeble and insubstantial, the effort of talking agitated her smoke-filled lungs and she broke into wracking coughing fits that hurt so badly tears streamed from her eyes.

Ryan held her face between his hands until her breathing returned to somewhat normal. "Nothing for you to worry about," his smile tried to be reassuring, but it did little to ease her jangled nerves. "You need to rest."

Nodding, this time she was going to allow herself to slide back into peaceful blackness when images started to flash into her mind. At first they were nothing more than disjointed fragments.

A headache.

Ropes.

A baby crying.

Isabella with a knife.

Blood everywhere.

Crawling down the halls.

Falling.

Fire.

Slowly, like jigsaw puzzle pieces, the images began to join together to form a picture. Isabella had knocked her out. Then tied her up in a small room. Brooke's baby had been there. Logan, too. He had told her that he and Gloria were her parents. Then Isabella had killed him. Stabbed him over and over again until the small room was covered in blood. She had passed out, awakening to find herself alone and no longer tied up. Summoning all her strength, she had dragged herself through the house in a desperate bid to escape before Isabella returned. But her sister had found her. And she had fallen down the stairs. Once again she had awakened from the darkness to find herself alone, lying in pain at the bottom of the staircase, unable to move, the house full of smoke.

Panic and adrenalin had her forgetting all about the pain, and she tried to push herself into a sitting position. Isabella and the baby could still be in the burning house.

Ryan's hands were on her shoulders, pushing her back so she lay against the grass, holding her firmly in place as she struggled in vain against him.

"I have to get inside," she heard her near hysterical voice insist. "Isabella could still be in there."

"I didn't see her," Ryan told her.

"The baby, the baby could be there."

"Brooke's baby?" Ryan looked confused.

"Yes, Isabella had it. They could still be in there. Let me go, Ryan, I have to go back inside, I have to see if they're still there. I can't let them die in there. Let me go, please," she begged.

"No, cupcake. I'm not letting you go anywhere. You're injured, you need to stay still until the paramedics get here."

More tears seeped from her eyes, "She killed him. Isabella killed him."

"Killed who?" Ryan asked, keeping his hands on her shoulders.

"Logan. She stabbed him. Over and over and over and ..." her mind stuck firmly on the image. Isabella bringing the knife up and then plunging it down, repeating so many times that blood streaked the ceiling and the walls and Isabella herself.

"Sofia," Ryan shook her gently. "Stop it. Stop. You have to calm down, you're going to hurt yourself."

But she couldn't calm down. She was completely out of control. "There was so much blood," she sobbed.

"I'm sorry, baby, I'm sorry you had to see that," he took her hand, squeezing it tightly. "I'm sorry you had to see Isabella kill your brother."

Shaking her head, ignoring the pain it caused. "Not my brother, my father. Logan was my father. And Gloria. She was really my mother. And I hated her, Ryan. All those years I hated her. Because she never acted like a mother to me. But now I understand why. Because Logan raped her. Her own stepson. He raped her and she ended up pregnant. How could she love me after that? Every time she looked at me it would have reminded her of what Logan did. And now she's dead and I'll never get a chance to know her as my real mother."

Although in her mind she was making sense, Ryan looked like he was struggling to follow her guilty ramblings. "Shh," he soothed, patting her hand. "Shh, cupcake. Just rest, try to calm down. I hear sirens, EMTs will be here any second."

All Sofia could do now was cry. Pain and grief and fear and the horror of the last few weeks mingled into her tears.

Then there was nothing.

Just nothing.

The next thing she registered was a mouth over hers, and a puff of air being forced into her lungs.

Then pumping on her chest. The movement making the pain in her ribs come back with a vengeance.

Somehow her eyes popped open.

The blurry circle above her slowly morphed into Ryan's terrified face. "Don't you *ever* do that to me again," he ordered shakily.

Sofia barely registered the medics who knelt at her side and began to tend to her injuries. Hardly noticed them starting an IV to give her fluids, or splinting her leg, or putting a collar around her neck, or the fact that the oxygen mask they'd put on her was helping her to breathe a little easier.

"Ms. Everette, we're going to give you something to help you sleep now, okay?" one of the medics told her.

Sofia wanted to ask Ryan to stay with her, to tell him that she couldn't handle being on her own right now, but she couldn't seem to make her voice work.

Somehow he read her mind. "I'm not going anywhere," he said, reclaiming his grip on her hand.

A sharp prick in her arm brought with it the merciful peacefulness that only unconsciousness gives.

* * * * *

3:38 P.M.

"How's Sofia doing?" Paige asked as he slid into one of the seats around the conference table.

"She's in surgery," Ryan replied. "Her leg was broken so badly they need to put in a metal rod to stabilize it as the bone heals."

Wincing, Paige asked, "What other injuries did she have?"

"Dislocated shoulder, cracked another three ribs, broken collarbone, a concussion, and lots of bruises," Ryan summarized. "Plus some mild smoke inhalation. Luckily, she was passed out and lying on the floor where the smoke was at its thinnest; otherwise, her smoke inhalation would have been a lot worse. There were two bad blows to her head. One from when Isabella hit her earlier, and another from when her head hit the floor when she landed at the bottom of the stairs. She, uh . . ." he paused to control the quiver in his voice. "She stopped breathing for a moment there." That had been the single worst moment of his life. Believing that it was happening again. That he was about to lose Sofia. That she was going to die right in front of him. That once more his efforts to save the woman he loved would be fruitless. But thankfully, this time the outcome had been different. His CPR had saved her life, and she had already been breathing again by the time the medics had reached them.

Reaching over to squeeze his hand reassuringly. "But she's all right now," Paige reminded him.

"How's she doing emotionally?" Belinda asked.

Ryan raked his hands over his tired face. It had been a long couple of weeks. The only thing keeping him on his feet right now was the knowledge that Sofia was going to be okay. That and the desire to know whether Isabella had been in the house when the building eventually collapsed. "She was pretty out of it when she came to out on the front lawn," Ryan answered. "She was weak, groggy from the pain, dazed, and in shock. She was rambling incoherently, something about Logan and Gloria being her parents."

"What?" the shock in Paige's face was mirrored in Belinda and Stephanie's.

"That's what she said," he shrugged helplessly.

"But she was in a lot of pain, maybe she was delirious, didn't know what she was saying," Stephanie suggested.

"I don't think so," he countered. "She said it again at the hospital."

"She was conscious?" Belinda asked with a raised eyebrow.

"In and out. More out than in," Ryan admitted, he had remained by her side until they took her into surgery. "Even when she was awake she wasn't all that lucid, but she said it several times. She was upset that she had hated Gloria all these years for never being a mother to her, and then to find out after Gloria died that she was her mother."

"Well *that* I wasn't expecting to hear," Stephanie looked miffed.

"I think that's an understatement," Paige chuckled. "How did Sofia find that out?"

"Best I could get out of her was that after Isabella knocked her out, she took her to a room in the attic. She already had Logan there, Brooke's baby, too. Isabella made Logan tell her that he was her father and that he'd raped Gloria, and that was how Sofia was conceived. Then Isabella killed him."

"So, she heard Logan's confession?" Belinda asked.

"Yes, Isabella's, too. Neither of those confessions do us any good unless we know what happened to them."

"I thought you said Sofia saw Isabella kill Logan?" Belinda pointed out.

"That's what she said, but I'll still feel better once we have a body." Ryan wanted this case closed definitively so there would be no one left to hurt Sofia.

"People have been searching the building for bodies ever since the fire was put out and it was deemed safe enough," Stephanie assured him. "Hopefully we have an answer ..." she trailed off as her phone began to chirp. "Speak of the devil," she smiled at him, then answered the call.

Ryan sat in agonizing anticipation as he listened to Stephanie's completely unenlightening side of the conversation. After enduring nothing more than 'yeahs' and 'okays', Ryan pounced on her the second she hung up. "Did they find bodies?"

"One," Stephanie replied solemnly. "Logan's in the basement."

His heart skipped a beat, "No sign of Isabella's body?"

"No," the CSU tech replied. "I'm sorry, Ryan."

That meant Isabella had already escaped before he arrived at the estate. That meant she was gone. Possibly forever. And there was nothing stopping her from killing more people, including Sofia.

"They could still find something," Stephanie told him hopefully. "The part of the building that collapsed has only been preliminarily searched. When they remove the rubble they could still find a body."

"Yeah," he nodded half-heartedly. The side of the house that had collapsed was the side near the front door, the side that coincided with the side of the basement where the fire investigators believed Isabella had started the fire. She would have known that. So no way would she have remained on that side of the building as fire consumed the house. Isabella was long gone and they all knew it. "Uh, I'm thinking of taking time off," he announced.

"How long?" Belinda asked, surprised.

He shrugged fitfully, "I'm not sure, a month maybe."

"Because of Sofia?" Belinda's scrutinizing dark brown eyes studied him calmly.

"Yes," Ryan replied truthfully.

"You didn't take time off after Katrina," Belinda reminded him.

"That was different. After Katrina died this job was all I had, it was the most important thing in the world to me."

"And now Sofia is the most important thing in the world to you," Paige said gently.

"Yes," he agreed. "And she's going to need a lot of help and support to get through this. I don't think any of it has really sunk in. Everything happened so quickly, I don't think it feels real to her yet. When it hits her, it's going to hit her like a bomb. And it's a lot to deal with in one go. Her paternity and maternity, the fact that she's the only member of her family left, that Isabella is still out there somewhere. She's going to need someone to help her deal with it all."

"And that someone is going to be you?" Belinda asked, calmly and non-judgmentally so Ryan didn't lose his temper.

"Yes, it is," he replied firmly. "And it's not just emotionally that Sofia is going to need someone, but physically, too. Her injuries from the fall alone are going to take her a while to recover from, and who knows what kind of long-term damage Isabella caused with the poisoning. Bottom line is she needs someone and I want it to be me. I want to make this work."

"All right," Belinda stood and collected her papers. "However long you need, you have."

"I'll miss you, partner," Paige stood, too. "Don't be a stranger; I expect a call every day to let me know how you two are doing."

"Anything you or Sofia need, call me and I'm there," Stephanie's hazel eyes shone with unshed tears. "Don't be away too long. We'll all miss you."

Once he was alone, Ryan realized he was surprised that he was so at peace with his decision. His job would be here when he came back, but right now Sofia had to be his priority. And to that end he was going to head back to the hospital, for the first time in a long time excited about what the future held.

* * * * *

10:57 P.M.

"Mmm," Sofia moaned tiredly, her head felt like it was full of cotton wool.

"Sofia?"

"Ryan?"

"Yeah, it's me," he gently picked up her hand and brought it to his lips.

"Where am I?" she was too tired to try and figure it out for herself.

"The hospital," he answered.

"I fell down the stairs," she recalled.

"Yeah, you did," Ryan confirmed.

"Did you find Isabella?"

"No, I'm sorry."

She sighed, so her sister was still out there somewhere. A threat to anyone who got in her way.

"We'll find her, Sofia, I promise," Ryan sounded sincere.

She didn't really believe him, but she was too weary to disagree.

"Can you open your eyes for me?"

She managed to accomplish this usually minor but at the moment mammoth feat.

Ryan beamed at her from a chair beside her bed and leaned forward to kiss her but hesitated, "I don't want to hurt you," he explained.

"I don't care if you do, just kiss me, please," she half whimpered. Sofia wanted to feel close to Ryan, would have melded their bodies together if she could, she didn't want to lose him like she'd lost everyone else.

Ryan complied, pressing a soft kiss to the tip of her nose. "It's the only place that doesn't look bruised."

"I feel like I got hit by a truck," Sofia offered up a feeble smile.

"Are you in a lot of pain?" Ryan's bright blue eyes filled with concern.

"It's not so bad, these pain meds they have me on are doing their job," she answered honestly, her pain was just a dull throb, there but manageable. "When can I go home?" Sofia longed to be in her own bed, in the security of her own home.

"I'm sorry, cupcake, but not for a while," he squeezed her hand apologetically. "I spoke with your doctors earlier and they want to keep you in for at least a week, probably longer. The concussion, broken ribs, broken leg, these are serious enough injuries on their own, but add to that the fact that your body was already weakened, and your doctors want to keep you here so they can monitor you, make sure you're healing okay. And make sure that the prolonged poisoning hasn't caused permanent damage."

She was disappointed and scared that Ryan would become preoccupied with other things and soon forget all about her. Fighting back tears, she shot him a watery smile instead. "Well, you can come visit me when you're not too busy with work."

He leveled her with a serious expression. "I took time off work, Sofia."

"Why?" she asked, trying not to get her hopes up too high.

"You know why."

Hardly daring to ask, "For me?"

"Yes," he stood, lowered the guardrail on her bed and perched beside her. "I'm not going anywhere, understand?"

Slowly she nodded.

"I mean, I'm not going anywhere ever, you're stuck with me forever now," he shot her an adorable grin, his dimples making him look boyishly handsome.

"Forever?" she attempted to hold back her tears but one escaped anyway, she could feel it winding its way down her cheek.

Wiping it away, "Forever," he promised.

"You know it's not going to be an easy road for me," Sofia cautioned. "I don't think anything that happened has really hit me yet, and when it does…" she trailed off, not wanting to think of that right now. But she knew it was coming, knew she couldn't avoid it forever. At the moment, thankfully, the anesthetic and pain meds in her system had her groggy enough not to have to deal with it, but that wouldn't last.

Ryan began gently stroking her hair, "I know, cupcake, and we'll deal with it together, every step of the way, a day at a time."

She was so grateful for his support that she couldn't hold back her tears, they streamed out now. "I have a lot to get used to. My brother was really my father. The mother I thought wasn't a mother really is. I'm the product of a rape. My whole family is dead. And the only member of my family that I really trusted was a crazed killer." It was Isabella's betrayal that hurt the most.

"There'll be time to work through all of that later, right now you need to rest, focus on healing."

Nodding, Sofia wanted to sleep, but was afraid of what her dreams would hold. She had been scared of bad dreams before; now she was utterly terrified.

Reclaiming his grip on her hand, Ryan said, "Close your eyes and let yourself rest," his voice had gone oddly hypnotic, and she found herself obeying. "If you have a nightmare, I'll be right here beside you holding your hand, so there's nothing to be afraid of."

Sofia allowed Ryan's comforting presence to calm her, and the rhythmic rubbing of his thumb across her knuckles to lull her toward sleep. Despite the nightmare her life had become, it had produced one wonderful, perfect, magical thing. And as she drifted off to sleep, Sofia prayed that it would be enough to get her through the days, weeks, and months ahead.

Jane has loved reading and writing since she can remember. She writes dark and disturbing crime/mystery/suspense with some romance thrown in because, well, who doesn't love romance?! She has several series including the complete Detective Parker Bell series, the Count to Ten series, the Christmas Romantic Suspense series, and the Flashes of Fate series of novelettes.

When she's not writing Jane loves to read, bake, go to the beach, ski, horse ride, and watch Disney movies. She has a black belt in Taekwondo, a 200+ collection of teddy bears, and her favorite color is pink. She has the world's two most sweet and pretty Dalmatians, Ivory and Pearl. Oh, and she also enjoys spending time with family and friends!

For more information please visit any of the following –

Amazon – http://www.amazon.com/author/janeblythe
BookBub – https://www.bookbub.com/authors/jane-blythe
Email – mailto:janeblytheauthor@gmail.com
Facebook – http://www.facebook.com/janeblytheauthor
Goodreads – http://www.goodreads.com/author/show/6574160.Jane_Blythe
Instagram – http://www.instagram.com/jane_blythe_author
Reader Group – http://www.facebook.com/groups/janeskillersweethearts
Twitter – http://www.twitter.com/jblytheauthor
Website – http://www.janeblythe.com.au

sic enim dilexit Deus mundum ut Filium suum unigenitum daret ut omnis qui credit in eum habeat vitam aeternam

www.ingramcontent.com/pod-product-compliance
Lightning Source LLC
Chambersburg PA
CBHW020738250626
47155CB00003B/813